Hans co

his gaze among the shoppers. "I give you, my friends, a word of warning."

Straightening her spine, Louisa prepared to remember every word. "What sort of warning?"

He lifted his chin and turned his head, looking again among the crowd in the center aisle. In the next moment, he focused on her. He cleared his throat. "Thieves and pickpockets roam this market."

"Oh, my." Widow Krause released her hand from the teapot. "Have you been robbed?"

"A minor encounter. I advise you to stay on your guard." He glanced over his shoulder.

Louisa moved one hand across her skirt. Skimming fingers above her pocket's opening, she patted the fabric until she touched the thickness of the second set of cloth pouches under her petticoat. She gave silent thanks for taking a few minutes at the boardinghouse to sew the majority of her funds, plus the precious passport and church papers, into the hiding place. "*Danke*. We will be careful. Will you?"

"I must go." Hans replaced his cap on shaggy, mahogany hair and hurried off into the throng.

"*Herr* Hoffmann is an unusual young man." Widow Krause poured tea.

Louisa stared into the crowd. Within two blinks, she lost sight of him. "Alfred does not trust him."

"And you? Do you trust him?" The widow leaned close.

She pursed her lips to delay an answer. When she looked into his face, she saw a friend.

Carol
Open the pages
and step into
the past.
Ellen Parker

New Dreams

by

Ellen Parker

New Dreams

Cover Art by *Tina Lynn Stout*

The Wild Rose Press, Inc.
PO Box 708
Adams Basin, NY 14410-0708
Visit us at www.thewildrosepress.com

Publishing History
First Edition, 2023
Trade Paperback ISBN 978-1-5092-4858-2
Digital ISBN 978-1-5092-4859-9

Published in the United States of America

Dedication

To our ancestors with the courage to board the sailing ships and set out to make dreams come true.

Chapter One

Bremerhaven, the German States, January 17, 1851

Louisa Mueller pulled her blue wool cloak close. Stepping from the guest house, she entered the dusk. A fine mist softened the edges of the landscape and created halos around the lanterns. A row of low, stone warehouses and stables faced the opposite side of the rutted dirt road. Beyond the buildings, the masts and spars of the great ships in the Bremerhaven harbor rose like a winter forest. She closed her eyes for a moment, breathed deep, and savored the mixture of salt water and wood smoke in the air. Another scent tickled her nose, and she smiled before she opened her eyes.

Sitting on a bench beside the door, Dietrich Mueller rested his arms on his thighs and held a wooden pipe in one hand. He looked small and tired in his thick, wool coat and a dark, flat cap covering his balding head.

"*Guten Abend, Papa.*"

"*Tochter.*" He patted the space beside him.

Accepting the invitation, Louisa settled on the bench and tucked her hands under her cloak. "Your pipe is a little piece of home."

"*Ja.* Are you homesick so soon?" He sucked on the long, slender stem before releasing a thin stream of fragrant tobacco smoke.

"A little." She confessed. "I want to remember my life in Westphalia. Tomorrow, we board the ship and leave the German states behind. I fear all the new things will crowd out the past." She stared straight ahead and allowed thoughts of the events which brought the two of them on this journey to tumble in her mind.

Two years ago, soon after her seventeenth birthday, her parents had received the first letters from family in America. Her Cousin Fredrick and his bride completed the journey to Elm Ridge, Illinois, and wrote interesting accounts of establishing a farm. According to her relatives, many *Deutsch* settlers moved into the area to open shops or start farming.

Conditions in Westphalia contrasted to the positive American reports. Poor weather ruined the flax two years in a row. Without money from the primary crop, the farmers had less to spend at the village shops, including the Muellers' bakery. This past year, the potato crop caught the blight, and the financial suffering became more widespread. Income at the bakery run by Dietrich Mueller and his younger brother dwindled until it could not support two families. Several months after Louisa's mother died of an early winter fever, the Mueller clan selected Louisa and her father to emigrate. The plan centered on establishing a bakery in Elm Ridge along the great Mississippi River.

She turned her face and studied Papa's familiar profile. "I enjoy sitting with you like this. I think of the many evenings in our apartment above the bakery. You smoked your pipe and read the newspaper aloud while Mama and I mended and listened."

"*Ja.* Good memories mingle with the sad each time I remember our snug rooms."

Beautiful and clever Mama. People remark about how much I look like her. But when I look in the mirror, I see a plain person with honey-blonde hair and blue eyes—not a beauty. She nodded. "*Ja.* I stack troubles on one side of the scale—joys on the other. Tonight, I want to remember the good times—Mama playing the violin while you and I sang—or *Grossvater* telling tales." She leaned her head on his shoulder and thought of Hermann's kiss. From the time she was a small girl, she knew *Herr* Wulff, the cooper, and her papa desired her marriage to the youngest of the three Wulff brothers.

One spring day, four months after Mama's death, she and Hermann left the beer garden together near the end of the afternoon dance. Past the candle shop, he pulled her one step into the alley. Before she understood his intention, he pressed his lips against her mouth. *Heaven on earth.* She frowned at the memory of the next portion of the story.

Three days later, the king's men arrived and took Hermann away to the army.

I shall remember my first kiss, Hermann's kiss, all the days of my life. A small part of Louisa dreamed of a miracle to bring him home to marry.

Instead, Hermann had died during an outbreak of measles in the army camp five months ago.

"I am surprised to find you sitting alone tonight." She lifted her gaze and counted lanterns glowing hazy on the ships through the mist.

"The others went to the tavern." He gestured with his pipe toward a building with a wide door and large chimney. "I wanted to enjoy the open air and feel firm earth under my feet on my final evening in Europe. Tomorrow morning, we board *The Flying Gull.* Many

3

weeks will pass before either of us sets our feet on solid land again."

"*Ja.* I find it difficult to imagine the distance left to travel. I apologize for complaining about all the walking." She flexed her hands under her woolen cloak.

Alfred and Bertha Meyer, a young carpenter and his bride, also from the village of Hamm, travelled with them.

Walking behind the cart carrying their trunks, she and the carpenter's wife knitted stockings. During the long miles, she made a good friend of the slightly taller, shy woman with a lisp. They talked of life on the banks of the River Lippe and traded stories of America. The first two nights in guest houses, she dreamed of knitting and walking, walking and knitting.

"Louisa."

She instantly gave Papa her full attention.

"I wish you to make a promise."

"Anything, Papa."

He laughed. "Don't be so eager to agree until you hear the request."

She glanced toward her worn, leather half boots. "What do you wish?"

"We are going to a new land, Louisa. We will find a new language and different customs. I want you to learn the English." He circled his pipe.

"Will I have need? According to Cousin Fredrick's letters, many in the community speak *Deutsch*, even the same dialect." Since Papa brought the passport home six weeks ago, he spoke often of learning English. Until this moment, she thought he referred to becoming familiar with a few words to use in the bakery. Now, she turned her face toward him and detected a sparkle in his eye. *Papa is enjoying our travels. I have not seen him this excited since Mama died.*

"Today, at the shipping company office, I met a schoolteacher, *Herr* Schutte. He lived in America two years, before he returned to marry. He, his bride, and her two young brothers will also travel on *The Flying Gull*. He plans to give lectures about life in America during the voyage. I asked about English lessons—you know I'm eager to learn the new language—he agreed to add several. Sixty days, or more, passage means we will need more than Bible reading and knitting to occupy the days."

Louisa, aware of a tingle beginning in her toes, released a soft laugh. "Papa in the schoolroom? It makes a curious picture in my mind."

"*Ja.* I will need to pay attention. I do not want to wear the dunce cap." Dietrich quickly stopped his laugh. "I hear from others at the ship's office that many Americans do not learn even simple things in another language. In my bakery, I will sell to both immigrant and American. Hearty bread and tender cake, we introduce Americans to good *Deutsch* food. Sell more loaves and sweets. *Ja?*"

She smiled. "You are a good businessman, Papa. I will learn English and work in the shop beside you."

"Until you marry."

"Perhaps I will not marry. I treasure Hermann's memory." During a slow blink, images from the dance floor and his strong arms guiding her among other swirling couples returned in startling clarity.

"You will find a good, young man and marry." He reached over and patted her knee. "Marry—give me grandchildren. It is the way of the world."

She pressed her lips. Let Papa think she would catch the eye of a young man. *I am an obedient daughter in her nineteenth year.* This emigration adventure filled too much of her mind to leave room for young men. She decided the more practical use of her time was focusing on being the best possible helper for Papa.

America, land of opportunity. According to Cousin Fredrick, hard work and determination made dreams come true in the new land. Phrases from the most recent American letter filled her with confidence. Perhaps, one day, her hard work would find reward. My own bakery—a dream, indeed. She tipped her head back and looked for stars beyond the mist.

Tomorrow, we board the ship. Louisa closed her eyes and imagined the letters she would write to record her great adventure. America—opportunity—a dream fulfilled for her and Papa.

****

Entering the narrow stall, Ulrich Kohle moistened his lips. "Easy, easy, my friend. I am not here to take away your fine ration of hay." He tugged the stopper from a short, wide-mouthed jar and pushed the worn, dark cork into his pocket. Speaking the opening line of a lullaby, he swiped two fingers across the surface of the pungent ointment.

"You are a lucky fellow, Blackie." Ulrich spread the medicine over the gelding's damaged skin. "I do not know how you managed to get the pebble pressed into your collar. But I cleaned your harness a short time ago and removed the source of your injury. I even added a little fine oil to my cloth during the final wiping to make the leather smooth against your hide. Now, you need to heal well during the night. Tomorrow, you work again hauling heavy wagons of barrels to and from the great ships."

The animal tugged hay from the manger.

After stoppering the ointment, Ulrich skimmed a hand once more down the draft horse's neck. "Good luck, my strong fellow. In the morning, I will make an effort to wipe your collar one more time before your driver settles it on your neck. Then you will see me no more. I am leaving this place and going across the sea. I seek a better life in America."

Half an hour later, after dusk turned to dark, Ulrich paused across the road from a tavern. Turning toward the water, he sighted ship masts and spars rising from the mist. *I sail tomorrow.* The Flying Gull *leaves on the noon tide.* He swallowed an unexpected lump of uncertainty rising in his throat. *I dare not become sentimental.* "America is a land of dreams." He watched his whispered words merge with the light fog. Patting an interior coat pocket, he felt the forged passport.

A muffled laugh escaped the tavern's small, square window and broke his somber mood.

Crossing the road, he hesitated beside the wide, wooden door. Straightening to his full five-foot-six-inch height, he skimmed one hand across his freshly shaven cheek. *I am neither handsome nor ugly—a good trait when you do not wish to be remembered.* A moment later, he opened the thick, black door and stepped inside the warm, smoky space. He spent a moment studying a half dozen men gathered near the fireplace. Similar to taverns throughout Westphalia, and other German states, men collected to tell stories, drink a little beer, and smoke an evening pipe. After a polite nod toward the group, Ulrich approached the man standing behind a tall counter. *"Ein Bier."* In the next breath, he requested a plate of supper.

A few moments later, he carried a full stein in one hand and a steaming plate of food in the other. Seeking out a table in a shadowed corner, he avoided any possible invitation to join the group. He sipped his beer and began to eat warm kraut, soft turnips, and spicy sausage. *Five years since I left my father's house.* The memory of his final night at the timber cabin on the edge of Selm sent a shiver up his spine. While his drunken father had shouted and crashed furniture to the floor, Ulrich stuffed a change of clothing into a bag and fled.

What have I gained in recent years? He glanced at his worn brogans and shabby trousers. *Honest work for two years brought me near starvation. Stealing allows me to eat better. But I'm weary of moving every few weeks or months to stay ahead of the authorities.* He blinked slowly and brought the man at the next table into sharper focus.

The portly man slumped against the high back of the bench. The table candle flared, and a silver watch chain glinted against a black waistcoat. A fine, low-crowned hat rested on the table beside an empty beer stein.

One of the men around the fireplace sang a ballad in a sweet, tenor voice.

Ulrich glanced at the group. *A welcome distraction.* He returned his attention to the dozing patron. Rubbing two fingers against his thumb, he shook his head. Last week, to the full moon, he'd sworn to be done with stealing. *I shall enter America an honest man.*

After draining his beer, he stood and adjusted his flat, wool, workman's cap. He stepped close to the sleeping man, drew a steadying breath, and darted his hand above a rounded belly. With practiced motions, he transferred the watch and chain to his own pocket.

"*Wa…wer?*" The stout man roused.

Ulrich quickened his steps toward the door. Pushing the sturdy barrier open, he sprinted into the evening mist.

"*Halten…dieb…halten.* Stop…thief."

Dashing across the road, Ulrich sought shelter among patches of high weeds and piles of fresh-cut wood. He crouched behind an untidy heap of fragrant beech and looked toward the tavern.

Three men, one carrying a lantern, hurried across the road. Pausing in the wild grass, they exchanged low words.

Ulrich held his breath and watched the tallest man point toward a low, wooden building. A few moments later, he moved behind another, larger woodpile farther from the shed. He sealed his lips and counted in his mind. Watching the search party move to his right, he held his breath and peeked around the edge of the jumbled fuel.

The tallest man held the light high as the trio waded through the weeds.

"I see something move." The stout man pointed toward the shadow of a warehouse.

"Quick—follow me." The lantern man strode across the uneven ground.

Ulrich shifted his weight when a muscle twitched, but he stayed in position behind the firewood. *Ein Narr. A fool I am. Not yet on the ship and I yield to*

9

temptation. Thieving brings me trouble—always.

Waiting and watching, he stayed hidden until the three men returned to the tavern and closed the door. In silence, he counted to one hundred. Finally, with glances toward the tavern and both directions along the road, he levered to his feet and moved away.

Several minutes later, Ulrich paused beside the stable door. Tipping his face to the sky, he searched for the half-moon in the waning mist. *Mein Freund.* He shook his head and shifted his gaze from heaven to earth. An honest man worked in the daylight, in full view of other men. *In America, I live as an honest man.* He moved his lips in silence while returning his gaze to the sky and a group of tiny stars peeking between drifting clouds.

Making as little noise as possible, Ulrich opened the small stable door and stepped into the hay-, horse-, and leather-scented space.

A horse snuffled.

A hoof tapped against a bare space on the stone floor.

Ulrich stood silent and blinked twice to adjust to the darker space. Taking slow, cautious steps, he stayed in the wide, central aisle until he reached the final stall. Turning left, he extended one arm and searched for the ladder to the loft. Climbing the worn, smooth rungs, he reviewed the evening's events. *In one moment of weakness, I destroyed my final chance to stay in Bremerhaven.*

After a short crawl across the hay-littered space, he reached the place under the eaves where he stored his meager possessions. He reached toward his bedroll.

A form fluttered past his face.

Ein Fledermaus. He slapped a hand to his chest and watched the bat escape through one of the small openings under the generous eaves. A short time later, Ulrich knelt beside his open valise. Reaching into his pocket, he removed the watch and chain. Holding the treasure by the chain, he examined it in the light leaking into the loft. *A good, thick chain. A plain timepiece.* He frowned. A pawnbroker would not give much coin for such an object. *I've no time to sell. I must board* The Flying Gull *before the ship leaves on the tide.*

Whispering a curse against his thieving, he inventoried the contents of the leather valise. *Another ill-gotten object.* He tucked his lip and remembered the summer day a prosperous man neglected his baggage in the pre-dawn. The satchel, made of strong leather, showed only a little wear. The quality of clasp and buckle, plus fine, even stitching, indicated quality workmanship and considerable expense. *A good valise is necessary to contain my possessions on the long journey.* He pushed the watch and chain deep under his change of clothes, extra shirt, and shaving equipment. Arranging the linen towel holding his food—three hard sausages, one white cheese, and a tin of thick crackers—on the top, he shook his head. The food, a supplement for the one hot meal a day provided by the ship, looked skimpy for two months.

After confirming his pockets still held the forged passport and his modest money supply, he settled onto his blanket. *My last night in Europe. From this time forward, I will be an honest man. I will work hard in America—the land where dreams come true.*

Chapter Two

Atlantic Ocean, thirty-second day of the voyage

Determined to keep her voice full of false cheer, Louisa adjusted the cup of diluted beer in one hand. Slipping her other arm under Dietrich's head, she blinked twice against forming tears. "*Bitte, Papa.* Please...one more sip. You need strength to fight the fever."

A soft moan escaped his dry, cracked lips.

"Oh, Papa. You must drink. You need to recover." She lifted his head another inch and dribbled a few drops of liquid across his mouth. *What will I do if I lose him?* If...? She closed her eyes for a moment and failed to banish the idea. Did they allow a young woman traveling alone to enter America?

Opening her eyes, she set the cup on the floor and stared into the gloom of the family quarters. Dozens of narrow bunks with aisles the width of a man's shoulders filled the room. Lanterns hung from the beams swayed in an echo of the ship's motion and contributed dim light to the space. Stale air pressed against her. With her next breath, the meager breakfast in her stomach curdled. The chamber pots were full to overflowing—again.

"Lou...Lou...isa."

She leaned forward until an ear remained a scant

inch from Papa's lips. "I'm here, Papa. Will you drink for me?"

"Too late. Too weak." He put a shallow breath between each syllable. "Promise me."

"Anything." *I will do anything possible.* She glanced to determine if a stranger could overhear.

At the far end of the room, a woman tended her son in another lantern's pool of light.

The other passengers were on deck, enjoying fresh air and mild temperatures.

The ship swayed like a rocking chair, indicating good sailing.

She shifted and touched a foot against one of the small trunks allowed in the room. Searching and finding Dietrich's hands under the blanket, she held firm to his thick, work-worn fingers. *Please, Lord, spare Papa. Today is the third day of fever. One more day.* The previous passengers usually died on either the second or third day.

"Continue…journey…dream." Dietrich trembled. "Learn…English…marry."

"Hush. You will recover. We will travel and work together." She pressed her lips the instant the mixture of wish and lie spilled from her mouth. Lowering him to the folded coat acting as a pillow, she suppressed a sigh. A moment later, she refreshed the cool, damp cloth on his brow.

Dietrich stuttered during his next breath.

A shiver raced across her shoulders. *Bitte— please—draw another breath.* Poor light and foul air made nursing difficult. *Tending Mama during her final days, I opened the shutters to give her cheerful daylight.* She prayed for mercy—and a miracle.

13

"No better?" Bertha, the young carpenter's wife, stepped out of the gloom.

"*Nein.* He only managed one sip of the beer." Louisa blinked at building tears. She belonged to the respected Mueller family. *Be strong.* Muellers did not cry in front of others.

"Go on deck. Get some fresh air. I will sit with him."

"*Danke.*" Louisa glanced toward the open door of the family quarters. "Is your husband on deck? I fear the time has come for me to have a word with him."

"*Ja—Herr* Meyer enjoys a warm day in the middle of winter. Today is fine sunshine with a breeze to fill the sails."

Louisa yielded the low stool and grasped the nearest chamber pot. "I will empty one. Perhaps it will make the air more bearable." A few minutes later, Louisa poured the foul-smelling waste over the side and rinsed the container with sea water from a nearby bucket. Re-securing her shawl, she surveyed the passengers enjoying the sunshine.

A few paces away, two young men stood talking.

She recognized the pair as half of a quartet often seen together. *May they be well.* She bowed her head and made the sign of the cross. Turning toward the ship's bow, she spied Alfred, Bertha's husband, among a group of men watching one of the constant dice games on deck. She walked close and touched his arm. *I cannot remember the words the doctor spoke to prepare us for Mama's final hours.* "*Bitte.* May I have a word? In private?"

"Certainly. Your face tells me Dietrich is no better." The carpenter, a sturdy man with wide

14

shoulders, led the way past a group of rain barrels to a quiet place near the rail.

"True…I-I begin to fear the worst." She tucked a few loose strands of hair under her dark bonnet. "May I travel with you and Bertha to St. Louis? I will pay my own way on the riverboat. I promise not to cause trouble."

He faced her, extended his arms, and lightly set his hands on her shoulders. "You will never be trouble to us, Louisa. Bertha welcomes your company. I invite you to stay in St. Louis. My brother and his wife will give you shelter until you can make longer-term plans."

"*Danke.* I appreciate your kindness." She released a small sigh. "Cousin Fredrick expects us…me…to join him in Elm Ridge. If…if necessary…I will send him a letter from New Orleans. I do not wish him to be startled if only I arrive." *Papa still breathes.* She pressed tight her lips for an instant. The plans and words of traveling without him came too easy.

She turned out of Alfred's light hold and grasped the rail. Staring toward the horizon, she imagined the waves going on forever. She blinked away more unwanted tears and tried to imagine all the miles and miles of water between the ship and America. Weeks remained before *The Flying Gull* would reach New Orleans. She drew a deep breath of warm, salted air.

Papa's dream. She remembered Dietrich sitting on the deck a few nights ago while smoking his evening pipe. After the next blink, the image in her head changed to Papa standing proud behind the counter in his own bakery. In the next moment, his figure was replaced with her daintier form. *My bakery? Is such a thing possible?* Could she use her skills to have her own shop in America? Did large, impossible dreams come true in the New World? Did the other passengers on this ship hold big dreams?

Alfred, standing beside her, braced his arms against the rail and shifted his weight. "Plans are settled. You will journey with Bertha and me to St. Louis. The discussion of you travelling north of the city will wait. Have you eaten today?"

"I had a bite at breakfast. I have little appetite." She set one hand on her stomach. The fresh air calmed her inner turbulence and gave her strength. "When I go below, I will eat some hard cracker."

After Louisa returned to the family quarters, she resumed her vigil. According to the candle in the lantern, two hours passed before Dietrich drew his last breath. She stared at his chest and prayed for one more slight rise of the thin blanket. Twenty…thirty…sixty. She counted seconds in silence and felt a wisp of hope fly away with each number. Ignoring the block of ice forming in her stomach, she clasped his hand and closed her eyes. *I loved you, Papa.*

Glancing in all directions, she counted only five or six others in the family quarters. *Each person here has their own concerns.* She drew determination with her next breath and reached beneath the blanket. Directing her hands under Dietrich's nightshirt, she sought, found, and removed the wide linen belt. Sewn inside the sturdy cloth, she fingered the precious passport, money, and church papers. She folded the fabric over and over until the bundle fit into her first set of pockets. Standing, she memorized his features. A moment later, she arranged the blanket over his hands and face. She raised a trembling hand to her face and wiped a few escaped tears. "I must go, Papa. I will ask Alfred to make burial arrangements. The ship's crew and the Lutheran pastor on board will give you a proper funeral."

****

Ulrich stepped into the men's sleeping quarters and held his breath against the smell of too many men living in close, windowless conditions. He ignored the rows of empty, narrow bunks built three high and sought out one particular bed. *Gute.*

Hans Hoffmann, a young man he'd become friendly with, now rested on a lower bunk.

Another friend, Max, sat beside him, holding a tin cup in one hand.

"How goes it?" Ulrich advanced another quiet step.

Max sighed and made the sign of the cross. "The same. Or worse. He refused the cup a few moments ago."

"I will sit with him." Ulrich stepped close and gestured for the slight youth to stand. "Go and stretch your legs on deck. You deserve to clear your lungs and enjoy part of a fine day. When I left them, your little brother was reciting multiplication tables to *Herr* Schutte."

Max smiled and handed the diluted beer to Ulrich. "Then I must go and rescue the good teacher. Once my brother, Ben, begins talking, he forgets to give a turn to the other. Shall I relieve you in two hours?"

"*Zwei ist gute.*" Ulrich nodded and eased down onto the traveling chest pulled into the aisle. The trunk made a convenient bench during the hours few people populated the room. Belonging to Hans, the modest container showed fine workmanship. Brass fittings, black paint, and a red horse's head on each end bestowed distinction.

After the sound of Max's steps faded, Ulrich leaned forward and studied the patient's face. The features were similar to those Ulrich saw each morning in the shaving mirror. Each of them had plentiful dark hair, thick eyebrows, and high cheekbones.

Hans opened his eyes, revealing fever-dulled brown irises. He moved a tongue coated with white film against cracked lips. "*Frrreund.*"

"*Ja.* I am your friend. The person others mistake for your twin." Ulrich offered the cup. "Drink—for your strength."

Hans managed one small sip. "Enough."

Removing the damp cloth from Hans's forehead, Ulrich refreshed the rag in a small basin. Performing the familiar task, he discovered dark thoughts crept out of his mind's corners. Hans carried a true passport, not a forgery. Hans Hoffmann, a common name, was not tainted by thievery. If...Ulrich allowed the idea to sprout. If Hans did not recover from the fever, he would have no need of official documents.

How many on the ship know me? Since boarding *The Flying Gull*, he'd been careful to avoid saying his name more than required. Continuing a habit developed during the previous five years, he refrained from speaking of his past. *Max.* The young man, and his slightly younger brother, would be aware if Ulrich followed through with the idea forming in his head. Perhaps a few silver *Thalers* would buy their silence.

Hans twitched in his sleep.

Pulling a stiff pin from his pocket, Ulrich knelt and picked the chest's plain lock. He lifted the lid and began inspecting the contents. On top, he found two changes of clothes and a pair of felt slippers. Below the clothing, he located a letter marking the Psalms in a Bible, shaving equipment, and a pair of spectacles. He held the reading glasses high in the soft lantern light. "I have never seen Hans wear these."

Deeper within the trunk, he ignored a linen shirt wrapped into a neat bundle and focused on cloth pouches protecting fine tools. Five hammers of different weights and head shapes filled one set of cloth pockets. An assortment of screwdrivers and pliers were stored in the others. Finding tin boxes of fancy brads, Ulrich tipped his face to the ceiling. *Ja, I remember now. Hans told us his father and uncles trained him and his brothers to be harness makers.*

Hans groaned and trembled with fever.

"Easy, easy, my friend." Ulrich closed the trunk without making a sound. Turning his attention to the patient, he touched Hans's shoulder and began to croon. "The moon rises in the east." The lullaby's words appeared to calm the fevered man. A few moments later, Hans lapsed into sleep punctuated with faint groans.

Ulrich lifted Hans's coat from a peg and searched the pockets. "*Gute. Gute.*" Ulrich nodded as he read and re-read the official description in Hans's passport. The stamps on this paper were genuine. The notation of "poor eyesight" explained the spectacles in the trunk. *I am a year and five months older now.* He recited the new birthday and pondered the exact location of Arnsberg, his new birthplace. A quick search of the coat revealed two more pockets, sewn shut. With the same tool used to pick the locks, he made quick work of opening the seams and transferring money into his own wool coat.

Detecting approaching footsteps, he froze. After a moment, he shifted his stance to present his back to an observer. He slipped his forged documents into the patient's coat pocket. Ulrich straightened and mouthed determined words. *No fear, my dying friend. In America, Hans Hoffmann will be an honest man. I will not ruin your name.*

Chapter Three

Emerging from the dim passenger deck, Louisa blinked against the morning sun. A steady breeze filled the sails and sent her bonnet ribbons into motion. She paused two paces from the ladder and stared at her shoes for a long moment. Soon, she heard the ship bells. For the passengers, the chimes signaled time for the morning prayer and funeral service. Among the crew, the sound sent them to a new set of tasks. *Papa is dead. My nearest relatives go about their lives in Hamm or Elm Ridge unaware their brother or uncle is now with God. Be strong. Do the family proud.*

"Come, Louisa. Alfred and I will stand beside you." Bertha extended a gloved hand.

Louisa nodded before walking beside her friend to the sunrise side of the bow. She estimated the group gathered around the young, Lutheran pastor and the two shrouded bodies at three dozen? *Two bodies?* She glanced at Bertha. "Who is the other?"

"A young man died during the night. His friends stand together by the anchor windlass."

Louisa adjusted her gaze and noted three young men. After a second blink, she swallowed a lump of grief. *I see these men often talk and take meals together...with another.* One man, perhaps twenty years old, stood with two younger boys. *Junge.* Clever families sent the youngsters to America before they reached army age. She shifted her gaze to the deck. *I believe the second corpse is the man who appeared twin to the eldest in the group, the young man wearing an ill-fitting jacket and in need of a haircut.*

The pastor removed his hat and stepped forward. "In the name of the Father, and of the Son, and of the Holy Ghost."

"Amen," the assembly responded in unison.

During the burial service, Louisa alternated her gaze between the wrapped bodies and the sky. Each covered corpse lay on a wide board supported by two barrels. *Which one is Papa?* She failed to find an answer in the high, fair-weather clouds.

I will honor you, Papa. With each glance at the shrouded figures, she stiffened her resolve to find work in a bakery. *I will learn English. I will become a proper American.* She envisioned herself older, after much hard work, owning a shop and training young women to be excellent bakers.

The pastor prayed in a monotone. First, he asked for mercy for the deceased. Then, he added a request for comfort for the survivors.

Louisa heard few of the specific prayers. She allowed her mind to drift into a review of past family burials. First, she remembered a small coffin. Her younger brother, Karl, died after a wound on his leg became infected. A few years later, *Grossvater* and *Grossmutter* died in the same winter—during Louisa's third year in the schoolroom. *Mama.* One year ago, after six days, her dear mama succumbed to a fever. She lifted her handkerchief to hide her lips. "Hermann, she muttered. "How terrible for you to die so far from friends and family." She shifted her gaze to the pastor a few paces away.

Smoothing a paper inserted into his small, black book, the cleric signaled with his left hand.

Four burly crew members, who had been standing respectfully near the shrouded bodies, stepped into position. One man counted in a soft voice. The group lifted the first board and carried the corpse the few steps to the rail. Holding firm, the men lifted the near end.

The pastor made the sign of the cross. "Dietrich Fredrick Karl Mueller, we commit your body to the sea."

"May God have mercy on your soul," the entire congregation responded.

Louisa managed a few deep breaths in the time the crew stowed the first plank and moved the second into position.

"Ulrich Adolph Franz Kohle, we commit your body to the sea."

"May God have mercy on your soul."

Moving closer to the rail, Louisa watched the second body slip between the waves. *What if...?* She peered along the side of the ship. The vessel cut through the waves, causing water to foam against the side.

Alfred leaned close. "The crew weights the bodies with rocks."

"*Gute. Gute.*" She swallowed her sudden fear of Papa bobbing like a cork in the ocean. Turning to the group of mourners, she listened to the words of a familiar hymn. She glanced toward the trio of young men standing awkwardly a half dozen paces away. A moment later, she joined the singing on the second verse. Music lifted her spirits from the depths and turned her thoughts away from the past to the present.

After the final blessing, the worshipers dispersed.

Bertha touched Louisa's elbow. "Come. We will walk around the deck and enjoy the fine sunshine. Fresh air will cleanse your lungs after your recent hours in the dank sickroom."

"*Ja.* Dear Mama taught our family sunshine is good for body and soul. I look for God's direction and sort my jumbled thoughts." Louisa studied her friend for a moment and considered sharing her bakery dream. Would the carpenter's wife understand? *Nein.* Each time the married woman spoke of the future, she centered her dreams on keeping a good home and caring for children.

Louisa blocked out her surroundings and focused her thoughts on the many changes she must make to honor Dietrich's dying request. *I must be extra careful on my journey to Elm Ridge. I need to find employment. Did Fredrick mention a bakery in his letters?*

At a bump against her elbow, she startled and blinked out of her daydream. "*Bitte.* Pardon me." Taking one step to the side, she increased the distance between her and the young man.

"*Nein*—my fault. I must learn not to gesture so wide when thinking." He touched the brim of his flat, wool, workman's cap and gave a slight smile.

Louisa sucked in a breath. *The friend—of the man buried with Papa.* Lowering her gaze, she nodded. *Polite.* She hurried her next step to draw even with Bertha. Glancing over her shoulder, she opened her mouth to speak but in the next instant sealed her lips. *Too soon. I'm too confused. If I see him again, then I will offer condolences.*

****

Hans, formerly Ulrich, turned and watched the two women walk between the rail and a collection of barrels. A dozen steps and the pair would reach the painted mark warning the passengers to go no farther astern. He stared after the shorter one, in the blue cloak and dark bonnet, until they halted. *Attractive, pretty face and figure.* During the funeral service, he preferred studying her instead of giving his attention to the pastor. According to Max, the young woman's father was the other man buried today. He blinked slowly and recalled the name. *Dietrich...Mueller. Next time I encounter, I will address Fraulein Mueller.*

Turning his head, Hans became aware of a man standing directly in front of him. *I saw him at the burial—standing near the late Herr Mueller's daughter.* He swallowed and opened his mouth. "Pastor gave a nice service."

"*Ja.* I've not seen you at morning prayers before. Were you a good friend of the young fever victim?"

"*Ja. Freund.* Close as brothers." The half-truth slipped easily into the mild air. He realized the man in front of him extended protection to the grieving daughter. Moistening his lips, he offered a hand. *Careful, I must use correct name.* "My name is Hans Hoffmann. I journey to St. Louis."

"Alfred Meyer." The muscular man gripped Han's hand brief, but firm. "My wife and I travel to the same city. My brother is established in the carpentry trade and writes well of the *Deutsch* community in Missouri."

Hans kept a pleasant, small curve to his mouth. St. Louis must be a very important place. According to overheard conversations, half the passengers on *The Flying Gull* planned to continue the journey from New Orleans up a large river to the Missouri city. *I must learn accurate information.* Rumors and tall tales overheard in Westphalian taverns are not enough. "Carpenter is a good trade. I wish you well."

Alfred studied Hans for a long moment.

Does he expect me to share a trade or skill? Herr Meyer does not appear to be the sort of man who would react kindly to the profession of thief. Hans pressed tight his lips before giving a tiny nod and stepping away.

A few moments later, Hans sat on the deck in a secluded place between the masts. He turned his thoughts to his new life. *I am an honest man. How best to learn facts about America? Ah*—he snapped his fingers—*Herr* Schutte's lectures. In the two sessions he'd attended, the English lessons proved difficult. But the stories of villagers, rivermen, and farmers, based on living two years among Americans in Ohio, were interesting and prompted memories of geography lessons.

With a plan for the immediate future in place, Hans went below. Several paces from the ladder, he turned to the side to allow a woman to pass in the narrow corridor.

"Young man." She halted mere inches away before adjusting the bundle of bedding in her arms.

"*Frau.*" He removed his cap and stood still. The note of command in her voice and a maze of fine facial lines indicated a woman a generation older and worthy of respect. *Did she know of his past life? Did she go to report him to the captain?* He steadied his breathing and stayed aware of every drop of sweat bathing his neck.

"A word of advice. You do well to pay attention to Widow Krause."

"I listen."

She tipped her head and stared into his face. "Dead man your friend?" She waited for his nod. "Take blanket from the sick bed and hang it in the sunshine. Give bedding a good beating, like your mother give carpet in the spring. Get the sickness out. *Verstechen?*"

"*Ja.* I understand."

"*Gute.*" The widow resumed walking toward the ladder to the main deck.

Hans stared after her. The advice made sense. A little sunlight and fresh air on the blanket before he claimed the bedding would banish some of the foul smell. He turned toward the men's quarters, wondering if simple sunlight would rid his mind of guilt from past sins. "No harm to follow the widow's advice." Stripping the bedding from the dead man's bunk, he followed the older woman's suggestion. He curved his lips into a brief smile. *Perhaps I see Fraulein—if she does similar task.*

He recalled her appearance from this morning's service. She stood small, delicate, and sad. Near the end of the service, the instant she raised her face during the final hymn, her eyes rivaled the sky for pure blue. He had sensed courage vibrating from the tilt of her chin. Her pert nose resided the perfect distance from inviting lips. Yes, without doubt, *Fraulein* Mueller was the prettiest woman on *The Flying Gull. Will she do me the pleasure to make acquaintance with Hans Hoffmann, an honest man?*

Chapter Four

Three mornings later, Louisa climbed from below decks and squinted at the bright, tropical sun. Dipping her head, she positioned her bonnet brim to block the majority of the sudden glare. A moment later, still blinking, she stepped to the side and observed the early morning activities.

Crew members coiled ropes and moved barrels among clusters of passengers. A shout punctuated the air from the group of gamblers and their audience behind the windlass.

Stepping off the ladder, Bertha panted. "I have entered bright summer."

"*Ja.* Today is warm like July—in late February." Louisa tipped her head and looked at the sails. The two large, square panels unfurled from the horizontal spars hung limp. "We have stopped."

"I thought something was amiss. I stumbled getting out of the bunk." Bertha led the way past knots of passengers to an empty place on the rail.

Louisa stared at the water. The ocean lay flat all the way to the horizon. The scene reminded her of the pond at the flour mill—but today's view was a hundred, no, thousands of times larger. *Does the still water extend all the way to America?* "What has happened?"

A crew member paused with buckets of sea water. "We are becalmed, ma'am."

She stilled as completely as the water surrounding the ship and puzzled the seaman's reply. Her life in a village beside a river did not acquaint her with nautical terms. "What does 'becalmed' mean?"

"We travel at the mercy of the wind."

She nodded understanding. "How long?"

Setting one wooden pail on the deck, he gestured toward the main mast. "No way to tell the length of the delay. Two years ago, I crewed on a voyage to Cuba. We didn't have a hint of a breeze for a week."

"An entire week?" Louisa swallowed a lump of swelling panic. Papa calculated their food supply to last for the typical span of sixty days plus a few. Only three days out of port, the ship encountered a storm and a delay of two days. If the wind did not return for a week, her food supply would run dangerously low. *Only one.* She exhaled. Her bag contained plenty of food. Sharing with the less fortunate would be the proper thing to do. Perhaps she would speak with one of the mothers with small children. A few slivers of ham and hard crackers each day would be appreciated.

Bertha cleared her throat. "I will add a prayer for a fair wind to my other concerns."

"As will I." She watched the sailor lift his burden and continue toward the ship's stern.

"Two days without a death among the passengers." Bertha pulled a stained handkerchief into view and wiped sweat from her face.

"*Gute.*" Louisa set a fist on her chest and rubbed at the pain left by Papa's death four days ago. Turning away from the rail, she studied her fellow passengers. Soon she recognized a tall, gaunt figure.

Wearing a stovepipe hat and green coat, the man

talked in the midst of half a dozen male passengers.

"*Herr* Schutte is on deck. I go now to speak with him."

Bertha walked beside her across the quiet deck toward the group.

Louisa drew a deep breath, called it courage, and halted two steps from the teacher. "*Herr* Professor Schutte, may I have a word?"

Doffing his hat, the man made a half bow. "*Guten Morgan, Fraulein.* You flatter me. I am a mere schoolteacher, not a professor."

"Forgive me. I am *Fraulein* Mueller, daughter of Dietrich, late of Hamm on the River Lippe."

"*Ja. Ja.*" His black, trimmed beard exaggerated the movement of his jaw. "I give you sympathy at the death of your father. He spoke well of you."

"*Danke.*" She stiffened her back and lifted her gaze from her hands to his face. *Remember the promise.* Moistening her lips, she opened her mouth before her courage fled. "It is not your sympathy which I seek. I wish to attend your lectures and English lessons. Papa…Papa brought back the new words each day, and we practiced together. Eight days since he…attended. I will not be far behind the others."

"I do not teach *Fraus und Frauleins*. Tending the home and raising obedient children does not require English."

"In America, they say all are equal." Louisa squeezed her hands so tight they ached. Ignoring the murmurs from the other men, she stared at the teacher's hat brim. *Papa…I must honor his deathbed request. Learn English. Become American.* She studied the teacher's lean face and reviewed the practical reasons for learning the new language. *Sell bread and cake to all—not only immigrant. Honor Papa's memory. Earn respect of my new neighbors.* Lifting her gaze to the cloudless sky, she imagined her name painted on a bakery window.

"Men do the business," *Herr* Schutte snapped.

"*Bitte.* I will not make a fuss in your class. I will be quiet as a cat and lap up your lessons like they were drops of sweet cream."

"I ask you to leave." He retreated a step and turned to his male companions.

Louisa breathed deeply and held her head high. "You have a bride, *Herr* Schutte. In the future, you might have a daughter."

He turned his face and peered from his ten-inch height advantage. "What does it matter to you?"

Grasping the knot of her shawl, she steadied her gaze on his face. "Would you deny wife or daughter the opportunity to keep a promise to the dying?"

He faced her full-on and wagged one finger. "I will not have you disrupt my class."

"*Nein.* I come to learn. I will join you in the small storeroom. I listen to the ship's bells. I will arrive when they chime four times." She held his gaze and bent her knees in a shallow, brief curtsey.

Moments later, returning to the rail, Bertha faced her. "What sort of trouble are you starting?"

"I'm keeping a deathbed promise. Since the day Papa came home with our passport, he talked of learning English to better sell baked goods to both Americans and immigrants. Mere hours before his final breath, he again requested I learn English. I invite you and Alfred to join me at the lessons."

"*Nein.* I have no need to learn English. Alfred's brother writes that *Deutsch*, much the same dialect spoken in Hamm, is common in many St. Louis neighborhoods."

Louisa shook her head and tapped gloved fingers on the smooth wood rail. She belonged to a strong, proud family. If necessary, she would face the unknown of *Herr* Schutte's class alone. *Study English. Learn of America. Work hard. Run my own bakery.* She stared out across the smooth water and prayed for strength without tears.

****

Wiping a stained, grimy handkerchief across his sweaty brow, Hans sighed. The tropics in February were hotter than Westphalia in August. He tipped his head and studied the running rigging. Sails and ropes hung limp in the still air. Listening, he heard none of the usual snaps, creaks, and groans from the spars high above the deck. Today the only sounds were shouts among the crew, conversations between passengers, and the rare scrape or bump of a bucket or tool. He closed his eyes and thought back to a year ago.

Last February, he had toiled in a stable. His duties involved long hours of hard, dirty work and little pay. But sleeping in the dry and warm quarters in the crowded loft above the animals contained little pleasures. *Contented horses make pleasant noise.* Every night he visited the tavern for supper and information. While other men drank and talked, Hans listened. He paid special attention to mentions of stored valuables, fierce dogs, and vacant houses.

Once or twice a week, when he felt confident in information dropped by others, he left the tavern early.

On those evenings, he picked a lock on an empty residence and filled his pockets with silver *Thalers,* jewelry, and small household items. By spring, he carried a heavy sack on his back. During his two-day journey to Essen, he refined a plan in his brain.

In the city, he sold the assortment of valuables and hired the forger. The day the fake passport was in his pocket, he left Essen. During the summer months, he continued to add to his pockets with honest labor supplemented by theft. Every week or two he moved, always closer to the great port of Bremerhaven. By the time he arrived in the busy city, he carried shaving equipment, an additional shirt, and a fine wool waistcoat in a newly acquired valise. Distributed among his various pockets, he had held enough *Thalers* to purchase a ticket to America.

Opening his eyes, he gazed out at the still water and the setting sun. With one hand, he patted the pocket containing his new passport. *My name is Hans Hoffmann. In America, I will be an honest man.* He lowered his gaze to worn leather shoes. In order to draw little attention, he'd not taken the other man's better shoes or coat.

The ship's captain kept the forged papers now.

He had personally handed them to the man at the time he reported poor Ulrich's death.

"Stop your thinking, Hans."

He startled and shook off Max's touch on his shoulder. "What would you have me do? Can I not spend a little time pondering at miles and miles of quiet water?"

"The gamblers are entertaining."

Hans considered his friend. Max and his younger

brother were aware of the identity change. For a few of the *Thalers* tucked deep in the red-and-black chest, they had promised to keep the secret. "Dice tend to roll wrong more than right. I don't have extra money to lose."

Max laughed. "I came to fetch you for *Herr* Schutte's lecture. I heard, on good authority, tonight's topics include California. I want to learn more of this place where gold nuggets lay in the streams."

"Rumors." Hans released the rail and stretched the stiffness out of his muscles. Several times in the past year he'd heard stories of gold without work in the American west. But men like *Herr* Schutte, who returned to Westphalia to marry or encourage others to emigrate, did not appear to be wealthy.

Max shrugged. "Texas—Missouri—California. Tonight, we ask *Herr* Schutte to show us the map again."

"*Ja.*" Hans wanted to study the great river on the map. If one of the towns before St. Louis looked pleasant, he might change his plans. By reading the letter tucked into the Bible, he learned the original Hans's brother lived in St. Louis. *If I go to the Missouri city, I must be careful to avoid any harness maker named Hoffmann.* He desired a place where he would not be noticed. *How long to learn proper use of the harness-making tools? Perhaps I will sell them and enter a different trade.* He smiled at his younger friend. "We go below and struggle with English again."

Hans counted the ship's bell while following Max to the passenger deck. *Three...four.* Within a few moments, he crossed the threshold of the storeroom. Two tallow candles burned in lanterns and a dozen men gathered among scattered barrels and crates. He found a place to rest one shoulder against a wall and breathed warm, still air.

"Good evening, gentlemen." *Herr* Schutte strode into the room and greeted them in English.

"Guten Abend, Herr Lehrer." The class greeted their teacher in unison.

"In English." *Herr* Schutte tapped a thin stick against a barrel's rim.

"Good evening, Mister Schutte." The voices stuttered and smeared over each other.

Herr Schutte rapped for their attention. "Again."

After the class spoke the proper words almost in unison, *Herr* Schutte slashed his stick in the air like a music conductor. "Better—tell me what day of the week today is."

Hans pressed his lips. *One day is like another aboard ship.*

The man beside him grumbled.

"Montag?" Max tipped his face to gaze at the floor.

"Today is Monday, the four and twenty day of February." Louisa followed her voice into the room.

Lifting one hand, Hans hid his smile. He studied her slender, straight back as she took a position in the front row. Taking advantage of the long silence, he memorized her appearance. He skipped a breath. *No bonnet or shawl.*

Louisa adjusted her arms, sending a slight movement to her shoulder. Light hair, in a smooth, secure bun at the top of her neck, reflected light from the lanterns.

She has courage.

Herr Schutte cleared his throat. "Very good,

Fraulein."

"Miss—in English you may address me as Miss Mueller."

Every male student inhaled in unison. Not one word escaped from over a dozen pair of lips.

Hans stared and held his breath.

Herr Schutte opened his mouth, closed it without a sound, and positioned his hands behind his back.

Holding his lips still, Hans shifted his gaze between teacher and new pupil. The quiet air felt delicate as glass. Instinct warned him the wrong word at this moment would direct all of *Herr* Schutte's silent anger toward him.

One of the other men coughed.

Men shifted their feet against the wooden deck, as if waiting for permission to speak.

"*Ja.* We will continue." *Herr* Schutte shattered the tension and appeared to gather his wits. "Together we recite the days of the week."

Hans replied with the group. Soon he recalled words from previous lessons and answered with a confident "Friday" to the question of which day came after Thursday.

After the entire class replied with the correct month to three questions in a row, *Herr* Schutte rapped his stick. "Good. Good. Raise your hand if you've heard stories of gold in California."

Sighing relief at familiar *Deutsch* words, Hans, like everyone near him, lifted one arm. He glanced at Max and his brother. *Eager gazes on both of them. A stranger might think California was a magic word.*

Herr Schutte unrolled a large map, pulled a pair of clothespins from a pocket, and pegged the sturdy paper to a thin rope strung between two hooks. "America is a large land. Travel is slow and difficult in many places. The ship will dock here, at New Orleans." He touched the end of his stick to a spot near the bottom of the map. "California is here." He moved the pointer to the left side. "How many in this room know the distance from Essen to Bremerhaven?"

"*Ja.*" Hans joined a soft chorus and nodded. He remembered walking, or begging a ride on a cart, between many villages on the route to the port.

"You can replace the days of your *Deutsch* journey with weeks in America. The West"—he traced a large circle—"contains many hazards. People travel in groups of wagons and leave in the spring. The great distance, and frequent difficulties along the route, delay arrival in the gold fields until the first heavy snows threaten to close the mountain passes."

Hans listened with one portion of his mind and continued to admire Louisa with the rest. At first glance, she appeared tiny and delicate. The longer she stood still and avoided turning her head, even the odd time a man called a question in rude language, the more he admired her courage and composure. *How does a young man become her friend?* He lacked experience with introductions and conversation with proper young women. He decided to be bold and considered phrases to begin an exchange. *Today—the moment class dismisses.*

After *Herr* Schutte removed the map, the men began to file out. Several students paused and gifted Louisa a respectful dip of the head and two fingers tapped to the brow.

Hans closed his eyes for a moment and hunted for

courage. *Hans Hoffmann is an honest man.*

Max poked him and pointed to the main deck.

Hans shook his head. He ignored the stifling air and stepped toward Louisa. "Welcome, *Fraulein* Mueller. Did you enjoy the lecture?"

"*Ja. Danke.*" She hid her hands in the folds of her skirt.

"May I be bold and ask you a question?" He waited for her slight nod. "Where are you going after we leave the ship in New Orleans?"

"I travel to join my cousin." She moistened her lips and shifted her gaze to the floor.

Polite conversation is difficult. He searched for proper phrases among the crude remarks common in the cheap taverns he frequented. "I-I would like to become acquainted. May I speak with you again?"

"A young boy, age five, died this afternoon. I will attend the burial and prayers in the morning." She tilted her chin and looked directly into his face. "If the weather is fair, my friend, Widow Krause, and I plan to take a walk after the service. Perhaps you would join us?"

"*Danke, Fraulein.* I anticipate our conversation with great pleasure." He touched his brow and gave her a half bow. Turning, he hurried along the passage to the ladder. Aware of a lightness to his feet, he scampered to the open deck and tropic evening. The prettiest *Fraulein* on the ship agreed to become acquainted. *Am I worthy of friendship with such a beautiful and intelligent young lady?*

Chapter Five

New Orleans, Louisiana, March 29, 1851

Hans perched the small, black traveling trunk on his shoulder and crossed to the ship's rail. An hour ago, *The Flying Gull* bumped against the New Orleans dock. The ship, secured by several thick ropes to stout posts, stood fast against the river current. The hatches to the lowest levels of the ship were open.

The crew, assisted by a few willing passengers, hoisted large traveling chests, stout barrels, and cargo crates out of the depths.

Reaching the rail, Hans set his burden on the deck and knelt on the smooth, painted wood. He wiped morning perspiration from his brow and studied the active scene. Voices called and sang between their ship and the shore. Men loaded and unloaded barrels of all sizes from carts and wagons. Giant bales of cotton waited outside a long, low shed.

He drew a deep breath and failed to identify more than a few of the scents swirling in the air. Yesterday, the ship followed the twisting channel through the delta heavy with marsh and mud smells. Today, river water competed with wood smoke and animal waste. Tipping his head toward the sky, he closed his eyes for a moment and concentrated. Yes, he smelled roasting meat. He swallowed the moisture in his mouth and willed his stomach to quiet. How many days since he'd tasted fresh pork or beef?

"*Guten Morgan.*" Max followed his words with a firm clasp on Hans's shoulder.

"A fine day, we set our feet on American soil before noontime." He glanced at the younger man. Max carried a familiar, scuffed valise. Until last evening, the bag belonged to Hans. But Max and his brother threatened to report the identity switch to the captain unless they received another payment. After some intense bargaining, Hans convinced the brothers the leather case was an ample price.

"New Orleans is large and noisy." Max set the luggage at his feet and placed his hands on the rail.

"*Ja.* Perhaps this Texas where you journey will be quieter."

"Our uncle wrote to us of a lively town. You should join us, Hans. You will find use for harness making and leather working tools on the frontier." Max touched the wooden chest with one brogan.

"*Nein.* I will try my luck in St. Louis." *Or Elm Ridge, Illinois. I do not believe Fraulein Mueller intended on telling me her exact destination.* Sealing his lips, Hans heated at the memory of yesterday's conversation with Louisa. Taking a cue from her, he continued to keep his actual plans secret from both Max and his younger brother. According to the map, Texas was several days journey from Illinois. But he did not want the brothers to find him months from now and demand more money. "I am eager to reach my new home. Unlike many, I will not stay long in this city."

Max's brother, Ben, squeezed his way to the rail on the other side of Hans. He pointed toward a draft animal on the levee. "What sort of beast is that?"

"Mule," *Herr* Schutte replied from his position four men away.

Hans stared at the team of long-eared animals. *Mule? I thought they were smaller—like a donkey.* He shook away the memory of animals pulling ore carts from the mine outside his home village. *One week was enough time working underground to last a lifetime.*

A deep steamboat whistle cut off all conversation.

A chorus of shriller whistles responded.

Hans turned and opened his mouth without emitting a sound.

A large boat with two tall metal chimneys spewing smoke and sparks moved past their docked ship. In a high cabin with windows on three sides, a man stood at a ship's wheel. Moving against the current, the steamship's full height came into view. Men moved with purpose on a deck no more than a few feet above the water. Two smaller decks, supported by slender posts, towered over the workers. The entire vessel shook in time to the belching engine. At the stern of the boat, a large, slatted drum churned the water into a wide wake.

Hans trembled. The noise was unlike any he'd encountered. The vibration from the boat assaulted his ears harder than the time he became trapped in a city clock tower at midnight. He fisted his hands and swallowed a clump of fear. An instant later, he detected determination rising from his toes. *I must board one.* Perhaps he could find a smaller steamboat, like one of the four tied to the levee, to take him north.

"They look important." Max pointed to a trio of men exiting a carriage.

The group, dressed in tall hats and bright coats, displayed an air of authority.

A moment later, the man carrying a slender case approached a ship's officer at the levee end of the wide boarding plank.

The other men carried a metal bound chest between them.

"*Ja.* I wonder if these are the men who decide if we can enter America?" Hans patted the pocket holding the passport with the genuine stamp. An hour later, Hans stepped in front of a table fashioned from a scarred board resting on two barrels. He handed his new passport, the one with the true stamp of the Westphalian eagle, to the man in the green coat.

"Name?"

"Johannas August Karl Hoffmann."

"Birthplace?"

"Arnsberg, on the River Ruhr." Hans conquered the urge to wipe nervous sweat from his brow. "I was born four and twenty, *nein,* five and twenty April 1830."

"Which date is it, young man?" The official steadied his gaze on Hans's face.

"Five and twenty—April—soon I be one and twenty years," he spoke the lie easily on the second try.

"Have you money?" The American waited for a nod, returned the passport, and pointed to the man with graying side whiskers. "See the banker if you wish American dollars."

Hans emptied silver *Thalers* out of his pockets and set them on the makeshift table.

The man counted out golden dollars and an assortment of smaller coins. "Welcome to America."

"*Danke. Danke.*" He gathered the unfamiliar money and distributed it between several pockets. A moment later, Hans strode across the deck, lifted the black trunk with the red horse head decoration, and continued to the gangway. Three steps across the levee, he paused. *Almost stumbled to my knees.* In the next instant, he adjusted his burden. America. *Hans Hoffmann, an honest man, will build a life worthy of the best dream.*

****

Turning a slow circle and peering toward the corners of the dim sleeping quarters, Louisa caught a whiff of tallow candle. Skimming her gaze in the semi-darkness, she noticed smoke from a recently guttered lantern. She tied her bonnet ribbons and lifted the canvas satchel containing a change of clothes, her toiletries, and the family Bible. For a long moment, she stared at the bunk where Papa died. She rubbed a tiny circle on her chest and remembered his final, labored breaths. Blinking, she banished sentimentality and turned toward the narrow passageway. *Auf Wiedersehen.*

A few moments later, Louisa emerged into bright New Orleans, late morning sunshine. A wave of new sounds and smells engulfed her. Lowering her face and blinking, she urged her eyes to adjust to the strong light. She gripped her satchel and walked to the levee side of the ship.

Gulls soared between the resting vessels and dived for food scraps on the cobbles. Dark men with short, black hair rolled barrels on and off low-decked steamboats expelling wisps of smoke. Patient draft animals hitched to wagons swished their tails. A man on a tiny boat lifted a basket of shellfish to his head before stepping to the levee. Wood smoke drifted across the scene like a familiar friend returned from a journey.

Louisa startled at a steamboat whistle. She set one hand against her chest in a futile effort to calm her heart. *America is noisy.* Moving her gaze closer to the ship, she realized a few of the passengers had disembarked.

Herr Schutte, in his distinctive tall hat and green coat, spoke and gestured with a wagon driver.

Is that...? Rising on her toes, she tried to keep sight of a man in a brown coat and flat cap carrying a small black trunk on his shoulder. *Hans?* A lump of sadness slid down her throat. *Will I see you again? America is so vast. I wish you well.* She lifted a hand to check for tears. Of all the passengers on *The Flying Gull,* Hans told the most interesting stories. At least half a dozen times, while she walked with either Bertha or Widow Krause, he entertained them with descriptions of residents of small villages. She sighed regret for the lost opportunity to bid him a proper farewell. *I must see to my own welfare. S*he turned and glanced at the long line of passengers holding hand luggage and small children.

The human string extended the width of the ship and curved toward the bow. Spotting her friends Alfred, Bertha, and Widow Krause near the end of the line, she tightened her hold on her satchel and marched toward them.

"Arriving in America is exciting." Bertha smoothed the wool cloak draped across her arm.

Louisa nodded to each of them. "*Ja.* Did you see all the people on the dock?"

"*Nein.* I have only heard the noise." Bertha moved a step forward. "Last night I dreamed of sleeping in a real bed."

"Sounds like a slice of heaven." Widow Krause pushed a large basket forward with one foot. "The first thing I plan, after we find a boardinghouse, is to wash my face with warm water and sweet soap."

Louisa smiled. "I want to eat a slice of rich bread with fresh jam. Since we entered the marsh, I've been looking at the flowering trees and getting hungry. The orchards at home do not bloom until May. Do you think we will find new berries in the markets?"

"The baker needs good, fresh bread." Widow Krause laughed.

Louisa widened her smile. Even her best friends did not need to know how many of her dreams on the ship were about the smells, sounds, and taste of bakery goods. She pointed to one of the birds perched on the ship's rail. "The gulls are brave." In due time, Louisa stood in front of the officials at the table. She handed over the single passport with the information for Papa and her. After a prompt, she recited her full baptismal name plus place and date of birth.

The man in a tight, green coat dipped a pen into ink and drew a single line through Dietrich's information before handing the paper back.

A short time later, Louisa stood with Bertha on the levee. *I stand in America—the land where dreams come true.* She moved one foot an inch to test the returning strength in her knees. *Solid ground. Weeks on the ship have confused my legs.*

Widow Krause talked with her married daughter on the other side of the trunks holding the bakery tools, household necessities, and the invisible memories of their European life.

Alfred and Widow Krause's son-in-law gestured with a Negro man in charge of a small wagon and a mule.

"*Deutsch Frau.*"

Louisa made out two familiar words from the driver's song-like speech. She paid attention to how many fingers Alfred displayed before pointing toward the baggage.

In a few minutes, the three men loaded the wagon.

Alfred fastened the tailgate. "*Gute. Gute. Alles an Bord.*"

The driver scampered over the front wheel and perched on the luggage. He gathered the reins and slapped them once. "Git up now!"

English? Louisa shook her head at the unfamiliar word...or words...she did not find a pause in the Negro man's phrase. She patted the pockets where her new American money rested. None of the words she heard from Americans this morning sounded like *Herr* Schutte's lessons. The speech around her swirled like people singing competing melodies. Stepping forward to follow the wagon, she felt one knee bend too much.

A few steps later, Louisa held her balance and followed the wagon beside the other women. She listened to Bertha and Widow Krause's daughter discuss the fine points of a good potato salad. She concentrated on the active city scene. Shouts, whistles, and animal neighs and brays attempted to overwhelm her ears. Food smells competed with river water for her nose's attention.

Two blocks from the levee, the wagon stopped.

Louisa stepped to the side for a view of the reason. Separating clinking chains from competing sounds, she shivered in the spring heat.

Six Negro men, naked except for trousers ending mid-calf, ran across the street.

Two white men on horseback followed close behind holding long whips.

Louisa stared after the group until they were out of sight. *I do not understand the need for whips and chains. Errand boys and servants work faster and harder with a little kindness.* The stories and letters which went to Westphalia spoke of opportunity. She straightened her spine and hurried to join the others. *I will work long and hard.* "Manners and kindness"—she murmured Papa's advice for treating bakery customers. She would practice steady, honest labor with drops of kindness to others. *I remember our dream, Papa. In this new land, I will make my own dream real.*

Chapter Six

Amid noise reminding Hans of men shouting political slogans over each other, he strode away from the New Orleans levee. He failed to find a single word from *Herr* Schutte's English lessons in any of the babble. The slightly softer words he overheard on the street confused him. *The language resembles neither English nor* Deutsch.

A mule brayed.

A bell tolled the hour.

Hans paused at an intersection, removed his flat, wool cap, and wiped his brow. Looking to his left, he spied a large, hipped-roof pavilion. *A market.* He drew a deep breath and savored the scent of roasting meat mixing with city smells of horse and dirt. Replacing his cap, he resolved not to think of food until he found lodging for the night. He adjusted the trunk on his shoulder and turned away from the market, following a street parallel to the river.

A few minutes later, Hans entered a small, quiet, hotel lobby. He glanced at plastered walls decorated with framed sketches of horses pulling fine carriages and steamboats spilling delicate streams of smoke. He stopped near the high counter, set the trunk at his feet, and addressed the clerk. "*Bitte.* Please. Room. One night."

"Aye." The clerk stood in slow motion from a

ladder-back chair at a small desk.

Hans turned his back to the generous window. *Hurry, man.* He called on all the patience he possessed to refrain from spilling an insult at the slender man in a limp, pale shirt and unbuttoned, black waistcoat. The sooner Hans was out of sight of the street, where other passengers from *The Flying Gull* could see him, the safer he would feel. He didn't want to share a room, or even a hotel, with Max or any of the others. Where he stayed, and when he left the city, would be his business—private business.

"Sign your name or make your mark." The clerk rotated a large register book.

Grasping a slender pen, he dipped the metal nib in the ink bottle. With only a heartbeat of hesitation, he wrote *Hans Hoffmann* in bold letters. *I am an honest man with a common name—nothing to fear.*

"Cash." The clerk rubbed a thumb across his fingers.

Hans pulled three small, gold coins from a pocket and displayed them on his palm. *"Ein Nacht."* He moistened his lips and found English words. "One night."

The clerk selected one coin and stepped away.

Waiting, Hans began to count the seconds. *A turtle crosses a road faster than this man of business moves.*

In due time, the clerk dropped two tiny silver coins and a key attached to an oval, metal fob in front of Hans. "Room four—up the stairs on your right."

Later, Hans gazed out the single, square window of his plain room.

A bricked courtyard lay below. A black pump, stone water trough, and a saddled horse hitched to a rail filled a large portion of the space.

He licked dry lips and thought of sweet, fresh water. Glancing around, he cataloged the objects in his room. The iron bed appeared generous at twice the width of the ship bunks. A cane-bottomed chair sat beside a washstand with chamber pot, basin, and pitcher.

Lifting the gray pottery ewer, Hans exited the room. He organized his limited English words and discovered *Herr* Schutte omitted many he wanted to use. After obtaining water, Hans set about the task of washing the sea voyage from his face, neck, and arms. While he shaved, steamboat whistles from a distance sounded a note of urgency. *Ja, ja. I have much to do.* His stomach rumbled. *I will find lunch at the market before I return to the levee and book my river passage north.*

He combed his hair and considered his options. Louisa travelled to Elm Ridge, Illinois. According to comments over the map two days ago, passengers continuing past St. Louis needed to change boats in the city. He could go ahead to the smaller Illinois town. *Louisa will be surprised to see me.* Or, he could stay in the larger city and avoid anyone named Hoffmann in the harness or leather trade. *Unless a town before St. Louis appeals to me.*

"No matter my decision, I will buy a ticket for St. Louis." He muttered plans for the immediate future and brushed a layer of dirt from his coat. Fishing the plain watch on a thick, silver chain from a pocket, he studied his final theft in Europe. *Foolish.* Shaking his head at his moment of weakness in the Bremerhaven tavern, he fastened the modest timepiece to his square-bottomed waistcoat. Turning toward the mirror above the washstand, he admired his reflection. *An honest man. A gentleman.* When his stomach rumbled again, he sighed. *Yesterday's soup on the ship contained no meat and few beans. The orange, small and tart, brought aboard during our brief stop in Cuba, was the best part of the meal.*

Wearing a shell of confidence over his mismatched clothes, he left the hotel and walked the few blocks to the market. The moment Hans stepped under the shelter of the market roof, large raindrops pelted the ground and made a noisy dance above his head. He glanced out the open sides and noticed little change in the tempo of the construction workers across the street. *Do Americans work through cloudbursts? Why don't they move quickly to put tools away?*

"You buy?" A buxom woman with gray curls escaping the edge of a calico bonnet pointed to baskets of carrots and turnips.

"*Nein.*" Hans gathered a few of his wits and English words before continuing. "No. Thank you." He walked farther into the market. Urged forward by the smell of spiced meat, he did not linger at baskets of familiar vegetables. His progress, uneven due to vendors calling customers to inspect produce and trinkets, remained aimed for the scent of an overdue meal. Pausing by a display of crooked, orange roots, he grasped one. He smiled at the small, Negro boy minding the booth. "What is this?"

"Yam—you want buy some?" The question emerged in one slow, continuous word from the lad.

Shaking his head, he dropped the root into a basket and reversed three steps. He felt his back bump against something large and solid.

"Look where you're going. Or get back on the boat. We've enough of your kind."

He snatched off his cap and turned to see a tall, sturdy man wearing a red-and-black waistcoat. A fine, braided, gold watch chain draped in a gentle curve. With a half bow, Hans started to apologize, realized he babbled *Deutsch,* and closed his lips. *The thief within me covets the chain and watch.* He swallowed. *Hans is an honest man.* Clutching his cap until his knuckles turned white, he found càlm words. "Sorry...so sorry...it will not happen again."

Hurrying away before the larger man could respond, Hans soon arrived in front of a stall where a hog shank roasted over a low fire.

The muscular man in charge of the booth rotated the spit a quarter turn and secured the handle in a notch. Fat droplets hissed against the heat of the fire, competing with the tapering drum of rain on the roof.

The smoke tempted Hans's mouth with a delicious, spicy, sweet aroma. He swallowed before any drool escaped.

Lifting a large knife, the vendor cut three long, narrow strips of meat into a shallow tin dish. With a smile, the man handed the plate to a customer.

"I want the same." Hans pointed first to the customer, then the meat, and finally to himself.

"Two bits," the merchant replied.

Bits? Hans reviewed the only lesson where *Herr* Schutte talked about American money. He understood a dollar was large, important, and similar to a *Thaler.* The caution not to lose the small dimes and half dimes returned to his mind. No mention of *bit* sounded familiar. Perhaps the man would be patient with him. He dipped his fingers into a pocket to retrieve the change from the hotel room.

Where is? He glanced to his waistcoat and discovered his silver chain and plain watch gone. He glanced at the vendor for an instant before he turned to look toward the wide aisle between the booths.

The thief, good at his trade, had vanished in the busy market.

****

Louisa stood in the street outside the boardinghouse and fingered her light shawl's knot. Two hours ago, she and five others from *The Flying Gull* rented rooms from the Prussian landlady. Now, standing in light, tapering rain, the group discussed where to find a hot meal. She straightened her spine until she stood her full height, exactly five feet, and faced Alfred. "*Ja.* I am sure Widow Krause and I will stay safe. The market is only a short distance."

"I think it would be better to all stay together. According to the landlady, we can eat where they speak *Deutsch* only a short walk in this direction." Alfred pointed away from the market.

Widow Krause poked a finger against her son-in-law's chest. "We will not get lost. You go your way. But I'm not going to stand out in the rain any longer."

"See you before sunset." Louisa turned away from the two couples and linked arms with the older woman.

"I hope you brought extra courage. I think I used my daily ration bargaining for the rooms and giving the married couples a little time alone." The widow guided them out of a rider's path.

Louisa smiled at the older woman. Widow Krause

showed plenty of independence from her daughter and son-in-law. Three days after Louisa started to attend *Herr* Schutte's lessons, the widow joined the class and demonstrated a sharp mind. During walks together on the deck, they held lively conversations about cooking, housekeeping, and observations of their fellow passengers. Louisa could imagine the widow being an outspoken matriarch. "I sewed a thimble of bravery into my pocket while we were at the boardinghouse."

"Ah. We are ready for adventure then."

The rain stopped a moment before they stepped under the market's protective roof.

Louisa paused at the first booth and shook the last raindrops off her shawl. Her winter capote felt heavy and hot in the New Orleans spring. *I will buy a summer bonnet before we leave the city.* She nodded and smiled at the woman selling long carrots and fat turnips from baskets. "Today we see what an American market is like."

"*Ja*... listen." Widow Krause extended one finger and tilted her head.

Holding her breath, Louisa paid attention to the words surging in the air. The pulse reminded her of musicians singing a complicated round. She caught one or two English words which soon vanished into the stew of noise. *French?* She surveyed the crowd and marveled. The patrons and vendors varied in size, shape, and dress, in addition to skin tone.

A plump white woman carrying a fringed parasol strode past. The lady's wide, blue, three-tiered skirt demanded room enough for two more slender skirts.

A slight, Negro girl, with a basket of produce on each arm, trailed behind the elegant woman.

"Look. Buy."

Louisa swung her attention to the saleslady.

Straw bonnets trimmed with bright ribbons filled the table. Pairs of thin, white summer gloves decorated with delicate, colored bows lay scattered between the capotes. "Beautiful." *I will not purchase the first bonnet I see—I want a fair price.* She touched a wide, sky-blue ribbon. "How much?"

"Three dollar." The young clerk displayed an equal number of fingers.

If a dollar almost equals a Thaler… Louisa hesitated and scrambled for English words. "Too much. Not today."

"Come." Widow Krause touched her elbow. "I want to follow the scent of warm, spicy food. I think the cooking is only a few stalls farther."

Louisa followed past three more booths. "*Halten.*" She gained Widow Krause's attention. "Have you seen such a thing before?" She peered at bags of tan objects the size of her little finger. Reaching, she tested the texture. "These feel a bit like coarse paper." She lifted her gaze to the American selling the goods and arranged her best English words. "What is this?"

"Goobers, ma'am. Best o' last year's crop." He touched his wide-brimmed straw hat.

"Goo…?" She stalled her lips forming the unfamiliar word.

"Goobers—some folks call them peanuts." He picked one from the sack and pressed an almost invisible seam. The thin shell popped apart and revealed two small nuts. "Taste."

Louisa lifted one of the treats with two gloved fingers. Popping the kernel into her mouth, she chewed and smiled. "*Ja. Gute.* Crunchy and sweet." She swallowed. Using a mixture of languages, plus pantomime, she addressed the American. "Good. Less hard than hazelnut. I buy handful."

Half a dozen booths and two strained conversations in English, *Deutsch*, and gestures later, Louisa paused by three round tables and seven cane chairs positioned between two vendors.

A customer carried a ceramic bowl of steaming food topped with a piece of bread away from a counter.

"Hot food, do you want to try?"

"*Ja.*" Widow Krause pointed across the wide aisle. "I see a tea shop."

A moment later, Louisa stood at a simple counter and pointed to the bowl of food purchased by another patron. "I want." She displayed two fingers—"*zwei.*" The steaming stew pleased her nose. She pressed a hand against her waist when her stomach rumbled with anticipation. Slipping one hand into a pocket, she fingered several coins. "How much?"

"Hav' dolla', Miss."

She puzzled over the reply. *One word? Or more?* She displayed one small, gold coin. "This much?"

The thin, Negro woman wiped the back of her hand across her brow and looked at the coin. "Dat too much." She lifted two empty bowls and turned to the bubbling kettles. "Jake."

The man, tending the fire, jerked his attention toward Louisa and nodded.

Louisa watched the woman put a portion of rice and a ladle of stew in each bowl before cutting a thick slice of bread for the top. A moment later, she warmed under the man's inspection.

He ambled to the other side of the narrow counter and looked at the coin in her hand. "How many?"

"*Zwei*...two."

Jake opened a metal cash box and exchanged her golden dollar for five tiny silver coins. He remained still, moving his gaze over Louisa, until the cook set the full dishes on the counter. "*Deutsch*?"

"*Ja.*" Louisa felt her cheeks heat.

He pointed to a tub at the end of the counter before addressing her in broken *Deutsch*. "Dish go there when you're done. Molly is good cook. Not good making change."

"Thank you." She tucked the small coins deep into her pocket. Widening her smile, she touched her nose. "Food smell good."

Jake smiled wide enough to display two missing teeth.

She lifted the bowls, turned, and spied Widow Krause setting a round teapot and two china cups on one of the tables. Stepping carefully to avoid an overturned chair, she joined her friend and placed the meals on the flat surface. "It would be more useful if *Herr* Schutte taught more about American money and less time naming the parts of the ship."

"The schoolmaster's lessons are all past. We learn quickly in a market." Widow Krause nibbled on the thick, golden bread crust. "*Gute.* What does the baker say?"

Louisa looked carefully at the texture of the bread before pulling off a small piece. She popped the morsel into her mouth and chewed. The simple flavors of wheat, lard, and salt blossomed. "Nice—"

"*Guten Abend, Frau und Fraulein.*"

Louisa turned her head toward the familiar voice. "*Herr* Hoffmann, this is a pleasant surprise. Have you eaten?" Aware her heart skipped in gladness at the sight of her friend, she touched one hand to her chest. *God gives me opportunity to bid my friend a proper farewell and good travel for the rest of his journey.* "Have you found lodging?"

Hans nodded and fingered his cap in his hands. "A few strips of fresh, roasted meat cheered my stomach. Tonight, I will sleep in a real bed." He continued to rotate his flat, wool hat and aim his gaze among the shoppers. "I give you, my friends, a word of warning."

Straightening her spine, Louisa prepared to remember every word. "What sort of warning?"

He lifted his chin and turned his head, looking again among the crowd in the center aisle. In the next moment, he focused on her. He cleared his throat. "Thieves and pickpockets roam this market."

"Oh, my." Widow Krause released her hand from the teapot. "Have you been robbed?"

"A minor encounter. I advise you to stay on your guard." He glanced over his shoulder.

Louisa moved one hand across her skirt. Skimming fingers above her pocket's opening, she patted the fabric until she touched the thickness of the second set of cloth pouches under her petticoat. She gave silent thanks for taking a few minutes at the boardinghouse to sew the majority of her funds, plus the precious passport and church papers, into the hiding place. "*Danke.* We will be careful. Will you?"

"I must go." Hans replaced his cap on shaggy, mahogany hair and hurried off into the throng.

"*Herr* Hoffmann is an unusual young man."

Widow Krause poured tea.

Louisa stared into the crowd. Within two blinks, she lost sight of him. "Alfred does not trust him."

"And you? Do you trust him?" The widow leaned close.

She pursed her lips to delay an answer. When she looked into his face, she saw a friend. At other times, observing him with others, he appeared a stranger. "I do not know if I trust him." She shrugged and lifted her spoon. "He tells interesting stories."

Chapter Seven

St. Louis, Missouri, April 19, 1851

Hans held firm to the bridle straps and watched the experienced teamster's hands.

A shout, followed by the thump of hammer against hot iron from the adjacent blacksmith, slipped into the spring morning's clamor.

The older man unwrapped the reins from the brake handle. Raising his left hand, he signaled the stable hand.

Stepping away from the harnessed team, Hans exhaled satisfaction. All of Mr. Covington's freight wagons were now on St. Louis streets. After a glance in each direction, he walked to the corner of the building and scanned the area again. *Gute. My ill-tempered American boss is not in sight.* Staying in the narrow alleys between the warehouses, stables, and blacksmith shops, Hans hurried toward the levee's northern edge.

A steamboat whistle punctuated the sounds of horses pulling wagons on cobbled streets and workmen calling to each other. A chorus of bells and shrill whistles replied.

Farewell and welcome. Morning and evening, the city focuses on the riverfront. When he reached a vantage point outside a small, frame building, Hans paused. Staring toward the levee, he focused on the boat at the end of the line.

A short, double-decked packet churned the water and backed into the river's main current.

Going north—to Iowa—with a stop in Elm Ridge, Illinois. Is Louisa a passenger today? After knocking bits of hay from this morning's work off his patched canvas trousers, he straightened and opened the plain door. Inside the office of Upper Mississippi Passenger and Freight Service, he encountered a stout clerk behind a rough-hewn counter. A large board listed towns, days, and prices. "*Guten...* Good morning. The boat"—he pointed in the general direction of the river. *I must find English words.* "Stop Elm Ridge?"

"Next packet's due to leave tomorrow. Do you want to buy a ticket?"

Hans shook his head. Clearing his throat, he repeated the same question from yesterday and the day before. "On boat today...*Fraulein*? This tall"—he held his hand close to even with his chin—"blue cloak, dark bonnet."

"Not today."

The stone of uncertainty deep inside his gut grew heavier. *How long did Louisa stay in New Orleans? What if she decided to remain in the southern city? Did she become sick from one of the fevers? Did she travel on the steamboat which exploded and burned three days ago south of Jefferson Barracks?* He forced his gaze away from the floor to the clerk's face. "*Danke.*"

Leaving the steamboat office, Hans sprinted toward the stables. Passing a log-and-stone warehouse, he slowed. He switched his attention to preparing a plausible story if he encountered Mr. Covington. The American stablemaster expected him to be cleaning stalls instead of running a private errand. *How do I explain the importance—to know Louisa is safe?*

"Got you." A strong hand wrapped Hans's upper arm. "Worthless, lazy *Deutsch*."

Hans attempted another step toward the stable, but Mr. Covington held fast. "I-I step away for a minute. A word with...blacksmith." He gestured with his free hand. "Teams all hitched and gone."

"Liar—no errand."

Hans looked at the cobbles and his worn, leather shoes. "I never lie to you again."

Mr. Covington pushed him away.

Struggling to stay on his feet, Hans swung his arms like a confused windmill.

"Stay away. No job. Never want to see your lazy, lying *Deutsch* face again."

Hans stood to recover his breath. Snatching his cap from the street, he gazed at the back of his boss, former boss, striding toward the stable door. *My trunk.* All of his earthly possessions, except for what he carried in his pockets, were in the stable's loft. He blinked at the memory of rolling his coat, with precious documents and money, in the thin blanket and storing the objects in a corner before sunrise. He sighed and settled his cap on his head. *Tonight. I return and claim what is mine.*

Half an hour later, Hans talked the foreman at a construction site into hiring him to carry brick. The cost of tomorrow's ticket to Elm Ridge would almost empty his pockets. *Land of opportunity.* He spat on the ground. *I am in same position, in an unfamiliar place, as three years ago—the summer I became a thief.* He followed another worker toward the new building's rear wall. *Hans Hoffman is an honest man—and poor.*

After collecting wages for the day's work, Hans refused an invitation to join two other laborers at the corner tavern. He slipped through alleys toward the levee. Perched on an empty wagon outside a warehouse, he waited for the sun to send the last light of the day over the city. He enjoyed a good view of the levee and counted resting steamboats. *Three and twenty tonight.* He focused on a large vessel.

Fading smoke from two tall, metal chimneys indicated a recent arrival. Giant, red letters below the pilot's quarters identified the vessel as *The Jupiter*. Three men, singing a bawdy drinking song, departed the steamboat.

Hans relaxed against the wagon's sideboard and listened to the cathedral bells call the faithful to prayer.

A nearby tavern door opened and added scents of beer and cooked meat to the calm air.

Urging his stomach to ignore the food's temptation, he peered toward Covington's Freight Service.

A driver, distinctive by his battered tricorne, exited the building and pulled the large door closed.

Hans nodded. *Gute, gute. The old man only latches the door.* Settling in to wait, he planned every step to give the least disturbance to the animals. A full hour later, after the moon rose above the trees across the river, Hans slipped from one shadow to the next. Reaching the stable, he paused for a long moment with his back against the unpainted boards and listened.

The familiar sounds of horses snorting and snuffling after a day's work seeped through the walls. No human voices disturbed the peaceful scene.

Careful not to startle the animals, Hans raised the

latch and opened the tall door enough to slide through. He moved slow and careful to the bottom of the ladder. Climbing three rungs, he risked a hoarse whisper. "Walter?"

"*Ja.*" The other stable hand, a short, young man from Saxony, peered over the edge. "Come—it's safe—for the moment."

Hans crawled across a thin layer of hay to the corner where the two employees shared sleeping quarters. Shifting into a cross-legged position, he faced his former co-worker. "I am sorry you had to do all the work today."

"Mr. Covington stayed angry for hours. I hurried the stall cleaning and avoided him." Walter glanced toward the top of the ladder.

Creeping toward the corner, Hans pulled his bedroll from the shadows and felt for his trunk. "*Mein Koffer.* Did you hide it?"

"*Nein.* Mr. Covington—this afternoon—while I put hay in the stalls—climbed to the loft and claimed it."

Hans's internal, invisible stone threatened to overwhelm him. *The tools—I planned to sell them.* Closing his eyes for a moment, he calculated how long he could have paid living expenses after selling them in Elm Ridge–or another town along the river. Searching his coat pockets, he sighed. The familiar shape of a pipe and tobacco pouch offered a little hope. "Is it all gone?"

Walter shook his head and wriggled over to a broken barrel. Reaching behind the busted staves, he retrieved a rough cloth bag tied with a thin rope. "I saved a little."

"*Danke.* You are a true friend." He clasped hands with Walter, grasped the sack, and took two steps toward the ladder.

The horses stirred.

A door creaked on tired hinges.

"Good evening, my beauties." Mr. Covington's voice drifted to the loft. "Lady Luck favored me at cards tonight. I've brought you a new companion. Yes, Caesar"—he addressed the only stallion. "She is a sturdy black mare. Now don't go snorting and showing bad manners. You'll have plenty of time to get well acquainted."

A thump of horse hoof against stall preceded a loud neigh.

"Walter," Mr. Covington bellowed.

"I'm here, boss." Walter scampered across the loft and down the ladder.

"Her name is Misty. Get her settled in the box stall at the end and stay with her. I'll spend the night in the office."

"Yes, boss. I be gentle with her."

Hans stared at the ladder, the only exit from the loft. The horses, all restless at the moment, would cover the sound of his escape. But the angry American remained close. He dared not risk being seen. *Snared.* He shivered and remembered an old fur trader in the tavern spinning tales of beavers and traps.

****

The afternoon sun floated low above the bluff by the time *The Jupiter's* crew tossed the lines to the eager hands at the St. Louis levee. The great engine faded to a whisper, and the captain clanged the bell to signal their arrival.

Louisa stood beside Bertha and wrinkled her nose at the sharp scent of fresh horse dung. An instant later, she moved her gaze from left to right and memorized her first impressions of the city.

The levee, by far the largest since Memphis, four days ago, slanted upward to a street of warehouses and other low buildings. Higher on the bluff, church steeples and a smooth dome marked important buildings.

She turned to the carpenter's wife. "Your new home is lively."

"*Ja.* Busy—much noise—and construction." Bertha pointed toward two lumber wagons. "Good business for Alfred and his brother, Heinrich." She lifted her tapestry satchel from the deck. "We follow my husband and listen while he bargains for a wagon to carry our trunks."

Turning toward the stern, Louisa waved farewell to an American woman, Suzanne.

Patient and generous, the fellow passenger taught English words to several of the immigrant women.

Kind. Under her breath, Louisa repeated the phrases required to buy a ticket to Elm Ridge. A short time later, she walked beside a wagon to the main portion of the city.

The teamster, speaking a mixture of *Deutsch* and English, pointed out churches, hotels, and the courthouse, notable with a smooth dome. Dozens of carts, buggies, and riders filled the streets while workmen, and a few women, hurried on narrow sidewalks.

"Here we be." The driver pulled the Percherons to a halt in front of a two-story, frame house with a wide, black door.

Louisa loitered beside the team while Alfred and

Bertha hurried forward.

In a moment, a robust man with fair hair and wide smile similar to Alfred's stepped out and engulfed the young carpenter in a hearty hug. "And this be your bride? Greta—*kommen,*" the stranger called into the house.

"Bertha." The rest of Alfred's words were lost under a woman's squeal of delight.

"Who is this?" Heinrich, with his hand on Alfred's shoulder, paused at the wagon and stared at Louisa.

Pulling her lips into a smile, she stepped forward and stated her name. "I'm the baker's daughter from Hamm. *Mein Vater*"—she glanced toward Alfred and cut the explanation short. "May I impose for a night's lodging before I resume my journey?"

"Friend? Travel from Hamm with my brother? Come inside. Soon we serve fine meal. My Greta will show you our spacious house." He lifted Louisa's right hand and pressed a quick kiss to the back of her new summer glove.

Louisa sealed her lips and remained calm during the extra moment he held her fingers. Using manners practiced with bakery customers, she held her mouth in a gentle curve. *I mix caution with manners in this house.* "*Danke.* From deep within my heart."

After a supper of a hearty beef-and-barley soup, dark rye bread, and simmered peaches, Louisa and the two couples settled into an evening filled with tales of the journey and the new construction in the city. Sensing a kindred spirit in Greta, Louisa drew her into quiet conversation and asked questions of the neighborhood she had glimpsed before entering the home.

"Ack. The hour grows late. Morn will come, and I will show you more things in daylight." Heinrich stood from the upholstered chair.

Several hours later, used to the rhythm of bakery life and rising early, Louisa left her cot in the kitchen and quickly dressed. Fastening the final button at the top of her dress, she stepped into the yard.

The first hint of dawn showed in the eastern sky. Horses and pigs snorted morning greetings to humans entering the sheds dotting the neighborhood. Three roosters competed for the loudest morning voice. The city emerged from the night and faced a new day.

She paused to regard the house of Heinrich Meyer, Alfred's brother.

The building exhibited generous proportions. Three windows faced the yard on the upper story and two from the lower. The gentle slant of the roof on the one-story kitchen portion softened the harsh line created by the second story.

She tipped her face to study the fading stars and hint of high clouds. *I have a fine day to start the next portion of my journey.* Returning to the kitchen, Louisa stirred the fire and added two pieces of wood. After ladling water into the coffeepot, she set the container on the stove. Determined to be a helpful guest, she gathered the coffee mill and tin of roasted beans from the shelf.

"*Guten Morgan,* Louisa."

She glanced toward her host. "*Guten Morgan, Herr* Meyer."

"*Bitte*—call me Heinrich. We are in America and you are my friend."

Nodding, she held questions inside. During the

several hours she'd known him, the elder Meyer brother gave the impression of a man generous with his affection. Like many men, he appeared accustomed to giving orders. The many small pauses in his speech, as if discarding the first word which came to mind, hinted he spent much time in the company of rough, ill-mannered workers.

Continuing to struggle with the tight lid on the coffee beans, she skimmed her gaze over her host. *The room, or I, has warmed since he arrived.* "I am a grateful guest. Your cot in the kitchen corner gave me the best night's sleep since New Orleans."

"Let me help you." He stepped behind her and reached for the tin.

Too close. When his chest brushed her back, Louisa held her breath. She leaned toward the table and yielded the coffee container.

In an instant, he popped off the lid with his strong fingers.

"*Danke.*" She reclaimed the beans and set the tin beside the coffee mill.

"Now for my reward." He set his hands on her hips and leaned in close. "A kiss from the pretty *Fraulein.*"

"*Nein.*" She tipped her face and studied the floor. His overnight breath of stale kraut and used tobacco overwhelmed her senses. *He is large. I am small. She listened to her heart pounding in her ears.* She did not give kisses to near strangers. *Does he forget his wife is in a bedroom upstairs?*

"I insist." He cupped her chin, raised her head, and turned her face.

"*Nein.*" She released the word like a storm speaks with a thunderclap. Jerking her face out of his grasp, she searched for a weapon. Labeling the coffee mill and a crockery bowl on the table as not promising, she turned her gaze to her left. In one swift movement, she snatched a towel hanging on a chair and backed toward the stove. "*Nein* kiss. *Nein* touch."

"I say otherwise." He reached and grabbed her wrist.

Louisa wrapped the towel around her free hand. Without turning her head, she lifted the heating coffeepot and swung the hot container toward the advancing man.

The hinged lid flew open. Scalding water leaped onto Heinrich's face and arm.

"Ach. Witch."

The container clattered to the floor and rolled under the table.

Louisa sprinted for the door and hesitated long enough to glance at the strong carpenter stumbling into furniture in his own kitchen.

"What is all the noise about?" Alfred burst into the room while still pulling one suspender to his shoulder.

Louisa held her breath. *A witness—the immediate danger might be past.*

"Witch." Heinrich pointed at Louisa before collapsing into a chair. "You have brought evil into this house."

Alfred looked at Louisa before settling his gaze on his brother. "What have you done, Heinrich?"

Louisa gathered her wits from the corners of the room. Recalling Alfred's patience and fairness during the long weeks of travel, she exhaled. She unwrapped the towel and tossed the cloth toward Heinrich. "Your demand for a kiss after opening the coffee tin is the only evil in this house."

"No harm in a kiss." Heinrich dabbed his face with the towel.

Louisa alternated her gaze between the brothers.

Heinrich's cheeks glowed red from both hot water and anger.

Alfred stood straight and stiff, intently watching his older brother.

Leave. This is a family quarrel. She turned and looked at the door, but she felt fastened in place. Glancing in the direction of the brothers, she sighted Bertha and Greta watching from the opening to the dining room.

Alfred cleared his throat and continued to stare at his brother. "Pack your things, Louisa. You, too, Bertha. We leave this house within the hour."

"Such a temper, little brother." Her host and assailant pushed to his feet.

"You are hopeless, Heinrich." Alfred shook his head and paced a small oval. "Father's beatings bounced off your thick hide. Mother's lectures hit a rock where your brain should be. Have you learned nothing after a journey to America and taking a wife?"

Louisa stiffened her spine and took the few steps to where her canvas satchel sat on the cot. Jerking the luggage open, she reached for her hairbrush and Bible. "I am the unexpected guest. I did not intend to provoke trouble between brothers."

Alfred sighed. "My brother and I have a strong disagreement with manners for many years. After we escort you to your boat, Bertha and I will find other lodgings."

She nodded, looked toward the hall, and realized

the other two women were gone. Listening, she heard footsteps and sparse words coming from one of the upstairs bedrooms.

"Do not fret, Louisa. I understand now to never trust my brother alone with a woman. He has neither manners nor honor."

Louisa finished her packing and tidied the blanket on the cot. During every motion, she felt Heinrich's steady gaze on her back. *I must be strong.*

****

Jerking upright, Hans listened. In an instant, he identified the sounds of the stable beginning a new work day below him.

Horses stirred in their stalls.

A trio of deep voices joined the slap of harness against leather and horseflesh.

Hans envisioned the scene of the drivers arriving, harnessing their teams, and leading the animals outside. *Will the normal sounds and activity in the stable cover my escape? The only man I need to fear is Mr. Covington.*

The stablemaster, coarse and stern, did not hold respect or affection from the employees. The American drivers often frowned and spat on the ground after the owner shouted a command.

Hans secured his bedroll and sack on his back and crawled to the ladder. After listening for a long moment, he peeked over the edge.

Walter stood in the center aisle and held a chestnut gelding's bridle strap. "Fair weather today."

" 'Bout time." The tallest of the drivers led a dappled mare in full harness into view.

"How many boats due today?" Walter tipped his

head and met Hans's gaze for an instant.

Interpreting the slight nod of Walter's head as an all-clear signal, Hans eased down the ladder. If one of the horses startled at his appearance, the morning would go badly for everyone. Stepping onto a generous layer of straw, Hans tugged on his cap and nodded at his friend.

Walter continued a mixed English and *Deutsch* conversation with the driver. Soon the two employees led the team through the south door.

Hans walked beside the gelding's shoulder, pressed his lips, and resisted stroking the fine animal's neck. One step over the threshold, Hans turned to the right, away from the watering troughs and empty wagons.

As the sky lightened in the east, Hans walked an indirect route toward the north end of the levee. He paused for a moment and stared at the ticket office for the daily, northbound packet. Directing his attention to the river, he confirmed a small sternwheeler tied to a dock. With a deep breath for courage, he walked into the office. "*Ein*"—he extended one finger—"Elm Ridge."

Yesterday's same stout clerk, in the same shabby coat, faced him across the stained counter. "Deck or cabin."

"Deck—wooder." He requested the cheapest fare. "How many days?"

"River's high and fast." The clerk spat tobacco juice into a spittoon. "Best guess is three days."

Hans set two small coins on the counter and lifted a red-and-black ticket. Purchasing three days of supplies would leave him little for lodging and food after arrival in the Illinois town. *I will eat little on the journey.*

Tucking the ticket into his pocket, he nodded once more at the clerk. "*Danke.*" An hour later, Hans stood on the deck of *The Perch*. He studied the St. Louis levee scene and blotted from his memory the stable on Second Street, distinctive by green slats in the three cupolas.

"*Guten Morgan,*" a tall, young man spoke and gestured toward two others dressed in plain coats. "My friends and I travel to Iowa, Fort Madison—where are you bound?"

Determined to be courteous without saying much, Hans smiled. "Not as far." For the next few minutes, he answered direct questions with the information matching the papers in his deepest pocket. *Each day, the name Hans Hoffman and birthplace of Arnsberg comes easier to mind.*

"We hear the land is rich—good to raise grain and cattle," the apparent spokesman continued. "For my part, I will plant a few acres in barley and wheat, build a snug house, and send for my younger brother before he's army age."

"*Ja.* Wise plan," the man in the black cap agreed.

"I do similar—however, I save money to bring *mein Schatz* to America." The shortest of the trio rubbed the back of his neck.

Hans closed his eyes for a moment and imagined Louisa. *Schatz. Sweetheart. I have never had the luxury.* A stray sound prompted him to open his eyes and study the three young immigrants. *The one with a sweetheart also wears an expensive watch chain.* Tucking his hand in his pocket, he rubbed a thumb across fingers. The motion did not satisfy the urge to steal. *Difficult to be an honest man.*

Clang-clang. The boat's bell signaled a warning to

board.

Hans stepped away from the other men and watched roustabouts carry two large trunks aboard. A slight woman, wearing a straw bonnet, black shawl, and brown dress, followed them across the deck and up the steps to the passenger cabins. *Was that?* He hurried forward and paused at the foot of the stairs.

"*Nein. Nummer zehn.*"

Hans smiled and felt his heart rise. *Louisa.*

Chapter Eight

An hour past noon, Louisa walked a circuit on the cabin deck promenade. Stopping to study the Illinois shore, she compared the descriptions in Cousin Fredrick's letters to the town of Alton behind them. She discovered comfort in the view of bluffs with sheer rock faces.

The horizon, full of crisp lines, contrasted with the landscape on her first days on the river. During the travel through Louisiana, the wide river and low banks implied the land in America required more boats than wagons.

She continued her walk and paused on the other side of the boat. The water ran clearer than in St. Louis. True, the river continued to hurry past while carrying tree limbs and other forest debris. But she noticed a change in the character of the current after the boat passed the mouth of the wide, Missouri River.

The steamboat lurched.

Louisa grabbed the rail. *I must pay attention and not take a tumble.*

A moment later, the boat whistle released two short blasts to announce a wood stop.

Returning to the shore side of the boat, Louisa prepared to watch the work party. Fuel stops were not a new sight, but she enjoyed observing the mixture of passengers and boat crew. Each time, the gang of men transferred a wood pile from shore to engine area. She recognized the captain by his wide-brimmed, rounded-crown, black hat.

Once ashore, the captain spoke for several moments with a man wearing dark, loose trousers and a tight, stained shirt.

A few minutes later, a crew member led the work party across the wide plank. She studied the men forming a ragged line from gangway to the wood. *It is a pity I cannot draw well.* Wait—the man third from the wood supply. *Do I see Hans? Or do my eyes play tricks?* She focused her attention on the man of average height with dark hair showing below a flat, brown cap. *He works steady—determined.*

Do you trust him? Widow Krause's question circled in her mind. *Alfred does not trust him.* But after the incident with Alfred's brother, Louisa did not give the carpenter's opinion great credit. Hurrying to her cramped cabin, she retrieved a paper of peppermints purchased on impulse on the way to the levee this morning. Tucking the sweets into her pocket, she headed for the stairs.

After the work party returned to the boat, the engine gave a great groan and pushed them back into the current. She ignored the tremble of the deck and threaded her way between passengers and freight toward the stern. Waiting for a clearer glimpse of the man's face, she moistened her lips. "*Guten Abend, Herr* Hoffmann."

He turned toward her and stumbled back half a step. Snatching off his cap, he curved his lips into a wide smile. "Louisa—it is you. You wear a new bonnet—my imagination did not play a trick. I saw you board."

"*Ja*. A few more days and I end my river travel." A thousand questions swirled in her mind, all wanting to escape at once. "I thought you planned to stay in St. Louis."

"The city did not agree with me. I decided to try my luck in a smaller town. You spoke well of Elm Ridge." He pointed at some sturdy crates. "Sit with me. We can compare our travels since New Orleans. How many days did you stay?"

Louisa took a seat on one of several barrels marked *Fort Madison*. While arranging her skirts, she considered her words. *I must not appear too eager. I need to remember the lesson in the Meyer household.* "We rested five days before getting on *The Jupiter* for St. Louis. Rain, with thunder and lightning almost every day, caused the deck passengers to huddle together. Our last day on board, the dry, sunny weather gave me great hope." *Yesterday? Was the grand approach to St. Louis under a beautiful spring afternoon sky only yesterday?* The confusion of the landing and the arrangements to get to Heinrich Meyer's house seemed like it happened at least a week ago. She counted the days in her head. One week ago, she stood with Alfred, Bertha, and the other passengers in rain and watched the steamboat pilot and crew work hard to avoid a fatal encounter with a snag. "What boat carried you?"

Hans accepted the peppermint she offered. "I hurried north. I was eager to be among a *Deutsch* community."

Moving only her eyes, she regarded him. *He is avoiding the question.* She sighed. Toying with the end of her wide, bright-blue bonnet ribbon, she decided not to press for Hans's secrets. She collected private experiences, including the incident at the Meyer household this morning. Trust proved to be a delicate virtue. She needed to take care selecting confidants. Today's painful experience, after Alfred's weeks of assurance she would find a welcome with his brother, soured her desire to make friends. *Two more days until I reach the safety of family.* She prompted Hans to speak again of his first experience with a wooding party. Perhaps the false courage she carried onboard would become real in Elm Ridge.

****

Two mornings later, *The Perch* whistled an alert to the wood seller on shore.

Hans stared through light rain toward the muddy bank and sighed. With slow movements, he removed his coat, folded it, and placed it on top of his sack.

The rain, announced with one of the violent American displays of thunder and lightning, had arrived before dawn. The dramatic overhead display, exhausted within half an hour, left a steady drizzle behind.

He joined the gathering knot of men at the shore-side rail. "Loading wood looks like a wet business today."

"You should be cheerful," the shortest of the three young men bound for Iowa addressed him. "Next town is Elm Ridge. You'll be off the river and out of the miserable damp by midday."

Hans considered the words. Yes, he experienced joy each time he thought of his destination. Once he set foot on land, he didn't plan on boarding a boat again. He could count on his fingers the nights spent on firm ground since he carried the leather valise aboard *The Flying Gull* in Bremerhaven. "You could change plans and try your luck ashore." He swallowed hard before a firm invitation escaped. While he answered to Hans Hoffmann more easily each day, he hesitated to trust any in the trio of young immigrants. "But I suspect your heart is set on Iowa."

"*Nein,* Iowa or Illinois are the same to me. The other passengers talk well of the farmland on both sides of the river."

The tallest of the trio shook his head and pointed one finger toward Hans. "I will continue to Fort Madison. The pretty *Fraulein* pays no attention to me. You, in contrast, she addresses with a kind voice. Have you not noticed the smile she wears in your company?"

Hans nodded. Since leaving St. Louis, Louisa drew him into conversation two or three times each day. He enjoyed every story she shared. Life in Hamm, whether she spoke of the bakery, the schoolroom, or the village streets, sounded interesting. He laughed during her tale of bargaining in the New Orleans market with her limited English and understanding of American money. From his viewpoint, she made a wise purchase in the straw bonnet with a bright-blue, cloth flower on each side. Glancing to the promenade on the cabin deck, he recalled her mention of watching the wooding party load fuel. Would she stand in the rain? Or would she stay dry and prepare for departure by checking all her possessions to be secure in the trunks?

"Step sharp, men," the boat officer shouted to the wooding party.

Hans followed the work party leader across the gangway and stepped on soft, decay-scented mud. He studied the wood piles and frowned. Instead of neat stacks of wood, this seller left the short logs in an untidy heap. He spied a few twigs with wilted leaves on the smaller logs. *Wet, green wood.* He shivered. Before the first chunk was onboard, he anticipated the hiss and snap of these logs hitting the firebox. The metal smokestacks would spew many sparks and dark smoke until the next fuel stop.

The men, prompted by the ship's officer, formed into a ragged line.

Hans planted his feet and removed a log from the top of the stack. An instant later, he passed it to the next man in the chain. Reach—lift—pass.

One of the Americans started to sing a shanty. Soon the men filled the air with a mixture of languages, unified by la...la...la on the chorus. The first pile of logs moved along the line and formed a stack near the firebox.

Moving up the slope, Hans selected a spot and reached for the first piece from the second heap. Reach—lift—pass. He paused to wipe a mixture of sweat and rain from his brow. Reach—lift—pass. He reversed a step and reached for the next chunk of wood.

A dozen logs shifted.

Hans lifted his right foot to move aside of the wooden avalanche. The mud under his left foot gave way. In an instant, he slid on the slick surface. Logs clattered and tumbled in all directions. *Plop.* Hans landed on his backside and raised his arms to shield his face.

Men shouted and added to the dull thuds of wood escaping down the slope.

"*Ack! Mein Fuss.* My foot. My foot," Hans cried

out in the sudden silence.

"Watch it. Careful now." Two men grabbed Hans by the upper arms.

Another pair of men lifted pieces of wood from his legs and feet.

Hans stood on his left leg, supported by the other men. Setting his right foot on the ground sent a pain flashing along his limb. *"Mein Gott.* My God." He swallowed gathering tears and forced a normal breath. "I hobble...with your help."

"Bring him here," Louisa shouted and waved.

"I sit. Catch my senses." Hans allowed the men to half-lift him to the top of a barrel. *"Danke. Danke."*

"You need tending." Louisa dismissed the others with a wave.

"I am fine. The shock of the thing has put me off balance." Hans lifted his cap and skimmed an arm across his brow. Glancing to the bottom of the passenger deck, he gave silent thanks for escaping the rain. He trembled. *Chill? Surprise?* Pressing tight his lips, he endured the pain when Louisa touched his lower right leg and repositioned his foot on top of another barrel. With his leg now extended, he inspected the damage through building tears. Instead of a worn leather shoe, he saw clumps of mud clinging to separate pieces of sole and upper. Any little movement of foot or ankle brought a new, stabbing pain to his entire leg.

"Water—to wash," Louisa demanded of the passengers clustered in a ragged circle.

Hans stared. Her delicate, steady fingers poised above his foot offered reassurance. He opened his mouth to protest her touch, but no sound emerged.

"I will inspect the injury. First, I need to remove

your shoe." She unknotted the wet laces and tugged the shoe free.

Pain, hot as fire, sped up his leg.

He clenched his jaw and shifted his gaze upward. *Count the painted boards. I must behave like a man.* Two deep breaths later, he turned his face and focused on the damaged, mud-caked shoe she set on a barrel. The brogan looked beyond repair. He sighed. He did not own another pair of shoes. The flimsy felt slippers, not suitable for a wet day, were lost with the trunk in St. Louis. Imagining his heart turned to a large stone, he contemplated arriving in a new town in bare feet. *Who will hire a shoeless man?*

"You need to visit a cobbler in Elm Ridge. My cousin included one in his list of businesses in the town." She dropped a wad of dark, wet, knit fabric beside the tattered shoe. "Your sock has a hole."

"I repair in good time." He shifted his gaze to the portion of her face visible beyond the straw bonnet's rim.

Louisa accepted a basin of water, slip of soap, and a small towel from another woman. "*Ja.* First, I wash the foot. Then I make a bandage."

Leaning forward, he watched the water remove bits of mud and dirt to reveal scraped skin. Blood seeped from several shallow wounds. A new wave of pain attacked, causing him to suck in a deep breath.

She pushed her fingers against the top of his foot and all sides of his ankle. "Nothing broken. Painful sprain, I think."

"*Ja. Gute.*" He struggled against the new pain released by her examination. "You bandage tight. I wish…I need…to walk off the boat."

Nodding, she continued to work. Twice she washed his foot with a generous coating of soap on the towel. Then she accepted a handful of clean, cloth strips from another woman.

"*Danke.*" Hans thanked the woman, wife to another man on the wood party. He winced as Louisa circled the cloth around his ankle.

"I bind tight. Tomorrow you must wash and bind again. Understand?"

Forcing a smile, he nodded. "You make a good nurse."

"God gives me too much opportunity." She glanced toward the shore and pressed her lips.

He watched her chest hesitate as if breathing was uncertain. *Don't be upset. I intended to speak a compliment.* He shut his mouth and looked toward the riverbank.

Once again, the vessel pushed against the current a dozen yards or more from a rocky outcropping. In another hour, or two, the boat would dock in Elm Ridge.

I need to change my plans for my first hours in a new town.

Louisa tied off the bandage and paused for a long moment. Straightening, she shook out her skirts. "Have you other shoes?"

"*Nein.*"

"Stay here. I need to fetch something from my cabin." She turned and hurried toward the steps.

Where does she believe I could hobble in my present condition? Hans bent low, fought dizziness, and unlaced his left shoe. *Another hole, soon more gaps than fabric.* He closed his eyes for a moment and wished others to think his outward pain from injury rather than embarrassment. What sort of man did not take the time to mend his socks? *A man without yarn and needle.* He studied his pale, bare foot and sighed.

I must walk off the boat. He planted his good foot on the deck and swung his right leg over the edge of his perch. Throbbing, dull pain resulted from the new position. He counted to fifty before pushing with his arms. Keeping his weight on his left foot, he stood and touched his right toes to the deck. *I can bear this amount of pain.* A cane or a crutch would be helpful. *Nein.* Cripples, old men, and prosperous gentlemen carried canes and walking sticks. *A workman seeking a job walks strong and sure. A desperate foreman might hire a man with a limp.*

"If the current holds, we will dock in Elm Ridge in one hour." Louisa approached, holding her hands behind her back.

"*Gute.*" He glanced at her face and forced a small smile.

She swung one arm forward and revealed a pair of wooden shoes with a red sunburst painted on the toes. "For you—to borrow—Papa's. You may use them until you find a cobbler to fix your brogan."

"*Danke.* Fine wooden shoes." He reached for one and set it beside his left foot. *Borrow. Hans...I am an honest man.* He made a silent vow to return the shoes. Until then, he would be grateful for such fine footwear to protect him from the hazards of everyday life. He pushed his left foot inside and discovered a perfect fit.

"Cousin Fredrick, in his most recent letter, directs me to hire Bergmann Livery to transport my trunks from the levee to the farm. I can ask for you to ride to the center of town."

"You are very kind. But I will manage." He eased his right foot into the shoe. One bolt of pain caused his lips to grimace before the nerves in his leg settled into an ache.

"With your chest from *The Flying Gull?*"

"*Nein.* I carry only a simple sack now." He gathered his damaged shoes and limped over to a different group of barrels. After he lifted his coat, he patted the canvas bag.

"But—"

The boat whistle interrupted all conversations.

Hans lifted his gaze to the shore.

The sun had broken through the clouds and sent shafts of welcome sunlight. At the top of a bluff, he observed narrow columns of white, wood smoke rising from dozens of chimneys. Buildings of log, frame, and brick clarified as the steamboat neared a small levee. Shifting his attention to the waterfront, he discovered wooden docks hosting an assortment of small boats. One long, low structure nestled against the sheer, stone bluff. *Elm Ridge, my new home.* He sensed the air vibrate with a promise for the future. *I am an honest man.*

"Wait for me on the levee. I will pay for your ride up the hill." Louisa extended a hand toward him and stalled with an inch gap between their fingers. An instant later, she withdrew her hand and rested it against her skirt.

Hans watched her cross the deck and climb the stairs. *I will not be indebted.* He glanced at the sturdy wooden shoes. Sighing, he realized he owed Louisa a great deal more than a fee to ride a wagon. With a determination to return the shoes soon, he donned his coat, bundled the muddy brogans on the outside of his sack, and limped toward the gangplank area.

He studied the view of Elm Ridge. A team hitched to a wagon of large barrels worked its way down a steep slope to the wharf. *I will make the climb—no matter how difficult. After I find a job and earn a little coin, I will return the shoes.*

"Good luck." One of the young men headed for Iowa clapped him on the shoulder.

"*Danke, danke.*" Hans straightened and pulled determination in with his next breath. *The thief died on the voyage. Hans Hoffmann is an honest man.*

****

Louisa waited beside the freight wagon. Ignoring the shouted messages between the boat crew and roustabouts, she studied the road leading from levee to the main portion of the town.

Several men, passengers from *The Perch,* hiked up the steep road carrying satchels or small chests.

Hans has already gone. She recalled her last glimpse of him from the cabin deck. If she closed her eyes, she imagined him limping across the levee with a pitiful sack across his back. *Will I see him again? Will he return Papa's shoes?*

"We go now." The driver fastened the wagon's tailgate and approached.

She accepted his offered hand and climbed to the high seat.

"We unload goods at the merchants—three stops in town. Fredrick Mueller farm will be final stop for today."

"*Danke.*" She arranged her skirts.

87

The teamster, *Herr* Weiss, clambered up on the other side, unwound the reins from the brake lever, and glanced back at the load. A moment later, he slapped the leather ribbons. "Git up."

Louisa turned for a last look at the boat.

Passengers stood on both decks while roustabouts and crew settled the new freight under shelter. The bell clanged and signaled time for all to be aboard.

My travels are almost ended. She breathed in the familiar scents of river, mud, and wood smoke. At each of the stops at businesses, Louisa stood and surveyed Elm Ridge from her wagon perch. She noticed a fine brick building, the tallest in town, and counted windows. *Hotel—I think.* She nodded at the familiar sight of a town square in front of the dominating structure.

The space, while not large, contained a flag pole, a row of low bushes, and at least two benches. A mixture of brick and wood structures, one or two stories tall, lined the other streets.

She moved her gaze to the north and encountered a tall smokestack spewing a dark cloud. Low buildings surrounded the chimney. For a moment, she imagined subjects bowing to the king. *Nein. This is America—no monarch.*

Emerging from a shop, the driver carried a bucket of water to a horse.

She pointed toward the black smoke. "What is that?"

"Foundry—good business. They make a superb kitchen stove. Ship their goods all the way west to St. Joseph." He stepped to the second horse, tipped his face to Louisa, and grinned. "St. Joe is the edge of civilization—where the wagon trains leave for Oregon. You heard of Oregon?"

She shook her head. The map from the lectures on the ship failed to clarify in her memory. "I hear talk of California and gold fever."

"*Ja.* Many young men catch such an illness. Tall tales, riches in every stream waiting to be claimed, circulate in every town." He stowed the water bucket and climbed back into his seat. "Now we go to Mueller farm."

Louisa absorbed the sights and sounds of Elm Ridge. *The streets are dirt—muddy spots from this morning's rain.* Wooden sidewalks bordered the businesses and a few of the homes they passed. The air vibrated with silent energy between the sound of shovels, picks, and hammers at construction sites. *New things in every direction.* She gave silent thanks the driver hummed a soft folk song between pointing out businesses and churches.

A block past the German Lutheran Church, a brick building with a single, square bell tower, the teamster turned the horses. Within a few moments, the town's bustle lay behind them.

Forest. Louisa studied the trees unfurling small, fresh, clean leaves. Twice, the woods gave way to cleared fields. She sighted a house among a cluster of sheds, and the driver spoke the farmer's name. She looked for landmarks, but soon all the trees began to look the same.

The driver directed the horses off the road to follow two rutted paths with a narrow strip of new grass between. "We on Mueller land now."

She leaned forward and searched for a fence or

building.

An instant later, a dog barked.

She spied a clearing with a frame house, three log sheds, and a fenced garden plot. She swallowed to prevent her pounding heart from escaping in joy.

"Whoa." The driver pulled the team to a halt.

"Anna," she called to a blonde woman coming around the corner of the house. Her cousin's wife carried a child on her hip. In an instant, Louisa gathered her skirts and climbed from the wagon seat.

"*Strup. Gute Hund,*" Anna called the dog without breaking stride toward the rig.

Louisa spied Cousin Fredrick coming out of the largest shed with a hay fork in his hand. She smiled at the wiry man with dark blond hair peeking from a flat, black cap. "Greetings."

"Welcome." Anna reached Louisa first and pulled her into a one-armed hug. "This is Karl. He is learning to walk and getting into all sorts of mischief. Karl, meet Cousin Louisa."

"I am glad to see you." Louisa hugged the woman with three more inches of height. Turning, she received Fredrick's hug. *Family, I feel safe for the first time since Papa took sick.*

He stooped and drew her close for a moment. Releasing his strong arms, he stepped back and looked toward the wagon beyond her. "Where…where is Uncle Dietrich?"

"Papa…Papa." She blinked at sudden tears and swiped with the back of her hand to check none escaped. "Did you get my letter? I sent it three days before we left New Orleans." She paused until he shook his head. "Papa died on the ship—fever."

"Oh, Louisa. You speak difficult news." Anna widened her eyes, stepped forward, and gathered her close again. "You must tell us the whole story—later. First, we put your things in the house and give you time to catch your breath."

"*Danke.*" Louisa closed her eyes for a moment and commanded her whirling thoughts to settle. In the New Orleans boardinghouse, she chose the words in her letter with care to avoid giving alarm. Now, the situation demanded she find the proper way to calm the panic in Cousin Fredrick's pale-blue eyes.

"I have not checked for a letter this week." Fredrick gestured wide before he took a few steps to join the driver at the rear of the wagon. "As you can see, we live on our land—an American custom. We go into town for church or to get supplies. We planned a trip tomorrow."

"*Ja.* Tomorrow, I take fresh butter to the store and trade for sugar. Over supper, we will discuss a plan in detail. I have much I want to share about the town." Anna glanced at the driver and then back to Louisa. "Ach—hold Karl. I fetch *Herr* Weiss' payment."

"*Mmma...mmma*"—Karl released a loud cry and reached for his mother.

Louisa tightened her grip on the toddler's body. "Hush—hush, little one." She adjusted her hands and began to sway. In less time than it took the men to unload the two trunks and one satchel, the child calmed and began exploring her face with his hands. "*Ja, ja,* you find my chin—and bonnet ribbon."

Anna returned and pressed a few coins plus a mold of butter into the driver's hands. "Send my greetings to *Frau* Bergmann. Tell her I will call for the cabbage starts tomorrow."

"*Ja. Danke.* I give message." The driver climbed to the wagon seat, gathered the reins, and ordered the team to start.

Louisa steadied Karl in her arms. Standing beside Fredrick and Anna, she watched the wagon bump along on the narrow track. She blinked at unexpected tears. Frozen to the spot, she stared until the rig disappeared from sight. *Another portion of life rolled up on the spindle.* Never again would she walk Hamm's narrow streets—or sit on the bank of the River Lippe. Gone were the sailing ship, moving at the mercy of the wind, and the steamboats pushing against the current of the Mississippi River. *Elm Ridge is my new home.* Shifting her focus to the clean, green leaves on a nearby shrub, she sighed. Grasping Karl's chubby hand to hide a tremble, she whispered determination to keep her final promise to Papa, "I shall do credit to the Mueller name. I will keep the dream. I will learn English and make good bread."

Chapter Nine

Creak. Thump.

Louisa startled awake. *A door? Where?* She opened her eyes, pushed against the cot, and stared out a small, square window. A few stars showed in a pre-dawn sky. *The bakery. My second morning in Elm Ridge.* In the next blink, she recalled arranging a few personal things on the shelves in the curtained portion of the bakery's storeroom. The faint scent of wood catching fire greeted her senses and eased fears.

"Du...du...du...du." A male voice leaked through the wall.

She eased out of bed and stretched. *My first workday in America.* Yesterday, at mid-morning, *Herr* Keil, the baker, had dismissed her inquiry for work as a helper. Hours later, after requesting work as cook or housekeeping at close to two dozen businesses, she returned. *Frau* Keil, alone in the shop, granted Louisa time to tell her story and hired her to be a chore girl. Her duties, the best she understood them, included keeping the upstairs apartment tidy, preparing the noon meal, and tending the garden.

The baker hums a happy tune. In the semidarkness, she dressed in a plain gown. Winding her night braid into a spiral at the back of her head, she smiled while inserting several pins. Pushing the blanket hung for privacy aside, she trailed her fingers over the tops of crocks and crates until she reached the workroom entrance. The familiar scents of yeast, flour, and sugar teased her senses before she opened the door. "*Guten Morgan, Herr* Keil."

He glanced from kneading soft dough. "*Guten Morgan, Fraulein.* I trust you slept well."

She nodded and studied him for a long moment.

Herr Keil was not a large man, but his shoulders and arms were muscular. He wore an apron over his plain shirt and canvas trousers. In the light of the two lanterns hung from the ceiling, his thick hair shown white and his generous mustache a vibrant red.

"I go upstairs and assist *Frau* Keil." She resisted bobbing a curtsey.

"*Ja.* She will be pleased you are ready to begin so early."

Louisa smiled briefly. Until the journey to America, she rose every day to the pre-dawn scents and sounds of bakers. The hours before sunrise belonged to preparing yeast treats for the oven. She understood the importance of starting work early and keeping a clean shop.

During a moment's pause in her sleeping nook, she grabbed an apron and slipped on wooden shoes. Louisa hurried up the outside stairs. Knocking twice, she turned the knob and opened the door. She stepped across the threshold into a large room.

A table surrounded by six chairs stood to her left in front of a corner cupboard. A small worktable, distinguished by a thick, scarred top, occupied a place in front of a square, cast-iron stove. A wide strip of blue carpet defined a sitting area, consisting of a settee, two rocking chairs, and a waist-high cabinet. A long, thick curtain hung beyond the seating arrangement.

"*Frau* Keil?"

"*Ein Minute.*" Charlotte Keil pushed aside a portion of the curtain separating the sleeping area from the main room, while fastening her calico dress's top button. "You are prompt—*gute*."

For the next hour, Louisa absorbed instructions from the baker's wife. She learned details of her daily responsibilities. Each day, she must prepare a meal—meat and vegetables—in the Dutch oven. Today, she was instructed to dust all the furniture and give the woodwork and floors a good scrubbing.

"*Verstechen?*" Charlotte ladled a little water over neck bones, onions, turnips, and carrots in the cast-iron kettle. "If you have a question, you only need to come downstairs to ask. Most of my time is spent in the front of the shop selling goods and visiting with the customers. Bernard, *Herr* Keil, is fussy about his baking area. Be sure to leave muddy shoes by the back door."

"*Ja.* Sensible rules." She glanced toward her black stockings. Following a lifelong habit, she'd stepped out of her wooden shoes before crossing the threshold.

"One more thing"—Charlotte added vegetable peels to the slop bucket. "Did you burn wood or coal in your stoves?"

"Coal for both heating and baking."

"Then I show you how to keep the fire constant with wood."

Louisa leaned over, lifted the poker from the wood box, and followed Charlotte's instructions. Within a couple minutes, she selected the proper size piece and prodded the fuel. The Dutch oven holding the noon meal and smaller, tin coffeepot of water warmed on the stove. "I will check firebox and add when this stick ready to crumble."

"*Gute.*" Charlotte glanced toward the shelf clock in the seating area. Next, she pulled open the sleeping area curtain and fastened a cloth loop on a hook. She paused at the mirror above the dresser and lifted a hairbrush. "Questions?"

"*Nein.* I empty garbage and fetch water for the scrubbing." Louisa snatched the containers and walked to the door.

During the morning hours, Louisa worked steadily. Comforting, familiar smells—fresh bread and sweet fruit—rose from the bakery and mingled with the scents of stew and lye soap. While scrubbing a stiff brush against the final window frame, she heard the clock chime eleven times. "Ach. I must set the table and serve *Herr* Keil lunch." She dropped the brush into the wooden bucket, wiped her hands on her apron, and rolled both sleeves to her wrists. In the next minutes, she set a place at the table with a plain bowl, small plate, spoon and butter knife. She was cutting a thick slice off a round loaf of yesterday's rye bread when *Herr* Keil's voice preceded him through the door.

"*Guten Tag, Fraulein.*" He hung his black, flat cap on a peg. "How are you getting on? Have you found what you needed?"

"*Ja,* I find soap, brush, and cleaning rags with no problem." Carrying his bowl, she went to the stove, lifted the lid, and ladled out stew. "Today *Frau* Keil put pork neck bones in the meal."

He grunted a reply and opened one of the three crocks below the kitchen shelves. Pulling out a fat, pickled cucumber, he smiled. "Best part of any meal."

After setting his stew on the table, Louisa retreated to the abandoned scrub bucket.

"Ach"—he gestured her to approach. "Do not pretend the frightened rabbit in front of me. Sit—tell me a little of yourself."

She stood at the far end of the table and recounted the highlights of her journey to Elm Ridge. "Fredrick Mueller is my cousin, the son of my late Papa's eldest brother." She glanced at the clock. *Twenty minutes?* "I have talked too long."

"*Nein.*" He pushed back his chair, stood, and went to the basin to rinse his hands. "Good for us to get acquainted, no?" He wiped his hands and began to talk of his past. "I journeyed to America a long time ago, twelve years." He gazed off to the far corner of the room. "My bride and I sailed from Bremerhaven in February 1839. Times have changed—from Prussia to St. Louis—and again in Elm Ridge." He snapped the linen towel before spreading it across the back of a chair. "Enough of the past for now. Did *Frau* Keil tell you about the whistles?"

More whistles? I heard three, no four, steamboats this morning. She shook her head.

"No? I explain. The village lacks a public clock. Therefore, the workmen across the entire town keep time by the foundry. The first blast dismisses men for lunch—an hour later, another calls them to return. *Frau* Keil takes her meal after the second signal."

"I understand. I will eat with her." Louisa stacked the dirty dishes and set them aside to be washed after the final midday meal. Twenty minutes later, Louisa went to fetch an additional bucket of water. Lifting the pump handle, she glanced toward Third Street at the exact moment a green freight wagon, pulled by a chestnut team, halted.

Without a word or wave, the driver climbed down, collected a keg from the wagon bed, and walked into the bakery building.

"*Nein—nein* flour from Black's Mill." *Herr* Keil's voice escaped into the yard.

Curiosity won over caution. Louisa set the bucket on the cistern cover and hurried inside. Taking a quick sidestep, she avoided a collision with the retreating driver.

Herr Keil, wagging a finger toward the delivery man's chest, followed the withdrawing stranger. Three more steps and both men were in the yard.

She walked cautiously into the baking area. A keg lay on its side against the wall. She ignored the two voices arguing behind her and continued forward. *Frau* Keil, partially visible on the other side of the set of pass-through shelves, served a customer. *Wait. Who?* A few more steps and she paused in the open doorway between the baking and sales areas. Moistening her lips, she nodded at the young man holding a half-eaten bun. "*Guten Tag, Herr* Hoffmann."

"*Fraulein* Mueller." He touched his cap with his free hand. Advancing one step, he smiled. "This is a pleasant surprise. Did you find your cousin and his family well?"

"All is well at Cousin Fredrick's farm. I enjoy the hours visiting with them and sharing stories of friends and relatives." Lowering her gaze, she spied bits of fresh dirt on Papa's wooden shoes. "Have you found work?"

"*Ja.*" He nodded and completed a swallow. "Construction—we dig foundation for new building. Few blocks…" He gestured toward the southeast.

Louisa shifted her gaze to *Frau* Keil. Many questions were evident on her new employer's face. "*Herr* Hoffmann and I became acquainted on the sailing ship. We arrived in Elm Ridge on the same packet."

Thud. The back door slammed and interrupted further explanation.

Herr Keil strode into the bakery, wearing a scowl. Muttering a string of curses, he washed his hands in a basin. He snatched a towel and approached the sales area.

Louisa moved aside, bumped a shoulder against the pass-through shelves, and eased closer to the large worktable. Alternating her gaze between the married couple, she guessed they passed a complicated message.

With a slight nod toward Hans, she turned in silence and exited the bakery. *A quarrel between the baker and a supplier is not my business. I am the chore girl. My thoughts need to center on cooking and cleaning.* Aware of a hurried, excited pulse, she formed her lips into silent words. *Hans found a job.*

****

More than a week later, Hans studied the clean, brick church building across the wide, dusty street. *An honest man attends worship.* Today marked the second Sunday after his arrival in Elm Ridge, and he'd woken with fresh determination to fit into the community.

Sitting on a high, stone foundation, the building welcomed people with a double, white door at the top of ten wide steps. A white, wooden cross topped a square bell tower.

He drew a deep breath and crossed the street. After walking a few yards, he paused to admire the horses hitched to farm wagons and buggies waiting in the spring sunshine. Reins looped around a long rail insured the teams or single hitches did not wander away. *Fine animals, every one of them looks well fed, with a healthy coat. One day I will own a good horse and a place to shelter him.*

Nodding toward a couple and half-grown boy at the foot of the steps, he followed them into the building. He paused two paces inside the door to adjust his eyes to the softer light. Standing in the narthex, he noted a row of coat pegs on either side of the sanctuary door. A locked offering box sat on a table in the middle of the center aisle between the rear pew and exit. He removed his cap, walked forward, and selected a seat in the second-to-last bench on the right side. Straightening, he moved his gaze among the pews looking for familiar figures.

Herr Keil shared a bench with *Herr* Hebing, the butcher, and three young, blond men. Jacob Thayer, his foreman, sat beside a youthful boy.

Shifting his attention to the other side of the aisle, Hans studied the women and children. *Frau* Keil's tall, slender figure occupied a spot beside three other women. *Louisa—unless another Fraulein wears a similar bonnet.* He curved his lips into a small smile. Beside her, a mother held a toddler on her lap. *Her cousin has a wife and son.* Returning his inspection to the men, he wondered which one was her relative. *What is the man's age? Did he have the same honey blond hair? Or was it lighter? Darker?*

The bell rang and called the last worshippers into the sanctuary.

An instant later, Hans focused his attention on a large, white-haired man.

Standing on the forward edge of the raised platform, the man blew a single note on a pitch pipe.

Singing master? Hans resisted the urge to seek a rear balcony during a quick search for organ pipes.

"Today we open the service with "Open Now Thy Gates of Beauty." You will find it on page eighteen of the songbook." The music master paused for a long moment before blowing a second note on his pipe. An instant later, he commenced singing and directing.

Looking toward the aisle, Hans spied three, thin, black books at the end of the pew. He lifted the top one and fumbled to find the correct page. During the second verse, he joined his soft monotone to the voices of the congregation.

As the group's "amen" faded against the white, plastered walls, the pastor replaced the musician on the platform. The minister's plain, black robe and clerical collar contrasted with the tall altar decorated with a scroll border around a painting of the ascending Christ. Following the lead of the other men, Hans stood, sat, and knelt. As the cleric recited liturgy and the congregation responded, long-buried memories stirred. Words familiar from the first fourteen years of his life formed on his tongue. He moved his lips in long-dormant patterns.

After a lengthy Bible reading concerning Moses and the Israelites wandering in the wilderness, the music master led another hymn. While the congregation settled on the pews, the pastor mounted the pulpit to begin the sermon.

Hans relaxed his shoulders. Within a couple of minutes, his mind wandered to the previous time he'd attended a worship service—five years ago. Two days after his mother's funeral, Hans had sat beside his father in Selm's stone church. The dim interior, due to a cloudy sky on the other side of stained-glass windows, fit his mood. *Vater* returned home late—and drunk—in the early hours. Resisting the temptation to move away from his parent, Hans endured the stench of too much beer and stale tobacco each time the older man exhaled in his direction. The odor soured his young stomach, but the memory of last night's slap on the face had held him in place.

Hans sighed and glanced toward the plain ceiling of Elm Ridge's modest German Lutheran Church. Concentrating on the pastor's words for a moment, he skipped his gaze over the worshippers in front of him and to the view of blue sky outside the clear glass windows. *Difficult years since I fled from* Vater *and his riding crop.* He blinked away the past and moved his lips in silence. *America. Hans Hoffmann is an honest man.*

Without warning, the congregation shuffled to their feet.

Hans snapped out of his daydreams and joined them.

After the final blessing, he nodded greetings to the familiar faces. Dropping one small coin in the offering box, he stepped back and lingered in the narthex. Today, he would make his own luck and have a friendly word with Louisa. Three times he'd caught a glimpse of her at the bakery. She always appeared to be in motion, busy with keeping the shop clean and tidy. *Frau* Keil hurried him along the instant another customer arrived. Twice *Herr* Keil glared when Hans paused at the opening to the workroom. He shifted his cap to the other hand and glanced at his repaired leather shoes.

Suddenly a dark blue skirt swaying above a pair of dainty black boots came into view. He raised his gaze and cleared his throat. "*Guten Tag, Fraulein* Mueller."

A tiny smile decorated her lips. "*Guten Tag.* Please allow me to introduce *Frau* Mueller, Anna, my cousin's wife. The little one is Karl."

"*Guten Tag, Frau.*" Hans gave mother and son a half bow.

"Who have we here?"

Hans shifted his gaze to a muscular man with blond hair and clear blue eyes striding toward him. He estimated the man two inches taller than his five foot six and noted a resemblance to Louisa in the hairline and shape of the jaw.

"Cousin Fredrick, this is Hans Hoffmann. We travelled together on *The Flying Gull.*"

Hans extended a hand. An instant later, he hid his wince at the power in the farmer's grip. He urged his tongue to be careful. "I am pleased to meet *Fraulein* Mueller's relatives."

"What sort of trade do you bring to our thriving town?" Fredrick spoke while guiding their group out the door and into pleasant sunshine.

Trade? Hans pressed his lips. Drawing a deep breath, he discarded lies from his answer. "At present, I work construction labor. I'm on the crew erecting a building at Sixth and Pecan. I understand it will be a fine, large business."

"*Ja.* I know the place." Fredrick nodded. "You work on a dry goods store with two apartments upstairs. The lot is owned by an American."

"Mr. Morris." Hans remembered the name of the man in a tall, black hat who'd brought the wages to the foreman yesterday.

Fredrick halted them in front of a team hitched to a black farm wagon.

Assessing the animals in a glance, Hans considered them handsome. With an open, flat palm, he presented his hand to the mare, a sorrel with a white patch centered above her eyes.

"Star approves of you." Fredrick nodded toward the horse. An instant later, he gave attention to his son clinging to his trouser leg. "Do you like horses?"

"I admire a good animal. This pair appears better than most to my untrained eye."

A steamboat whistle drifted high and sharp from the river.

Both horses perked their ears and raised their heads, but they held their feet in place.

"Calm is good." Hans skimmed one hand down the mare's neck.

Fredrick rose on his toes and scanned the lingering parishioners. "Pardon me. I see a man I wish to talk business with."

Anna lifted the little boy before he could follow his father. "Always farm business with my Fredrick. He works hard toward his dream of a dairy. Perhaps next year, he can begin to deliver fresh milk in the town. Last year we had two cows. God willing, we will have five healthy milkers and their calves by the end of next week."

Easing away from the team, Hans remained quiet for a long moment. His experience with farming was limited to scattered weeks of honest labor stacking rye for threshing or digging potatoes in exchange for food and shelter. "It sounds like difficult work." He turned his attention to Louisa. "Will you walk with me? To the corner and back, while Fredrick is doing his business."

She glanced at Anna. "I think…"

"Thank you for the offer," Anna spoke promptly. "Karl and I will follow to make it all proper between two almost strangers. With my son's tiny steps, we will soon fall behind."

"*Danke.*" Hans doffed his cap to Anna. Turning, he offered his arm to Louisa.

She set her hand on his elbow and broke the silence after half a dozen steps. "Today we are going to the home of friends for dinner and a visit. Often, if the weather is fair, Anna packs a picnic. The family spends the afternoon visiting and dancing at the beer garden."

Joy mixed with hope, rare emotions for him, swelled in his chest. "Food and conversation in sunshine sounds like a pleasant way to spend a day away from work."

"They have a small band. Do you enjoy dancing the polka?"

He lightened his step and imagined holding Louisa in his arms and twirling. "Will you teach me? I try to be a good student."

Chapter Ten

Louisa paused and checked the fire under the large kettle. Adding one slender stick of wood, she glanced at the sky. *A fine, May morning—four weeks already in Elm Ridge.* She hummed a dance tune while observing the chimney smoke rising straight into the Friday morning air. The weather promised to be warm and dry after yesterday afternoon's brief storm. *One more bucket of water.* Walking the few steps to the pump above the cistern, she reviewed *Frau* Keil's instructions for laundry day. *First wash day in Elm Ridge. I must trust* Frau *Keil's information.* She pumped a final stroke, lifted the bucket, and added the contents to the warming kettle. A moment later, she hurried into the building to retrieve the wooden tub and washboard.

"*Nein.* Your price is too high."

Louisa jerked to a stop inside the back door. *Herr Keil seldom raises his voice or speaks English. The baker tends to hum folk tunes or work in silence.* Shrugging, she listened to the tone of the conversation and reached for the laundry tub hanging above the large storage crocks.

"I'll smear your name. I have the power." A deep voice ended each English word crisp.

"I now buy at Gordon's Mill. Agreed purchase from you is complete—poor quality," *Herr* Keil replied.

Louisa held one rope handle of the tub and peeked around the open door.

A medium-height, slender American in a dark suit and tall hat gestured with a walking stick. "He won't sell you a speck of poor cornmeal after I'm done."

"Go." *Herr* Keil jabbed the air with his index finger extended toward the stranger. "Out of my shop. I bake in Elm Ridge five years. You…you are newcomer. You take advantage of the late miller's name. You destroy reputation of the business. I don't know where my sense travelled the day I agreed to buy even one speck of flour from you. I should tell the other merchants the sort of business you did in St. Louis."

Holding her breath, Louisa imagined short bolts of lightning passing between the men. She did not understand the words, but the anger was clear.

"The keg of rye flour delivered last week appears light. Tell me—are your scales honest?" The baker pushed the butter crock toward the worktable's center.

"And who will people believe—*Deutsch* with queer ways—or a man descended from a brave veteran of Yorktown? You've not seen the end of this." The stranger pivoted and strode from the bakery without even a glance or tip of his hat to *Frau* Keil and the early customer.

"*Bitte.*" Louisa stepped into full view. "Excuse me for overhearing. The American—who is he?"

"Mr. Black—a vile man. He owns Black's Mill. Trouble is his close companion." *Herr* Keil opened the oven and removed a pan of wheat buns. "No concern for you, *Fraulein*—see to the washing."

With a respectful nod, she snatched the washboard and fled into the yard. Operating the bakery was not her

107

business. *My duties are housekeeping and gardening—nothing more.* Worries of millers, brewers, and other suppliers belonged on the capable shoulders of *Herr* Keil. *I am chore girl—not the baker's daughter.*

During the next three hours, Louisa boiled, scrubbed, rinsed, and hung laundry. She filled the single line strung from the building to the tall corner post of the garden fence with bedding, undergarments, and towels. She rubbed the final apron against the sturdy washboard and recited a recipe for plum cake under her breath.

"*Guten Tag.* A fine day to wash." *Frau* Hebing, the butcher's wife, greeted her from the next yard. Dressed in a gray frock and white apron on her stout frame, the woman set a tin pail under the pump spout.

"*Ja.*" She glanced at the sky and breathed a quick prayer *Frau* Keil's confidence the laundry would dry before sunset was well-placed. "Is all well at the butcher's household today?" After the neighbor gave assurance of everyone's health, Louisa voiced a concern. "Tell me, in the summer, does it rain enough to keep good water in the cistern?"

Frau Hebing paused her pumping, wiped her hands on her apron, and stepped closer. "Some days I forget you are new to America." She glanced toward the butchering shed with the hoist at the peak. "The weather will be hot soon. Today, not to worry—beware the days the heat arrives early. Hot before noon brings strong, noisy storms before sunset."

"More storms?" Louisa widened her eyes at the older woman's words. During her less than two months since docking in New Orleans, she had witnessed more thunderstorms than during an entire year in Westphalia.

She decided to ask Fredrick and Anna more questions about the weather during tomorrow's visit to the farm.

"*Ja*—spring and summer rain come with God's fireworks. But Illinois is a good land. America is a fine place for our three sons to grow into men. Although I worry every day for Werner." Speaking the name of her youngest son, she changed her tone from cheerful to serious.

Louisa twisted the scrubbed apron once more to remove soapy water. Satisfied at the result, she dropped the garment into the rinse tub.

Two of the butcher's sons worked in the shop with their father. Named Benedict and Claus, the brothers looked so much alike she had to ask for a name each time she went over to fetch an order for *Frau* Keil. At this moment, she recalled seeing the third one at church, but not in the shop. "Werner—is he the youngest?"

"A dreamer, he is. Unlike his brothers, he has no interest in the butcher shop or sausage making. Books, tinkering with machines, and more books—takes after *mein Vater*. A good man, my father, much respected, but schoolmasters collect more kind words than coin. I fear my son will follow dreams rather than a trade able to support a family." *Frau* Hebing raised her hands and glanced to the sky. "Where do you suppose he spends a fine late spring day?"

"I cannot begin to guess." Louisa poked the long, wooden stick into the pot over the fire. Fishing out a pair of trousers, she transferred the garment to the scrubbing tub.

"He does not work in the shop. Nor does he repair the garden fence or put a new rope on the hoist. No, he takes his book and goes to get a lesson from the pastor—Latin. What use will he have for such a language?" Placing hands on her hips, she shook her head. "I am satisfied with *Deutsch* and enough English to get along with my American neighbors."

Pressing tight her lips, Louisa organized an idea into a question. "Do you know anyone, a lady, who would teach me English?"

The butcher's wife frowned. "I learn from our customers." She reached for the bucket handle, hesitated, and touched her chin. "Do you know Mrs. Cook at the hardware?"

Louisa nodded. "Twice, I have errand in the store."

"She is a good, kind woman with much patience." *Frau* Hebing lifted her water bucket.

"*Danke.* I will go across the street and speak with her before they close the shop today." She eyed the laundry and estimated the time to finish the last few garments. In the next moment, she recalled her impression of Mrs. Cook. *She is a pleasant woman. The day I purchased a darning needle, she explained the American coins.*

"Good luck to you. I must go inside and finish my morning work."

Louisa rinsed the bakery aprons. Lifting one from the small tub, she wrung out most of the water and snapped the garment out to its full shape. She stepped to the garden fence and suspended the apron over the boards.

Grunt—grunt—snort.

She turned her gaze toward the sound. "What?"

Half a dozen young pigs wandered across the Hebings's yard toward her.

"*Nein. Nein.*" She plopped the clean apron across the fence without a care for the shape. An instant later, she waved both arms and hurried toward the animals. "Go—go—home—away."

The young hogs ignored her and continued into the bakery's yard. One pig bumped against the wash tub.

Soapy water sloshed over the side an instant before the washboard slipped out of sight.

Another animal grabbed the corner of a bedsheet on his way under the line and pulled the cloth to the ground. A moment later, the thin rope fell from the garden post.

"Ach. Ach."

With a few parting grunts and one squeal, the pigs dashed off across Third Street and between two buildings.

"All my work." She placed her hands on her hips and stared at the wet laundry scattered on the ground. Every garment from the line lay dirty again from mud and pig's feet. Turning at the sound of a deep laugh, she ignored the heat rising in her cheeks and faced *Herr* Keil. "*Nein* joke this is."

The baker became solemn in one blink. "I laugh at the pigs. Always they visit on wash day. *Ja,* other times the swine inspect our yard. But only if the garden gate is not latched do they cause mischief."

She shifted her gaze to study the destruction in the yard. The chaos could be put to right easy enough. The clothes would wash quickly before the mud and fresh stains dried. But the time to repeat an easy scrub and rinse would make it difficult to complete her other chores.

Herr Keil strode across the yard to the tall garden

post and re-fastened the rope.

"*Danke.*" She gathered garments from the ground. "I give this quick wash and pray our swine friends find another place to play."

He adjusted the apron across the fence, shook out the folds, and arranged the wet linen flat. "Louisa, you have worked four weeks for us now without complaint. I watch your skill with the housework and listen to your mild words. I think tonight…when I mix the bread sponge…you may sift the flour."

Standing in the yard, her arms filled with damp clothes, she resisted the urge to hug the baker. Demonstrating such emotion would be improper and risk him changing his mind. Instead, she nodded, grinned, and urged her heart to stay within her chest. "*Danke.* Sifting flour…a pleasure…a great pleasure."

****

As the sun approached the zenith, Hans paused to wipe his brow. In the next instant, he lifted the pair of boards and set them on his shoulder. He marveled at the progress on the new dry goods store. Yesterday, late in the afternoon, the workers secured the final rafter. He paused for a moment and admired the organization of the work. *Herr Thayer directs the work better than a schoolmaster organizes an assembly.*

Today, skilled carpenters and informal apprentices hammered wide boards to the studs, enclosing the sides and ends of the building. The frames for two doors and five windows on the first floor were complete. *Herr* Thayer, the foreman, a man of average height and weight but possessing a commanding voice, positioned another board on the second-floor joists in preparation for installing the diagonal pattern. Near his scaffolding, the young stonemason, *Herr* Giesel, shaped a large, chimney rock with mallet and chisel.

The foundry whistle drowned out the shouts between the workers. The signal caused laborers to cease work, set tools aside, and begin the one-hour lunch break.

"Going to the bakery for a glimpse of your girl?" Ernst, a helper recently promoted to apprentice, removed his carpenter's apron containing precious nails and folded it on top of a keg. In the next instant, he removed his cap and shook abundant dark hair.

"*Nein.*" Hans shook his head to repeat the answer. Today, he planned to visit the *Holzschumacher,* wooden shoemaker. *I need to purchase my own wooden shoes.* Each morning, slipping into the borrowed shoes, the weight of guilt grew heavier in his core. Construction wages were steady and sufficient for his current needs. He glanced to the sunburst on the toes, knocked a little loose dirt off the left shoe, and sighed. *An honest man keeps a promise. Especially to...* He skipped a breath at the memory of his hands against Louisa's frock as he assisted her into Fredrick's wagon Sunday afternoon. Moistening his lips, he faced Ernst. "Business errand."

A few minutes later, Hans brushed another bit of dirt from his shirt and stepped into a small shop on the north side of the town square. He was greeted with scents of fresh sawdust and a trace of turpentine. Walking over to a narrow shelf, he inspected several pairs of new shoes waiting for customers to claim them. *A good business.* Glancing around for the proprietor, he called. "*Guten Tag.*"

"*Ein Minute.*"

Hans relaxed his shoulders and paused in front of a clock in an intricately carved case.

A moment later, a man of middle age followed his strong, clear voice into the room. "How may I help you today?"

"Are you *Herr* Fischer? How much for a pair of shoes? Like these." He pointed toward his feet.

"*Bitte.* I take close look." The shoemaker gestured for Hans to remove his footwear. An instant later, *Herr* Fischer bent over and retrieved one. Adjusting a wide, black suspender with his thumb, he held the shoe in front of his face and examined it. Running his fingers over the outside and then the inside of the shoe, the craftsman nodded. "These are in excellent condition—good workmanship. Why replace?"

Hans drew a calming breath. *Truth is best.* "Borrowed—agreeable fit. Time to return to proper owner."

"Ah." *Herr* Fischer opened his mouth and smiled with his eyes. He named a price and the amount of deposit. "Take two weeks to make."

Swallowing, Hans calculated how much he needed to hold back from his next two Saturday wages. *Keep my tavern supper small—skip one day.* "*Ja.* I pay. You make pattern of my feet?"

A moment later, Hans stood with his left foot on a square of brown paper while *Herr* Fischer traced his foot with a piece of chalk. *Gute.* He contained a smile at the sight of no holes in his socks.

"How long in Elm Ridge?" *Herr* Fischer signaled Hans to change position.

"Four weeks." Hans blinked surprise. The answer left his lips easy. How long since he'd stayed in a small village this long? One year—two—more? *I am an honest man.* He sighed. Elm Ridge appeared an attractive town. He earned fair wages and felt a trace of kinship with his co-workers. Attending church proved more pleasant than his memories. Last Sunday, Fredrick invited him to join the family picnic at the beer garden. After a pleasant lunch, Louisa gave him a dancing lesson. He silently prayed for sunny weather and a chance to hold her in his arms again this week.

"Newcomer—explains why I've not seen you before." The shoemaker examined the pattern and straightened. "I craft you a fine pair. You give me your deposit and name."

Swallowing, he discarded the wrong response rising in his throat. "Hans Hoffmann."

****

One hour before the bakery's closing time, Louisa stepped into the sales area. Like many midafternoons, *Herr* Keil was gone on errands, and few customers came in the door. "*Bitte.* May I have a word, *Frau* Keil?"

"Louisa—you startled me." The taller woman stabbed her needle into pale linen inside the embroidery hoop. "Please, call me Charlotte when we are alone."

Moistening her lips, Louisa nodded. "I want to study the English. My papa desired to learn. As he lay dying, I promised to find a teacher and take lessons. During these few weeks in the bakery, I understand English is useful." She clasped her hands at the front of her apron and held her gaze on her employer. "Mrs. Cook, at the hardware, is a kind lady. I wish to go across the street and ask if she will teach me. The wash is brought inside, except for a few things not dry. The

115

upstairs floor is swept. I will not take long."

The older lady smiled from the high stool behind the sales counter. "You are ambitious, Louisa. You must be careful not to scare away the young men."

She opened her mouth and closed it without a sound. A denial would not be believed. Her friendly greetings to the young German men at church and at the beer garden could be seen as seeking attention, even courtship. Glancing to the ceiling, she imagined Hermann's cheerful eyes and robust laugh the day he informed Louisa's family he was off to the army. One more blink and the blond man's image was replaced by Hans's dark brown hair and gentle gaze. "I do not think—"

"Good afternoon."

Louisa snapped her attention toward the speaker.

A slender young woman dressed in a fashionable green gown and matching bonnet stood at the open door. The stranger held a small boy's hand. The *click* of the latch behind her punctuated the air. "Is this the bakery of Bernard Keil?"

Charlotte set her embroidery aside. "*Ja. Herr* Keil is not here. I am *Frau*. Have you come to buy a treat for your son?"

At these words, Louisa shifted her attention from the lady's face to the boy. Estimating by his size and the way he looked at the display case with wide eyes, she guessed his age at four, certainly no more than five.

The child looked at the world through soft, brown eyes matching his mother's. Above a smooth, oval face, straight, copper-colored hair covered his head.

"My business is with your husband. Will he return soon?" The woman lifted her chin, and her bonnet ribbons fluttered.

Louisa shifted her attention back to the mother with her brown eyes and a few caramel strands of hair visible. What sort of business did an American lady have with *Herr* Keil? She returned her attention to the child. *He stands odd.*

The boy moved toward the glass display of cookies and turnovers.

He limps. The unnatural angle of his left foot became obvious to Louisa the instant he moved forward.

Charlotte set her hands on the edge of the counter and leaned toward the stranger. "Who are you?"

"Yes, I suppose you have a right to know." The woman smoothed her skirt. "Tell Bernard...tell *Herr* Keil...Polly Black from St. Louis recently arrived in Elm Ridge and works at Mrs. Clark's dress shop."

"Polly..." Charlotte's voice faded. She stared at the boy.

Louisa hurried behind the counter and cupped her hands around *Frau* Keil's elbow.

The baker's wife, with skin paled to the color of fine flour, clung tight to the edge of the counter.

"*Frau* Keil, are you ill?"

Shaking her head, Charlotte tipped her face toward the floor and gathered a deep breath.

Tick...tock...tick. The bakery clock sounded loud over the silent women and child.

"It is the surprise of the thing." Charlotte eased to the stool and rested her arms on the counter. "*Herr* Keil has spoken of you. I will tell my husband where you may be found." She glanced to the street and then to the boy. "What is the name of your son?"

117

Polly reached out and touched the back of *Frau* Keil's hand. "Joseph—my son's name is Joseph. I do not mean to cause you trouble."

"Not trouble." Charlotte sat very still and studied Polly.

"Joseph." Louisa went in front of the counter and squatted near the boy. "*Geblack.*" She pointed to a sugar cookie. "You like?"

He nodded before he tipped his head to look at his mother.

"You may have one. Remember your manners." Polly returned her attention to Charlotte.

Louisa reached into the back of the case and removed one flat, circular cookie dusted with cinnamon sugar.

"Thank you." Joseph took one bite and smiled. "It is good—very good."

"We will go now. Tell your husband I look forward to either a note or a visit." Polly extended her hand to Joseph. Walking slowly, she guided her son out the door, to the sidewalk, and across the street.

Louisa stood in the middle of the sales area and watched the pair. The afternoon sun sparkled on Joseph's hair. *The boy's hair matches the color of* Herr *Keil's mustache.* She swallowed the thought before it fully formed. At the moment, her mind could not find a happy explanation.

Charlotte cleared her throat. "We will close for the day. Please put the sign in the window. Then you may go and speak to Mrs. Cook about English lessons."

For three ticks of the clock, Louisa continued to look out the large window at the street. The conversation overheard this morning returned. "*Frau*

Keil, is Polly Black a close relative of Mr. Black—the miller?"

"Black is a common name among Americans." Charlotte went into the workroom and soon returned with two large tins to store the leftover cookies and small baked goods. "You dare not say a word about this…situation. To anyone. *Verstehen?*"

"*Ja.* I not say a word." She pressed her lips. *Listening careful to every word is not a sin.*

Chapter Eleven

Sunday, Hans lingered in the pew after the final blessing. He nodded a silent greeting to Louisa as she headed toward the exit. Today, he remembered the responses better. Soon, if his courage held, he would sit forward—toward the center of the sanctuary. A few minutes later, he walked through the church's front door and down the steps.

"Join us." *Herr* Thayer gestured.

Hans greeted his foreman and smiled during introductions to fourteen-year-old Johannes and Hilde, a girl of ten or eleven. "Fine weather today. I think I will spend some time at the beer garden."

"Is the attraction the beer, the music, or the pretty girls?" Jacob fumbled in his pocket and withdrew several peppermints. He presented the candy on an open hand to the children but directed his words to Hans. "Reward for enduring the sermon in silence. Pastor tends to become tedious."

"*Ja.*" In his experience, all religious lectures presented an opportunity to let your mind wander to either the past or the future. Today his thoughts definitely dragged him forward. He'd spent many minutes of the sermon imagining a conversation with Louisa during a dancing lesson.

A steamboat whistle drifted from the river.

Hans shifted his gaze to a clump of four women

standing on the church lawn. Louisa, the prettiest girl in town, stood talking to *Frau* Hebing and two others. The sight of her, in her dark-blue Sunday dress and straw bonnet, caused his heart to thump louder. He touched his plain cap and stepped back from Jacob and the youngsters. "Excuse me."

"Don't spend all your money in one day." Jacob chuckled.

"No worry." *I know to the penny how much I dare spend at the beer garden today.* Long months without steady income taught him to be frugal. Yesterday's wages, after paying his landlady and setting aside *Herr* Fischer's fee for the wooden shoes, were sufficient to buy one round of beer today and supper each night. Glancing once more at the ladies bidding each other farewell, he headed toward Fredrick's team and wagon.

Greeting each of the horses with soft words, he displayed a flat hand for their inspection.

"*Guten Tag, Herr* Hoffmann."

Hans startled at Fredrick's voice and the sudden weight of a hand on his shoulder. *I am an honest man— no reason to fear a clasp on the shoulder.* After a quick swallow, he found his voice and greeted Louisa's cousin.

"Good weather today."

"*Ja.* Today is a fine spring day. I am thinking of going to the beer garden." Hans continued to pat the mare. A warm collar gathered and surged up his neck each instant he stood under Fredrick's inspection.

"I invite you to join us. My Anna packed a picnic. We have plenty to share. You may buy the beer."

"*Danke.*" Hans returned the other man's steady gaze. Did the farmer trust him? Many times, he

121

observed behavior in Fredrick which signaled the protectiveness of an older brother. Or rather, how he imagined a concerned brother behaved. *I put aside both lying and thievery. Have I managed to stay with the truth in all our brief conversations?*

"*Herr* Hoffmann. It is a pleasure to see you."

Louisa's voice comforted his ears and gave courage to his tongue. "*Bitte.* This is America. You are my friend. Please call me Hans." He glanced toward Fredrick.

She alternated her gaze between the two men and ended with a slight head shake. "Too soon, *Herr* Hoffmann. Will you join us at the beer garden?"

"Invitation already given and accepted, Louisa." Fredrick scanned the clusters of worshipers lingering at the base of the steps.

"*Gute.*" She smiled directly at Hans.

"Perhaps you agree to give me another dancing lesson." Hans felt a warm blush race across his face.

"*Ja.*" She lowered her gaze from his face to his feet.

He skimmed a sweaty palm across the bottom of his coat. "I remember the shoes. They are best for work. Soon *Herr* Fischer will craft a pair, and I will return your property." He pressed his lips. *I am not a thief.* Today he remained uncertain if the phrase would be truth or lie, present or past.

****

"I trust you." Louisa held her smile in place. She failed to banish Alfred's question regarding Hans. Nor did she forget the gentle, yet direct, manner in which Widow Krause phrased the inquiry in the New Orleans market. At each meeting, Hans, while gentle and kind, shielded his past. She reminded her heart to be cautious. Instead of directing her thoughts to others' secrets, she tried to concentrate on the privilege of living at the bakery and sifting flour with *Herr* Keil. "Ah, Anna and Karl are here. Shall we ride in the wagon?"

After a journey of several blocks to the southern edge of town, Fredrick pulled the team to a halt. Couples, families, and a few single men populated the street between the wagon and Althoff's Beer Garden, an open-air tavern and music hall.

Hans scrambled from the wagon bed and turned to assist Louisa.

"*Danke.*" She straightened her skirts. "*Bitte*—hand me the blanket and picnic basket." A short time later, Louisa helped Anna spread the cloth and set out the food.

The men went to get everyone a beer, and little Karl practiced pushing to his feet after each fall.

"You are very thoughtful today." Anna lifted a bowl of potato salad from the basket.

Louisa smoothed a corner of the blanket. "I keep thinking about something *Herr* Keil mentioned while he prepared the bread sponge Friday evening—a confidence." Until she had sifted half the measure of wheat flour, she did not know her employers had been married a mere four and a half years. She hid her surprise, but she listened carefully to the story. *Six years* Herr *Keil worked for another baker in St. Louis. I noticed a sadness in his face when he spoke of the cholera which took his first wife.* Since the revelation, her mind swirled with half a dozen explanations for his move to Elm Ridge. How did the mysterious Polly Black and her red-haired son relate to *Herr* Keil? Long

123

silences and tension hung in the air between Bernard and Charlotte since the appearance of the seamstress. Louisa alternated between temptation to ask—and certainty the delicate situation consisted of only private concerns. *Let others have a secret or two—my employer's past is not my business.*

"Don't get involved in keeping secrets for others. Mysteries lead to trouble." Anna handed her son his favorite toy, a wooden horse.

"I believe everyone holds at least one secret." *I told no one about Hermann's kiss.* Louisa pulled a more cheerful topic forward. "Mrs. Cook agreed to teach me English. My first lesson is Tuesday, after I finish my housekeeping chores."

"English." Anna shook her head. "I find everything I need in the *Deutsch* community. Fredrick learns a few words at the American store when he checks for letters."

Louisa held her response inside. She and Anna held a variation of this conversation every Sunday. Perhaps Anna's life did not require conversation with Americans. But Louisa intended to live in town and become a businesswoman. She wanted to read the signs in shop windows, whether they were written in *Deutsch* or English.

"For you, my pretty *Fraulein*." Hans half-bowed while keeping two beer steins level. He presented one to Louisa.

Giggling, she wrapped both hands around the drink container. "*Danke,* kind sir. Listen to us, we sound like characters in an ancient tale."

"I desire to be polite to my dancing mistress. Perhaps she will remember small kindnesses and ignore when I tread on her toes."

"After lunch, we will discover how much your brain and feet remember from two weeks ago." Louisa took a sip of beer before settling on the blanket.

Hans sat and studied her for a long moment. "In school, I did poor with the examinations."

"Your classroom performance does not concern me." She spooned a mound of potato salad on a plate, added three thin slices of cold, roasted pork, and handed him the meal. Serving her own lunch, she thought of all the things she did not know about Hans. *Did he keep secrets? Or did she not ask enough of the proper questions?* She knew he had a difficult childhood, and his mother died when he was fourteen. She took the first bite of tart, spiced potato. The flavor, with a hint of bacon, brought memories of learning to make the dish under her mother's watchful eye. "Tell us of progress on the building."

"Tomorrow, the crew starts the roof." He chewed a bite of meat. "Lots of windows. Business downstairs and two apartments above. Americans build large."

Fredrick swallowed. "Not only Americans. Think of the church—the building will hold three times the number of current members."

"*Ja.*" Anna wiped a speck of food from Karl's cheek with her handkerchief. "Wise planning to make church with extra room in a growing town. Since Easter, a new family or two arrives every week."

The three-piece band started to play before Anna and Louisa packed all the lunch dishes away.

"Go." Anna swished her hands at Louisa. "Already your foot is tapping."

"Hans?" She turned her head toward him and

realized he stood with a hand extended to assist her.

"I apologize in advance for stepping on your feet."

She laughed. "Come. We will review before we join the circle."

Reaching the edge of the pounded earth dance area, Hans squeezed her hand, stopped, and faced her. "Are you sure you want to risk dancing with me?"

"I am certain." She glanced toward her arm and gave silent thanks for long sleeves covering the gooseflesh prompted by his touch. "Remember, listen to the steady beat from the tuba." She gripped her skirts and displayed her feet. "One…and two. Large step—quick step."

He nodded and watched her half boots below the dark blue hem. "One…and two. Three…and four." Counting above a whisper, he started to move his feet.

The tuba sounded the low note.

Hans took a large step, then a quick step. "Large step—quick step."

"Listen carefully and start again."

He drew a breath and stepped to his left. Counting in a soft voice, he stayed in rhythm.

"*Gute.* Now hold my hand for the dance." She opened her arms, as if for an embrace. The instant his hands touched her, heat radiated into her hand and her hip. Listening to the band, she nodded the beat and counted. "Begin…now. One…and two. Three…and four." After counting another cycle, she guided them into a wide gap between two swirling couples. Familiar with dancing all of her life, she moved her feet with joy. "A little quicker. Listen…follow the steady throb."

A quarter of the circle later, Hans bumped into another man. "*Bitte,* forgive me."

Louisa tugged Hans to continue the polka step instead of pausing in further apology.

"I…off…I apologize." Hans looked at his feet. "I am not good at dancing."

"*Nein.* You student. Listen to the music and begin again. Hear it?" She moved on the next beat, urging Hans toward the empty center of the circle.

The band stopped and announced a break.

"You are a good teacher." Hans panted. "You encourage my feet to remember many years ago, the few times my mother danced with me."

She continued to hold his hand and eased them out of the dancing area. "How many years ago did you dance with her?"

"*Vier*—" He pressed his lips and shook his head. "*Sech Jahr.*"

Louisa hid her surprise. *I asked a simple question. Did he forget when his mother died—or his own age?* "Not so long for me. God took Mama the winter I was eighteen." She sighed. "Mama and Papa taken one year apart, almost to the week."

"*Ta…ta…ta.*" Karl toddled toward her with his arms outstretched.

"*Tante*—soon you will find the word, little one." *Anna is correct. I will be more aunt than cousin to her children.* She gathered the child into her arms and glanced over her shoulder to Hans before turning to face her relatives. "Dance the next set with your wife, Fredrick. We will keep Karl out of mischief."

"*Danke.*" Fredrick touched the brim of his town hat an instant before the band played a tuning note.

Louisa settled on the blanket and began to rock Karl in time to the music. She steadied her gaze on

Hans before speaking. "Will you stay in Elm Ridge? Or will you take the packet and move upriver after the building crew disbands?"

Straightening his legs, he leaned on one elbow. For a long moment, he gazed at the clear sky. "I will stay…find a different job. Illinois—Elm Ridge—is a good place. I meet nice people—pretty dance teacher."

Louisa turned her attention to the child as heat flashed up her neck and over her face.

Chapter Twelve

Late Tuesday morning, Louisa snatched the calico sunbonnet from the peg and paused in the doorway between storeroom and bakery workspace. Tapping one finger against a hanging dishpan, she gained *Herr* Keil's attention before speaking. "The table is set for your midday meal. Kraut and sausages are on the stove. I will be in the garden."

"*Gute.*" The baker brushed melted butter across a pan of hot rolls without lifting his face.

A glance through the pass-through shelves confirmed *Frau* Keil worked in the sales area. Louisa caught a glimpse of a customer's bonnet, turned, and hurried out the back door. She followed several wide, flat stones to the garden gate. Pausing, she breathed in the scent of growing plants. Releasing a sigh, she felt the heavy weight of unspoken words between her employers slide off her shoulders. *The tension started with Polly Black.* Leaving the gate open, she walked to the raised bed at the far end of the garden. She squatted and pulled tiny weeds emerging between the young cabbages.

"A small boy with red hair," she muttered while dislodging the unwanted plants. "What business does an American seamstress have with a German baker? She appears much younger than *Herr* Keil." For at least the third time this morning, Louisa calculated the marriage date of the baker and guessed at the age of the boy. *I doubt he attends school.* Moving to the other side of the planted space, she began to thin the carrots. While she kept her fingers working, her mind re-played the cryptic conversation during last night's flour sifting.

Herr Keil spoke less than most evenings. He did not hum the folk tunes. Friday, not so many evenings ago, he told a story set in St. Louis. During most of the hour in the workroom yesterday, he frowned and gave directions between muttered complaints concerning Mr. Black's flour.

"It is not my business," she spoke to the vegetables and moved to the next raised bed to clear weeds between the emerging turnips.

"*Guten Tag, Fraulein.* What is not your business?"

She raised her gaze toward the garden entrance.

The butcher's youngest son, Werner, stood with one hand resting on the gate post and holding a slim book in the other.

"*Guten Tag, Herr* Hebing. Private concerns of other people. I must learn to watch my tongue. A gossip is not a trustworthy person."

"I hesitate to use such a harsh word to describe you, a mild-mannered *Fraulein.*"

She looked at the tender plants without really seeing them. Heat pooled at the base of her neck and threatened to surge over her face. *How does a person stop blushing at any kind word from a young man?*

Like his brothers, Werner was a tall, handsome man with a pleasant round face and curly blond hair. He wore a well-fitting, plain coat and one of the low-crowned, wide-brimmed straw hats favored by Americans.

A good dancer. She recalled his confident steps during the set they danced late Sunday afternoon. Swallowing, she risked another glance toward him. "Have you been to a lesson?"

"*Ja.*" He lifted the book for an instant. "The pastor teaches me Latin. I will need the language in college."

"University—do you go soon?" She estimated his age at three or four and twenty. *Today is poor time to ask questions concerning advanced schooling in America.* A moment later, she recalled his mother's stray words on the topic of Werner's education.

"First, I need more money. The best schools are expensive and far away."

She nodded and resumed pulling weeds. Additional portions of *Frau* Hebing's comments returned. "Will your family help you?"

"Papa tells me to find a school close to Elm Ridge. But I have my heart set on an engineering school in New York."

"New York sounds very far away." She closed her eyes for a moment and visualized the large map *Herr* Schutte used during his American lectures aboard *The Flying Gull.* If she remembered the states correctly, New York sat on the Atlantic coast. How many days journey by steamboat and overland from Elm Ridge? "You have a grand dream."

"More important, I have a plan." He glanced toward the butcher shop before returning his gaze. "I save money from little jobs for either American or *Deutsch.* Soon I will have enough to travel."

"Engineer." She thought of the many mechanical marvels she'd seen since leaving her village. "Do you enjoy fixing the sausage machine? Are you clever with gears and levers?"

Werner laughed. "From a small boy, I tinker and repair. Now I want to design and build large things. Have you seen the Iron Horses? Can you imagine great stone bridges carrying steam trains over American rivers?"

She shook her head and hid the fear dancing along her spine. The only time she'd watched a locomotive cross a bridge, the noise and trembling prompted her to gasp a prayer. The American rivers were larger and wider than the waterways on the journey to Bremerhaven. "*Nein*—*s*uch a mighty bridge sounds impossible."

"Have you dreams, *Fraulein* Mueller?"

"*Ja*—but none so grand." She removed a stubborn weed and pushed a lump of dirt back into the garden bed. "I promised to my papa…the day he lay dying…to learn English. Mrs. Cook, the kind lady at the hardware store, agreed to give me lessons. I want to learn how to speak, read, and write. Two lessons a week, I begin today, after my chores are finished."

"Excellent. Perhaps, by the end of summer you will speak English well enough to bargain with the American merchants." He pushed off the gate post and looked toward the butcher shop. A moment later, he turned in her direction, touched the brim of his wide hat, and gave a hint of a bow. "*Auf Wiedersehen, Fraulein.*"

End of summer. Louisa allowed the phrase to circle in her mind. Midsummer Day was still three weeks in the future. Glancing at the tiny vegetables, she refused to set a time for speaking good English. The lessons on the ship did not teach her much practical in daily life.

Counting, the most useful thing *Herr* Schutte attempted, faded without someone to correct her mistakes.

She stood, dusted her hands on her apron, and moved to the next raised bed. Two rows of weeding later, she heard the butcher shop's door thump. She glanced toward the noise. Staying silent, she observed Werner pump a pail of water and carry it inside. *The young* Herr *Hebing is unlike other men his age.* She recalled, and repeated, Fredrick's Sunday evening comments regarding the butcher's family. "Youngest Hebing boy is smart. He will make a good husband for a clever girl."

"*Nein, nein, nein,*" she muttered to the discarded weeds. "Do not push me into a marriage, dear cousin. I'd rather be the spinster running the smallest bakery in town than tied to the wrong man." An image of Hans relaxing on the blanket at the beer garden sailed into her memory. He intended to stay in Elm Ridge. He worked steady on the construction crew and told interesting stories. *Does it matter that he cannot keep the beat of the music? Do I trust him?*

****

Hans swung three boards to his shoulder and drew a long breath. *We begin afternoon work.* He glanced toward the fair Wednesday sky and climbed the scaffolding. With a clatter, he shrugged his burden to the completed portion of the roof.

"We need short boards for the pattern." One of the skilled carpenters tucked the order between hammer blows.

"*Ja.* Next trip I bring short." Hans paused for a breath and took in the view. From this height, he could see all the way to First Street over his right shoulder and along Sixth to the Lutheran church a bit to his left.

"Today, man."

Snapping out of his daydream, Hans hurried to the lumber wagon. In a few minutes, he resumed the work rhythm developed this morning. Hoist the rough boards on his shoulder. Carry the lumber up the scaffolding. Deposit the material on the completed portion of the roof for the two skilled carpenters and one helper to nail into place. The work was repetitious and physically demanding. He wiped sweat off his forehead and began another cycle.

Thud—thud. Two boards fell the last few inches to the area of completed roof.

"Getting hot." Hans wiped his brow. Drawing a deep breath, he paused and checked the view.

Across the street, a man in a flat, black cap walked with his head bent.

Lost in his thoughts? Glancing left, to Sixth Street, he sighted a team pulling a wagon filled with grain sacks. *Not right.* He blinked. *The off horse walks half a step ahead of the near horse. Does the driver not pay attention?* With a shake of his head, he shifted his weight to step toward the first layer of scaffolding. *What?* Motion at the edge of his vision prompted Hans to shift his attention.

A tall man, wearing a wide-brimmed straw hat, exited the soap factory across the street and bumped the man in the black cap.

Losing his balance, the shorter man fell into the dusty street.

A steamboat whistled.

The horses neighed and bolted. The near horse

galloped over the prone figure before the wagon rolled across his body.

"*Halten!*" Hans shouted and scampered to the ground. His feet barely contacted the earth before he dashed to intersect the team. "*Halten. Halten,*" he called the *Deutsch* command to the team as he sprinted.

A few yards after drawing even with the near horse, Hans snatched at the bridle. For an instant, he hung with both feet above the street. He touched earth and ran backward as fast as his legs could move. "*Halten. Gute Pferd.* Good horse. Halt." With each word, Hans lowered his voice a notch.

The team slowed to a brisk walk.

"Easy, easy, my friend. The boat will not harm you."

The near horse snorted and flung foam from his mouth.

Hans gripped each animal's chin straps and continued speaking in soft *Deutsch* until the team stopped. "*Gute Pferd.* Good horse." He released his hold on the off horse and ran one hand down the neck of the snorting, chestnut gelding. Glancing toward the wagon, he met an angry stare from the American driver. Mindful not to scare the horses, he released the strap with his right hand and backed a step.

The American driver cursed a long collection of words without drawing a fresh breath. Then he spat a stream of tobacco juice straight ahead toward Hans. "Person would think Duke's never heard a steamboat before."

"Take care, my pretty." Hans puffed soft words between greedy breaths. *Do American drivers not care if their team runs wild in harness?* Giving the horse a quick pat on the cheek, he stepped away from the yoke and eased to the side. Instantly, he memorized the shape of the blaze on the gelding's face and the height of the stockings on his rear legs. Drawing courage with his next gulp of air, he addressed the driver in *Deutsch*. "The team pulled uneven before the whistle. Did you not see the man in the street?"

"I don't speak your queer German—or *Deutsch*—or whatever language you's spouting. Now get out of the way." The driver lifted a long driving whip and flicked it over the team. "Git up now."

Hans braced his hands on his thighs and blinked. *No tears.* He ground his teeth. Every scar on his back quivered.

Chapter Thirteen

Lifting the full water bucket, Louisa counted each step from the pump to the bakery's back door. "One...two...three...four...*funf*— Ach. Now I must start again with English numbers. One."

"Louisa," *Frau* Keil shouted.

She stopped so quickly water sloshed onto her skirt. In an instant, she jerked her attention toward the baker's wife.

Standing in the doorway, Charlotte Keil twisted her hands in her apron.

"*Ja.* I come." Louisa hurried the final distance and stepped out of her wooden shoes across the threshold. "*Ja—ja—w*hat is the trouble?"

"*Fraulein.*" A muscular man dressed in workman's shirt and trousers stood one step inside the bakery workroom.

Hans, pale and trembling, peered around the older man's shoulder.

I see him at church...name?

The spokesman clutched his flat, wool cap to his chest and nodded as *Frau* Keil claimed the plain wooden chair.

Louisa blinked and looked at the pair of men again. *Herr Thayer is a carpenter. I remember his name now. Why is he in the bakery?* She opened her mouth and stopped the words when she deciphered the command in the carpenter's blue eyes.

"I bring sad news to *Frau* Keil. I wish you to be near."

"The shop"—Louisa took two small, quick steps toward the sales area. "What if we have a customer?"

"They...they told me...to lock...the door." *Frau* Keil glanced toward her lap.

Louisa looked first to Hans, then *Herr* Thayer, and finally at Charlotte's unnaturally pale face. Taking the other woman's hand in hers, she squatted beside her employer. "What is this sad news?"

Clearing his throat, Jacob Thayer began. "I am construction foreman at a new store on Sixth Street where Pecan crosses."

Louisa nodded. *Foreman. Ja.* "Two Sundays ago, Fredrick, my cousin, pointed you out after church service. You installed windows at his farm house one year ago—tight—keep winter outside. Now you direct work...and *Herr* Hoffmann. I understand a little—not all."

"We bring news of a terrible accident. *Herr* Keil...fell...in front of a runaway team and wagon." *Herr* Thayer shifted his gaze to his feet.

Charlotte lifted one hand over her mouth.

Louisa felt her heart skip a beat. Forcing her lungs to work, she looked toward *Herr* Thayer. "Have you called a doctor?" She continued to rub her thumbs across Charlotte's hand. Holding her gaze on *Herr* Thayer, she selected careful words. "Will your crew bring him home?"

Hans worried the rim of his cap. "We are sorry, *Frau* Keil. Your husband died of his injuries before we could give him aid. We beg forgiveness for bringing the sad news."

Staring at her work-roughened hands, Louisa froze. *Dead? Herr Keil?* She hid a stutter in her breath, forced a blink, and glanced toward Charlotte's face.

An unnatural calm rested on *Frau* Keil's features for an instant before her lips trembled.

Herr Thayer shifted his stance. "I sent a man to fetch the Lutheran pastor. I hope you approve."

Louisa soon gathered enough wits to press a handkerchief into Charlotte's hand. "*Ja*—the preacher is a good man."

"Bernard"—Charlotte spoke her late husband's Christian name through a hiccup. "He went this afternoon to speak with the pastor. Oh…my last words to my husband were unkind. How? I-I…cannot beg his forgiveness."

"*Herr* Keil was a good man." Louisa focused her attention on Charlotte's hands. Swallowing unshed tears, she glanced at the men. "Did you see it happen?"

Hans nodded.

Tick…tock…tick.

Louisa studied Charlotte's somber face. Did today's planned visit to the pastor concern the mysterious Polly Black? Or was it a routine matter? Did *Herr* Keil prepare the communion bread? *The nature of the call on the pastor is not my business.*

Hans moved his feet and the sound of wooden shoes against the smooth pine floor broke the silence. "There are many things I wish to tell you, *Fraulein.* Now is not the proper time. *Frau* Keil should have comfort from the pastor. May I speak with you this evening?"

Removing her hands from *Frau* Keil's, Louisa

stood and faced both men. "*Ja.* This evening is good. I will let you out. The pastor will arrive soon. We have much to do."

After unlocking the bakery door for the men, she checked the street for the preacher. Stepping inside, she turned the key and hurried to Charlotte.

"He…he did not know." Charlotte lifted the handkerchief to first one eye and then the other. "Five and a half years ago…all his years in Elm Ridge…he did not know. Only a few days…and now he is gone."

Louisa pressed her lips. She failed to make sense of her employer's words. But the woman had received a terrible shock. Confused speech should be excused. She turned her thoughts to the bakery. Fetching one of the large tins to store the unsold items, she studied the pass-through shelves. "We give Pastor Belker the final rye loaf?"

Tap-tap-tap.

Nodding, Charlotte stood. "Get the door, Louisa. I think *Frau* Hebing is the first of many visitors."

A short time later, after Charlotte, *Frau* Hebing, and the pastor had gone to the apartment, Louisa continued to tidy the bakery. *My world changed today. Will* Frau *Keil continue the business? Will she let me be her assistant?* Glancing at the bowls and utensils stored in their usual places, she sighed. *Regular customers depend on our bread. I make half size sponge this evening.*

Closing her eyes for a moment, she visualized *Herr* Keil mixing salted water, bubbling yeast, pale lard, and sifted flour into dough at the sturdy table. The baker took great care and placed the troughs in the exact position near the empty oven. In the morning, the dough, tripled in bulk, was ready for kneading and the second, shorter rise. *I will miss his stories of St. Louis…and careful instruction of baking in Elm Ridge. I wonder what Hans wants to tell me?*

****

After Hans deposited a bundle of short boards on the roof, he paused to wipe sweat from his brow. Since the accident earlier this afternoon, the entire crew worked in near silence. He glanced both ways on Sixth Street. *Do I wish for the angry American with the mismatched team to drive past again? Or do I feel relief they are not in sight?*

"Day is done." *Herr* Thayer struck the iron triangle hanging from the supply wagon's tailgate. "Good work, men. Same time tomorrow."

Within a few minutes, the carpenters and apprentices gathered near the wagon. While the other workers stored their tools for the night, Hans and Ernst secured a canvas over the remaining lumber. Twice, Hans opened his lips to speak and thought better of the idea.

"Exciting day." Ernst swatted sawdust off his jacket before slipping his arms into the sleeves. "Shall we walk together to the tavern?"

"*Nein.*" Retrieving his coat, Hans flapped the garment twice. *My shirts and jacket get tighter at the shoulders each week. I must ask the laundress if she can alter.* He looked at his co-worker and shook his head. Most evenings he took his meal at the small, friendly business on First Street. The tavern served a hearty stew at a cheap price. Today he sought answers to questions circling in his mind since the accident. "I have an errand."

A short time later, Hans paused on First Street and studied the large, plain building with half a dozen, small windows at shoulder height. The sign proclaimed *Bergmann's Livery and Freight Company,* exactly the place he wanted to be. He crossed the street and approached a workman leading a sturdy, black gelding toward the watering trough. "*Guten Abend.* I wish to speak with *Herr* Bergmann. Where might I find him?"

"Third stall on the left." The man gestured toward the wide-open stable door.

"*Danke.*" Nodding to the stable hand, Hans hurried the final steps into the building. He found the correct stall within a few moments and paused in the wide, center aisle. Breathing in the familiar scents of hay, horse, and leather, he stayed silent while a slight man finished inspecting the right front hoof of a small, dappled mare.

"No luck if you came to board your ride." The man straightened and adjusted one suspender.

"*Nein.* I do not come to either board or rent an animal. Are you *Herr* Bergmann?" After the man confirmed his name, Hans introduced himself and described the chestnut gelding. "Do you know this horse?"

Herr Bergmann shrugged, exited the stall, and double-checked the latch. "What does it matter to you?"

"This animal, a fine *Pferd*, was half of the team driven by an American in the accident this afternoon." *Not lie. Others have no hesitation using the word for the event.*

"The wagon which killed the baker?" The stablemaster removed his cap and swiped an arm across his balding head. "Did you see it happen? All I hear is rumor."

"*Ja.* I see from the roof of new building. Ran like devil chased me to stop the team. The driver was unpleasant man." Hans gripped his cap while memories danced across the scars on his back. *A good driver does not need to use the whip.*

"You want to know if I sold a chestnut gelding to an American." *Herr* Bergmann led Hans along the aisle, pausing to open two stalls on the way to the far end. "I sold an animal like you describe three days ago. He's a saddle horse. I got a good price. Odd thing, the buyer spoke little *Deutsch*—expected the beast to know English."

"Would the horse be accustomed to steamboat whistles?"

"Hard to say. I owned the gelding only one day."

Hans clamped tight his jaw to stay silent. In a few sentences, the stable owner explained a great many things. The information increased his pity for the horse. The change from saddle to draft work was difficult for a great many animals. If the horse, trained in *Deutsch*, suddenly heard commands in English, he would become terribly confused. *Why did the driver show so little concern about the accident?* He closed his eyes for a moment to recall the instant before the steamboat whistle. *Herr* Keil was bumped, or pushed, into the street. *I feel a trace of doubt at the word accident.*

"Are we done?" *Herr* Bergmann straightened a harness hanging on a peg.

"You have been most helpful." Hans settled his hat into place. "One more question. The American—do you remember his name?"

"Armstrong—at least that's what he told me to put

in my record book. Half the drifters give a false name."

Hans swallowed and looked at the tips of his wooden shoes. *Herr Mueller's shoes.* The casual comment about a false name sent his blood racing to his toes. *"Danke...* I go now and let you finish your work. You have fine animals—a well-maintained stable."

Fifteen minutes later, dusk was settling over the town. Hans climbed the stairs to the bakery apartment. At the top, he paused and looked west for a long moment. Lanterns glowed from the river, indicating a boat seeking a place to tie-up for the night. Drawing a deep breath, he tapped on the door.

"Guten Abend." Louisa opened the door at his first knock and gestured him to enter. "Have you eaten? We have potatoes fried with onions and bacon."

He pressed his lips to stop his mouth from drooling at the warm smoky and spicy smells of their supper. *"Nein.* I went on an errand after work."

"Then come, sit, I will fix you a plate." Louisa swirled toward the stove.

He removed his cap and greeted the two women sitting in front of half-eaten suppers. His heart felt a little easier when he recognized the butcher's wife. *I think a neighbor at such a time should be a comfort to the new widow.* "I apologize for bringing such sad news today."

Frau Keil paused tracing a circle on her spoon handle. Lifting her gaze, she looked him straight on. "Bernard...*Herr* Keil...was a good man. Will you be at his funeral service? The pastor and I decided on three o'clock tomorrow."

"I will need to ask *Herr* Thayer." Glancing around the large room, he noticed a row of pegs near the door.

The one beside the new widow's Sunday bonnet was bare. *Herr Keil's place?* He kept his hat in his hands and stepped behind a ladder-back chair.

"Sit...eat." Louisa carried a plate mounded with hot, fragrant potatoes and two slices of rye bread. After she set the meal in front of him, she fetched a glass and filled it from a small beer keg.

"Bitte." Frau Keil pointed to the place setting. "The news is beginning to settle. I want you to tell us everything you saw from the roof."

Hans sat and reached for the jam pot. *A fine ladle. Heavy silver. Expensive.* He lifted his gaze to the whitewashed exposed rafters. *Hans Hoffmann is an honest man.* Ladling raspberry jam on a slice of bread, he gathered bits of courage and sorted words. "Today I carried boards to the roof. I saw a team and wagon on Sixth Street."

"Go on..." *Frau* Keil pushed a piece of potato from one side of her plate to the other.

Hans recounted the events with an emphasis on stopping the horses. He told the story without giving details as to how *Herr* Keil came to be sprawled in the street. *I do kindness to let her believe her husband tripped.* He took a final sip of his beer. "The American started the team again and continued along the street."

"The wagon." Charlotte lifted a cup of tea but paused it away from her lips. "What color? Did you see a design on the tailboard?"

He chewed and swallowed a bite of flavorful bread crust. "Green, the wagon was painted green. On the back"—he blinked and recalled an image of the vehicle moving away—"three bags painted in white."

"Ahhh. Black's Mill." She leaned against the chair

back and curved her lips into a faint smile. "A snake changes his skin, but not his character."

Hans watched the two ladies on the other side of the table exchange a silent story in a single glance. For a long moment, he stared at his plate and puzzled over *Frau* Keil's words. Lifting his gaze, he saw an invitation to continue. "Others in the crew rushed to aid *Herr* Keil. However, even the short time to cross the street proved too late. *Herr* Thayer directed men to move the body and cover your husband with a canvas before sending a message to the pastor and letting me accompany him to the bakery."

Charlotte took one sip of tea and set her cup in the saucer without moving her gaze from his face.

She knows I'm not telling the entire story. He did not want to add to the widow's burden by telling of the American driver's rudeness. "*Herr* Keil was a kind man."

"*Ja.* Good baker. Decent husband. Married four years and seven months—happy times."

Hans blinked twice to hide his surprise. According to comments from another customer last week, the baker was forty years old. He'd estimated the Keils's marriage to be a dozen years long.

"You may close your mouth, *Herr* Hoffmann. You are a new resident in Elm Ridge. I was a widow, five years, before Bernard moved here from St. Louis." Charlotte released the hint of a laugh. "I worked in the laundry. He brought in the aprons, towels, and other clothing at a regular interval. Each time, we talked a little more. A full year after he arrived, we married. Little by little, each time a bakery boy caught *gold fever* or some other nonsense, he taught me more of the business and the baking."

Pleased the widow had found her tongue, Hans finished his meal while she spun stories of life with her husband. He listened to tales of Sunday afternoon buggy rides and several misunderstandings with English-speaking customers.

"Ach. I have talked too much."

"Nein." Louisa touched Charlotte's left wrist. "Remembering the good times is proper."

"The *Fraulein* is correct." *Frau* Hebing pushed her chair from the table and stood. "The hour grows late. I will clear the dishes and clean the kitchen. Louisa, did you say something earlier about making bread sponges?"

"Ja." She glanced toward the clock. "This is good timing. Small batch each of wheat and rye for morning customers—I think."

Hans stood. *"Bitte,* if you do not object, I will accompany you."

"Go"—*Frau* Hebing made a swishing motion with both hands. "Young people need time for a private conversation."

Louisa turned a charming shade of red.

Would her Cousin Fredrick forbid the private time? Give a deep frown and sigh? Fixing a neutral expression on his lips, Hans nodded once more to *Frau* Keil. The situation did not allow for a chaperone. He gripped his cap tighter than necessary before walking to the door. *Louisa is a respectable young woman. I will speak, but not touch.*

"Gute." Louisa handed him one of the wooden buckets sitting under the coat pegs. "I will direct you in work of bakery boy."

147

He smiled and followed her out of the apartment. The older women had given him a great gift, and he intended to use it to speak of today's events—all of them. Instinct told him he could trust Louisa with this mystery. *Who plotted and killed the kind baker? What did she know of Black's Mill?*

Chapter Fourteen

The morning after *Herr* Keil's funeral, Louisa stood at the worktable, stirring soft butter and precious sugar in a large crockery bowl.

The tantalizing odor of finishing rye bread seeped from the oven and mixed with the comforting scent of buttered wheat loaves cooling at the far end of the table.

She glanced at the clock and frowned. *I did not allow enough time.* Beginning work at the same hour the deceased baker began his morning tasks failed to consider her less-experienced hands. *The first dough was ten minutes late into the oven.* Each step in the careful routine ended a little later, until now, forty minutes late, she began the first cakes.

"Fifteen minutes until the door is unlocked." In rapid succession, she cracked four eggs into a small bowl and checked them for bits of shell or traces of blood. Confirming the eggs were good, she gave them a quick stir before she slipped them into the butter-and-sugar mixture. She began to beat the first phase of the batter with the wooden spoon. Flicking her gaze to the waiting bowl of dry ingredients, she shook her head. The wheat flour left too many lumps in the sifter. "Poor quality. Damp. I understand why *Herr* Keil refused to buy again from Black's Mill."

Thump. Thump. Thump.

She turned her attention toward the noise at the

front door.

A slender man wearing a tall hat stood on the other side of the glass.

"Bakery is closed. Return on the hour," she called from the workroom.

"Now." He rattled the door.

"Let him in, Louisa. *Herr*...Mister Black knows neither manners nor patience." *Frau* Keil paused at the boundary of storeroom and workroom. An instant later, the widow shook a clean apron and began to fasten it over her brown-and-white-striped dress. Her hair, pulled back and secured in a low bun, looked tidy and normal. Dark crescents under her eyes hinted at little or no sleep.

Giving her hands a quick wipe on her apron, Louisa snatched the key from the hook behind the sales counter and went to the door.

The impatient Mr. Black pushed the door open before she pulled the key from the lock. "Where is Mrs. Keil?"

Charlotte entered the sales area while securing the final pin to the top of her apron. "*Guten Morgan, Herr* Black."

"Don't use your guttural talk with me. I know you are capable in English." He advanced until a mere palm's width remained between their shoes.

Rude. He does not even remove his hat. Louisa slipped into the workroom. She had loaves to remove from the oven. *I will work and stay silent.*

The pass-through shelves and doorless opening allowed all but the softest conversations to reach the baking area.

"The bill is due."

"The amount is in dispute," *Frau* Keil replied in slow, clear English. "My husband took a letter to the mill a week ago. He offered a fair price."

"The proposal is refused."

Thump.

Louisa startled at a sound much like a fist against the counter. Gathering her nerves and wrapping a towel around her hand, she opened the large oven.

"Pay—all—now." Quick thuds punctuated the words.

"*Nein.*"

Tick...tock...tick.

Charlotte shattered the pressing silence with a string of rapid *Deutsch.* "The flour is poor quality. We ordered fine. You send us coarse with more lumps than hairs on a cat."

Louisa curved her lips into a tiny smile. She placed the hot bread on the clean end of the table and set the pan of cinnamon buns into the oven.

Thump.

"What did you say? Speak English."

While Louisa brushed butter across the warm loaves, she listened to Charlotte speak in slow, loud English words. She did not understand the comments, but anger coated every word.

"Poor flour," *Frau* Keil repeated. "Price is higher than Gordon's Mill."

"You'll pay for more than flour. I'll own this place—fancy oven and all. Tomorrow noon—full payment."

Crash.

Louisa jumped. Turning toward the front door, she stared at the quivering panel. *I expected the glass to shatter.*

"Trouble, trouble, trouble. He does not even allow Bernard time to settle in his grave before stirring up problems." Shaking her head, Charlotte entered the workroom and removed a white, china mug from a hook. "Have we coffee, Louisa?"

"*Ja.*" She reached for the coffeepot beside a pan of simmering apple slices on the stove. Filling the mug, she arranged her words. "Can he take the bakery?"

Charlotte accepted the drink and blew across the hot liquid. "He can cause trouble. *Herr* Hebing and his son, Werner, suggested I hire a lawyer."

"Will an attorney be expensive?" *Papa complained of the fee both times he had business with a lawyer.*

"Do not worry, Louisa. You are hired baker. Concern yourself with the kneading, mixing, and oven temperature. I will deal with the bills and rude Americans."

She nodded and pressed her lips. Her thoughts were a jumble, and she did not want to add to *Frau* Keil's problems. She grasped the bowl with the beginnings of the cake batter and began to stir. "Two cakes today, topped with sweet apple. Tomorrow, I fix cherry tarts."

Setting her coffee beside the cooling loaves, Charlotte began to gather the tins to stock the glass case with cookies and turnovers baked earlier in the week.

A minute later, Louisa heard the first regular customer of the day enter the shop. She continued her work but failed to banish *Herr* Black's threat to take the business. *What would happen to Frau Keil? I can live with Fredrick and his family until I find different work. I never hear Frau Keil speak of relatives—will she find shelter?*

Mapping out the businesses of Elm Ridge in her mind, she included the small, American bakery on Cherry Street. *Too much English. I'm not ready.* She glanced at the clock while greasing the cake pans. *Papa's money—seed for his Illinois bakery—must not be wasted.* With new determination to polish her skills in baking and learn the buying and selling of supplies, she poured batter into the first pan.

Is it possible for me to aid Frau Keil? Perhaps Hans will have an idea—or be able to answer questions about Mr. Black. She pushed the problem to the back of her mind to simmer, but the questions insisted on creeping forward as she worked. *Hans is not certain Herr Keil's death was an accident. Who pushed him into the street? Why?*

****

The foundry whistle's distinctive sound sliced through the air. Before it faded completely, the carpenters placing the shingles stopped their work.

Hans shrugged the bundle from his shoulder and pushed it away from the roof's edge. "Noon—we do much work this morning."

"*Ja.* Today is good. Better than the hot sun." *Herr* Thayer pointed to the clouds in various shades of gray before tucking his hammer into a loop on his short, leather apron.

Nodding, Hans hurried down the scaffolding. Yesterday, the crew worked and sweated to get the final roof boards in place. By noon, he had felt a storm building.

Heat continued to build even after *Herr* Thayer left for the funeral in mid-afternoon.

The church bell still tolled for *Herr* Keil when dark clouds swept in from over the river with thunder, lightning, and rain.

Switching his thoughts to the present, Hans shrugged into his coat. *I will apologize for not attending the service.* A few minutes later, Hans stepped inside the bakery. He removed his cap and glanced toward *Frau* Keil. *Gute, she is busy with customers.* Lifting his mouth into a smile, he nodded at Louisa. The blonde *Fraulein* in the dark dress and linen apron excited him more than the tray of ginger cookies in her hands. "*Guten Tag.*"

She curved her lips into a generous smile and returned his greeting. "Will you do an errand for us before you return to work?"

"I have most of an hour before the next whistle."

Frau Keil beckoned him to the counter and reached into her pocket. Displaying a folded piece of paper, she leaned forward. "Do you know Mrs. Clark's dress shop?"

A seamstress? "Sign of needle and thread?"

Charlotte nodded. "Next to Mr. Fox, the cooper, and same corner as the vacant wheelwright shop."

Many evenings, walking from the German tavern on First Street to his room at Mrs. Winter's house, he passed the business. "*Ja.* Easy walk from here."

"I wish you to deliver my message to the girl named Polly. Wait for a reply. I think she will give you a note." *Frau* Keil extended the paper.

"*Ja.* I wait long as I dare for my job." He accepted the paper and tucked it inside his cap.

"*Gute.* I pay you with sweet lunch." She handed him the largest of the spiral cinnamon rolls on the shelf.

"*Danke.* I hurry." Walking along Third Street, Hans puzzled over *Frau* Keil's request and chewed the sweet roll. *Did she need a new dress to tell others she was a widow? I think the wide, black band pinned on her arm symbolizes mourning. No profit to argue. The baker's wife treats me with kindness.* He swallowed the final bite of his lunch, wiped his hand on his trousers, and opened the dress shop door.

A small bell above the door announced his entrance to an unfamiliar world. Bolts of cloth filled the shelves, and lace lay displayed across a felted board. He skimmed his gaze in the majority of a circle and cleared his throat.

"Good day, young man." A plump woman stepped out from an alcove. She wore a pale dress under an apron holding more than a dozen pins. A trace of peppermint lingered in the air around her.

Hans gave a half bow and removed his cap. Fingering the note, he hunted for English words. "Good day. I have…"—he displayed the note—"for girl named…Polly."

"Ah…wait here…I will fetch her." The lady disappeared behind a dark drape.

After nodding, he studied the space. A faint memory of entering a shop similar to this at his mother's side returned. *Many years, a lifetime, since Mama visited a dressmaker.* He spied a dish of bone buttons on the counter and smiled. *I learned to count with Mama's button box.*

"Who are you?"

Hans glanced toward the voice.

A small boy with bright-red hair stood less than three steps away.

155

"Joseph. Please leave the gentleman alone. You have a lesson to finish." An attractive woman, appearing a few years older than Hans, arrived behind the boy.

"Yes, Mama." The child glanced to the floor before moving away to the curtained doorway.

He limps. In a blink, Hans recalled Louisa's concerned words and odd story as she prepared the bread sponges the night *Herr* Keil died. She'd told him a woman with a crippled boy arrived at the bakery several days before. After the lady's visit, the words between *Herr* and *Frau* Keil changed from light to formal. Every exchange she overheard between the married couple carried more unspoken messages than voiced words. *How many red-haired boys with a turned foot live in Elm Ridge?* He drew a breath and gathered his wits. "Polly?"

"Yes." She stepped to the side and put the counter between them.

"I bring note—from *Frau* Keil." He extended the paper.

Accepting the stationery, she unfolded the message and frowned. "I do not read *Deutsch* well."

Hans pressed his lips and studied his hands. Unless the woman asked him direct, he would not admit he did not read *Deutsch* well, either.

"Can you wait? I need to find paper and ink."

Before his lips formed a single word, he watched her turn and vanish behind the curtain. Looking for a clock, he spied one on a high shelf. *I can wait ten minutes and still walk to bakery and construction site before whistle.* An instant later, movement outside the shop window caught his attention.

A team walked past pulling a freight wagon. The driver held the reins with both hands. The whip rested in a holder beside him. *Bergmann's Livery and Freight Company* lettered in black against the tan side board identified the business.

Hans recalled his recent conversation with the stablemaster. Watching the scene in the street, he moved his lips in near silence. "*Herr* Bergmann talked to me like a fair man. His driver appears to treat the horses well."

"Excuse me."

Hans turned toward the voice and studied Polly.

"I won't be writing a note. Can you give *Frau* Keil a message? Spoken?"

"*Ja. Deutsch?*"

She widened her smile enough to show even teeth. A moment later, clear, slow *Deutsch* words emerged. "Tell *Frau* Keil I will come to the bakery tonight— seven o'clock."

Hans sighed relief before he repeated the message back to the young seamstress. "I deliver every word. Prompt."

Chapter Fifteen

Saturday afternoon, strong sunlight bathed the generous bakery window and exposed every bit of dirt and dust to view.

Louisa coaxed a scrap of dried mud out of a corner with the broom before glancing at the clock. *Five more minutes, then I can lock the front door and turn the sign.* "Running a business is difficult," she whispered to the empty rooms. Today, after the baking was finished and the customers slowed to a trickle, *Frau* Keil left Louisa alone in the bakery. She silently praised God for small blessings. Each of the recent customers spoke fluent *Deutsch.* All, except one, presented the correct change. She made a mental note to ask Mrs. Cook to again explain American money during her delayed English lesson. Worrying her lower lip, she thought of the coins. *When one coin is called by two names, I become confused.* The bakery price list appeared simple until she tried to match the numbers with the money on a customer's palm.

"*Guten Tag,* Louisa." The butcher's wife entered the sales area.

"*Frau* Hebing, a pleasure to see you." Louisa propped her broom in a corner. "Have you come for bread? We have two nice loaves of rye from this morning."

"*Nein.* Or maybe." She worried her hands on her

gathered skirt. "I come to ask if you have seen my son, Werner."

Shaking her head, Louisa arranged her lips in a serious expression. "*Nein.* Not today. The last time I saw Werner was…at *Herr* Keil's funeral." She recalled the tall, young man standing with the other pallbearers at the graveside. With a bowed head, he stood still as a tree, not even moving his shoulders when the rain arrived with a sudden swoosh. *I think I saw tears mixed with rain on his face before I left the graveside.* "Do you think he fell asleep doing a lesson at the parsonage?"

"I fear worse."

"What do you fear?" *Frau* Keil stepped into the room, closed the door, and loosened her bonnet ribbons.

"Werner is gone. His second set of clothes, his books, and a leather satchel are missing from his room. He…he didn't appear for breakfast. *Herr* Hebing and I joked about our son going on an early errand to avoid sharpening the knives. I did not enter his room and discover his things missing until after midday meal." *Frau* Hebing withdrew a paper from her dress pocket. "Gone…without a word…except for a note."

Louisa accepted the folded message and held the paper to take full advantage of the light. She read aloud. "*Gone on my adventure. Sorry for all the trouble I leave behind. Werner.*"

"Trouble? What sort of problem? Did he steal from the business?" *Frau* Keil snatched the note.

"*Nein. Herr* Hebing and I counted the cash box twice. The other money…all our funds are where they belong. He is a good son." *Frau* Hebing paced a small circle between the counter and the door. "He is devout.

Serious. Not prone to mischief—even when a young boy. I hoped for a time he would find a trade to hold his interest. I fear my dream of my youngest staying close is gone."

Louisa clenched her hands together and thought of her conversation with Werner in the garden. *He spoke of Latin lessons and an engineering school in New York. How many days past? Four? Five?*

"Do you have relatives he might seek out? Does he have his own money?" *Frau* Keil walked to the door, locked it, and turned the sign in the window.

Frau Hebing sighed so hard her shoulders trembled. "He earns some money doing errands—odd jobs. Americans hire him because he can read and write both *Deutsch* and English."

"Do you know which Americans?" Louisa failed to picture the scholarly, fine-mannered young man among the rough characters coming and going on the steamboats. "Did he write papers for some of the business owners?"

Frau Hebing rubbed fingers and thumb in the gathers of her skirt and shook her head. "He didn't speak of his employers. Last night, he arrived home late and went directly to his room. Considering what I found, he packed his case and left. But why did he not bid his parents and brothers a proper farewell? Secrets do not sit well with me. What does he need to hide?"

"He is a good son. He will write. You must be patient." *Frau* Keil wrapped a loaf of rye bread in a clean towel and handed the food to the butcher's wife.

Errands for Americans. Soon I will have enough money to travel. Louisa stood still while a shiver danced across her shoulders. Hans claimed to have seen a tall man wearing a wide-brimmed straw hat push or bump *Herr* Keil into the street. Werner was tall and owned a hat like Hans described. *Ja, half the Americans wear the same type of hat.* The rest of the description circled like a lost puppy. A team pulled uneven. A loaded wagon. A horse bolted at a steamboat whistle. An animal which responded better to *Deutsch* than English. The symbol for Black's Mill on the wagon. A disagreeable teamster. *Why didn't the driver return to offer aid?* "Does Werner know *Herr* Black—at the flour mill?"

"Let me deal with Mr. Black, Louisa."

One glance at *Frau* Keil's face and she understood the topic was closed.

A few minutes later, muttering about Werner, *Frau* Hebing left the bakery.

Louisa reclaimed the broom and finished sweeping. Working, she listened to *Frau* Keil put the leftover baked goods into the tins.

"Louisa—you know the danger of gossip?"

She exchanged the broom for the scrub bucket and brush. "I know where my business ends. I can keep a confidence, *Frau* Keil."

"You may call me Charlotte in private." She gestured for Louisa to sit on the small bench in the workroom and claimed the one, plain chair. "Today, I went to speak with a lawyer. Soon after Mr. Black arrived in Elm Ridge, Bernard paid for legal papers to secure the business in event of his death. Today, I read the papers and asked questions."

A will? She blocked the words and waited for the older lady to continue.

"All of the equipment, including the oven, plus

161

everything in the storeroom, belongs to me. *Herr* Hebing owns the building. For the present, my rent is fixed at an affordable rate. I will continue to live in the apartment." She glanced toward the sales area and street beyond. "You must not tell this to anyone, especially *Frau* Hebing. The butcher's wife is a good friend and kind neighbor, but she cannot keep a business deal quiet."

"I understand." Louisa expected her heart to float out of her chest. They could continue running the bakery. *Frau*...Charlotte...had a safe, comfortable place to live. *I will work to polish my baking skills until I make the best bread and cake in Illinois.*

"One more thing." *Frau* Keil stood and inspected the smaller dough trough.

"I listen."

"Bernard told me stories of his time in St. Louis. During his years in the city, he suffered when first wife died of cholera. After due time, he courted Polly Black. Before the nuptials were performed, her brother returned from travel to the West and forbade the marriage. Yes, this man is the disagreeable Mr. Black at the flour mill. He threatened Bernard with a pistol if he did not leave the city. I do not know the exact threats involved—but my husband came home anxious the day he learned Leo Black purchased the smaller of the two flour mills in Elm Ridge. Polly's arrival, with a child, troubled *Herr* Keil. The afternoon of the accident, he was going to the pastor to seek advice."

Scraps of information, floating around in Louisa's mind, began to arrange themselves like quilt pieces. Mr. Black certainly knew of the crippled boy. *Did events in St. Louis cause him to charge so much for poor flour?*

Was he blackmailing Herr *Keil—forcing him to buy from his mill?* "The mill, the seamstress, the boy…it is a…difficult situation."

"*Ja.* Complicated."

"*Frau*…Charlotte. Why did you welcome Polly last evening?"

"Were you eavesdropping?"

"*Nein.* I merely noted the time she arrived and departed."

Frau Keil nodded. "I do not wish to judge Polly Black by her relatives. What are you thinking, Louisa?"

"What if…no, I need to think on this before I speak." What if Mr. Black, *Herr* Keil's accident, and Werner's sudden departure are all tangled together? She weighed discussing the topic with Hans against breaking Charlotte's confidence. She would think and pray on the problem—without a direct word to another. "Men do terrible things for money."

****

Carrying a warm stew bowl in his left hand and a full beer stein in his right, Hans crossed the tavern's main room. He stopped at a small table where a co-worker, Ernst, sat finishing his supper. "A good crowd tonight."

"Saturday—workman's payday." Ernst pointed toward the bald accordion player shrugging into his instrument.

Hans settled at the table. After a few bites of his meal, he met his friend's gaze. "How did you fare today?"

"Dismissed. You?"

"The same." He tore a mouthful of dark bread from the chunk served with the meal. Late this afternoon,

163

when *Herr* Thayer handed out the wages, he released half of the crew. Only the skilled carpenters and two or three apprentices remained to finish the interior of the large store. "Have you plans?"

Ernst took a swallow of beer and ran a thumb along the stein handle. "I think I will ask at the foundry. They are always in need of men to shovel coal."

A shiver danced across Hans's shoulders. His father, before drink ruled his life, worked in a coal mine. At age thirteen, after a week loading carts by flickering light, Hans swore to the moon and stars to work above ground. Unloading coal at a factory sounded little better than shoveling the fuel from ground to cart inside the mine. One of the other men at Mrs. Winter's boardinghouse arrived home each day with face and clothes coated in fine, black dust. He stopped at the pump and washed the worst of the foundry grime away before setting foot inside. "It sounds like hard, dirty work."

"*Ja.* Pay is steady. Work all year."

Hans ate in silence and thought about the money. Today, during the lunch time, he'd gone to *Herr* Fischer's shop, paid for his new wooden shoes, and taken the borrowed pair to his room. Tomorrow, after church, he would return Dietrich Mueller's clogs to Louisa. *Hans Hoffmann is an honest man—a poor, unemployed man.* He mentally counted the money remaining after paying next week's rent. "Are any other construction crews hiring?"

Ernst shook his head. "You might find work on the levee."

"Loading boats and wagons is outside work— better than dim, hot factory conditions." He pushed the empty bowl to the center of the table. *When did I become fussy about work? I should accept any honest labor.*

"I saw you stop the team the other day." Ernst leaned close. "Well, the last of it. Can you drive?"

Hans pressed his lips. No employer wanted to know his experience driving horses. If possible, he would forget about the time he *borrowed* a team and wagon long enough to steal a small salt keg. For a long moment, he tallied his honest jobs in Westphalia and St. Louis. "I have worked in a stable."

"Gute. Ask *Herr* Bergmann for a job. I heard a rumor one of his stable hands ran west last week."

Nodding, Hans remembered his conversation with the stablemaster. The older man treated him with respect. The animals he'd seen at the stable, or pulling the tan-and-black wagons along the streets, appeared well fed and groomed. "I will think on it."

Ernst nudged his arm and directed his attention toward the door. "Newcomer—I think fresh off today's boat."

Hans lifted his gaze toward the stranger approaching the tavern keeper.

The man stood a little taller than Hans, had a slender build, and a stiff posture. His dark suit and striped vest appeared tailored from quality cloth. A black, low-crowned hat completed the portrait of a man of means.

"A stateroom passenger, I think. Difficult to imagine him on the wooding party."

Ernst chuckled and packed his pipe.

Hans leaned back, listened to the music, and allowed his thoughts to drift to Mr. Armstrong, the thoughtless American who did not control his team. Hans's inquiries among the many business owners and residents of Sixth Street prompted sad head shakes. The mention of *Herr* Keil, the baker, brought out respectful words from all the *Deutsch* plus the few Americans Hans questioned. *Mr. Black is new in Elm Ridge and not well-liked.* Two of the Americans Hans spoke with mentioned the miller's dislike of immigrants.

"Guten Abend. Tell me, sirs, is the food good in this tavern?"

Hans lifted his gaze to the newcomer standing beside the empty stool at their table. *"Ja*—decent— affordable."

"Your name, sir?" Ernst gestured for the stranger to sit.

"Wulff—Otto Wulff." He set his stein on the table and extended a hand.

Hans stilled his lips while Ernest introduced them both. For an instant, when he crossed his gaze with *Herr* Wulff's, he sensed more than casual interest. He skipped a breath and willed the weight in his chest, similar to encountering a constable while carrying stolen goods, to ease.

"Perhaps you gentlemen can help me. I seek a man headed to Elm Ridge earlier this year. Do you know of Dietrich Mueller?"

Hans tightened his grip on his nearly empty stein. *Why does a stranger ask for Louisa's father? Fredrick has not mentioned an acquaintance immigrating this year.* He moistened his lips and steadied his voice. "Dietrich Mueller is not in Elm Ridge."

"Ah. You know him?" *Herr* Wulff stared at Hans over the rim of his drink.

166

"I have heard the name." He shrugged. "What more can you tell of this man?"

"*Herr* Mueller is a baker by trade. He travelled with his daughter." Otto ran his tongue across his upper lip before smiling.

Hans nodded and risked a glance at Ernst. *Not a word.* Returning his full attention to *Herr* Wulff, he arranged words that were neither lies nor the entire truth. "I hear of him. We both sailed on *The Flying Gull.*"

"Are you certain he is not in Elm Ridge? My informant told me he planned to join relatives in this area."

Swallowing hard, Hans stared back into pale, steady eyes. "I tell the truth—Dietrich Mueller does not live in Elm Ridge."

"Ah. A pity. I looked forward to a familiar face from my home village." *Herr* Wulff shrugged. "All is not lost. Since stepping off the packet at noon, I have learned the town has need of my services. One Illinois town with a *Deutsch* community should be the same as the next to a man like me."

Hans drank the last drops of his beer and wiped a sleeve across his mouth. The music from the accordion and violin gained volume, but the silence at their small table pressed on him like the weight of a foundation stone. With a nod to Ernst, he pushed out his stool.

"*Herr* Hoffmann."

He met Otto's gaze.

"I have managed to sort out who you resemble. Do you know Adolph Hoffmann…from the village of Arnsberg…currently of St. Louis?"

"*Nein.*" Hans willed his knees to obey, cease their

tremble, and stood.

Herr Wulff appeared to ignore Hans's distress. "I am good friends with Adolph. Less than three days ago, I enjoyed his company in St. Louis. I will tell you something odd. He has been expecting his younger brother, Johannes, to join him this spring. He has not heard a word since his brother set out for Bremerhaven. Adolph is from a family of leather workers and harness makers. He was eager for his brother to join him in a growing business."

"Much can happen on such a journey. Our ship experienced both a storm and a becalming." Hans gathered the empty bowls and prayed his hands would stay still enough for them not to clatter. The letter, tucked into the Bible and saved from the black trunk, bore the signature *A. Hoffmann*. The message inside the book, addressed to Johannes, rather than the familiar form of the name, was signed in a different hand. He searched for comfort and found a drop in knowledge that both Hans and Hoffmann were common names among the immigrants.

"Ja. Ja. You speak the truth about hazards on travels. Our ship survived a wicked storm, and many passengers caught the fever. I worked both day and night among them."

"Did you tell us your trade?" Ernst rejoined the conversation.

"Trade?" *Herr* Wulff stiffened until his back was straighter than a schoolmaster's. "I am a physician— trained at university and practiced two years in Essen. You know the place?"

Hans fumbled the crockery and managed by a whisker to avoid an accident. *Bitte, I do not desire the attention of the entire room. Essen...I beg my mind to forget my adventures in the city...especially.* He closed his eyes while a memory of the authorities nearly capturing him visited. *I was fortunate the silver stolen from the lawyer's home was small and easy to hide.* The incident scared him enough to flee the instant the forger completed his work. Drawing a deep, quiet, breath, he eased from the table. "Welcome to Elm Ridge, *Herr* Doctor Wulff."

A few moments later, Hans stepped into the dark and tipped his head to the sky. He caught a glimpse of the moon between the clouds and estimated the time. *Near midnight—Louisa sleeps at Fredrick's farm Saturday nights.* He walked steadily to his boardinghouse and glanced often at the sky. "I must warn her. I fear the physician seeks more than the location of Dietrich Mueller."

Chapter Sixteen

The next morning, Hans alternated his gaze from the distant church steeple to the rough plank sidewalk. *I must hurry.* With every step toward the building, he grew more self-conscious of the bundle under his arm. *Better I leave the wooden shoes at Mrs. Winter's and fetch them after service. Too late now—first bell will ring at any moment.* The more he thought of *Herr* Wulff, with his pale eyes holding secrets, the less he wanted to give the newcomer an opportunity to speak with Louisa before he informed her of last evening's events.

He arrived at the foot of the church steps at the same time Fredrick lifted little Karl from the wagon. "*Guten Morgan.*" He glanced in all directions before he touched his cap to *Frau* Mueller. "Is Louisa well? I expected she would be with you."

Fredrick smiled wide. "Ah, your true intentions are showing at last."

"No disrespect. Your company is pleasant. I learn much of dairy farming from our conversations." He continued to seek Louisa among the gathering congregation.

"My cousin stayed in town last night. She was reluctant to leave *Frau* Keil alone so soon after the tragic accident. *Mein Frau* agreed. Listen to the women…makes life go smoother. *Ja?*"

"I must…I want to speak with her before the service." Hans looked along the street. The instant he spied *Frau* Keil and Louisa walking toward them, he skipped a breath. "I be back quick."

A few moments later, he paused two steps in front of the women. Taking off his cap, he gave a slight bow. *"Guten Morgan, Frau, Fraulein.* Please may I have a word before you arrive at the church?"

"Have you found the wagon driver?" Louisa unhooked an arm from Charlotte's elbow.

"Nein. Nein. I want to speak of a different matter."

"We must not delay." *Frau* Keil stepped forward. "Soon they will ring the bell. Can you talk and walk at the same time?"

Hans nodded. Stepping beside Louisa, he set a determined pace. "Last night, while I ate my supper at the tavern, a stranger, a man fresh from the daily packet, inquired after Dietrich Mueller, a baker."

"Papa? Who would do such a thing? Acquaintances from *The Flying Gull* know of his death. Fredrick is our only relative in America." She halted and stood at the edge of the street until *Frau* Keil touched her arm.

"This man gave the name Otto Wulff and claimed to be from your village. Yet in the next breath, he described himself as a physician from Essen."

Louisa frowned. "Otto Wulff—I know one person by the name. He left Hamm many years ago. *Herr* Wulff, the cooper, and my father were great friends. Otto, the oldest son, attended university, married, and lives in Essen. Papa and I spoke with his parents the evening before we started for Bremerhaven. They did not say a word about him preparing to emigrate."

"This man is tall…slender…wears fine clothes."

"Pale hair and faded eyes?"

Hans nodded. *All night I puzzle why a physician seeks your father. Your clear description adds to the confusion.* "You know him then?"

"I do not have time to speak at great length." She grasped the edge of her light shawl. "Years ago, when a schoolboy, Otto Wulff did not practice kindness."

Arriving at Fredrick's wagon, Hans remembered the package. Removing it from under his arm, he presented it to Louisa. "For you, I return your papa's shoes. *Herr* Fischer finished my pair this week."

"*Danke.*" She accepted the bundle and appeared to weigh it in her hands before she placed it in the wagon. With deft movements, she covered the package with the picnic blanket. "I am glad you returned the shoes, *Herr* Hans Hoffmann. You show honesty in all your dealings with me."

A warm swirl lightened Hans's heart. Louisa, a woman of importance in his life, called him honest. He curved his lips in a smile. *One day, when you and I are in private, I will confess my birth name.*

****

Standing, Louisa added her clear, alto voice to the opening hymn. Following the familiar responses of the liturgy, she focused her attention on the silver altar cross to keep her thoughts on the worship service. The instant she sat and the pastor began the first of the scripture readings, she lost the internal battle. *Otto Wulff. In Elm Ridge.* Glancing toward the men's pews on the other side of the center aisle, she did not see any newcomers. She pressed her lips. Otto would sit near the back. In Hamm, before he left for university, he, and his friends, sat in the last pew and spent much of the service whispering to each other.

When Pastor Belker started to preach, she closed her eyes, bowed her head, and allowed a memory to blot out the present. She had worn her hair in braids during her second year in the schoolroom. One day, while she hurried through the narrow alley toward home, she was startled when Otto stepped out from between two buildings and blocked her way.

He demanded a password.

She hesitated.

He tugged a braid.

"Amen," she blurted the word and had dashed toward the bakery.

A weight settled on her lap.

She opened her eyes and smiled at little Karl. Setting one finger against his lips before he babbled one of his new words, she returned her attention to the present.

Later, with the words of the final blessing still in her mind, Louisa stepped into the central aisle to exit the sanctuary. The instant her gaze intersected Hans's, she curved her lips into a small smile. In the next moment, she froze her mouth into a mixture of surprise and disapproval. She swallowed her emotions and lowered her gaze. For a moment, she busied her hands in finding her coin for the offering box. *Does he recognize me? I have changed during these last six years.* Arriving at the foot of the steps, Louisa felt Anna's hand on her elbow.

"What is the matter with you? You've turned pale as bleached linen."

"None of your concern. I…an unexpected person at the service. It has been a difficult week." She swallowed a lump of sadness at the sight of *Frau* Keil's bonnet with new, black ribbons.

"Shall I ask *Frau* Keil to join our picnic?"

"*Nien.* She is invited to dine and spend the afternoon at the Weiss household."

Half an hour later, Louisa spread the blanket for the family picnic in the beer garden.

"Where is your mind today, Louisa?" Anna opened the large basket and handed Karl a spoon. "Are you worried about your place at the bakery? You will always have a home with us, if *Frau* Keil sells the business."

"*Danke.* The bakery is not my worry." She lowered her gaze. *Anna does not know the Wulff family. She will find it difficult to understand.* "*Frau* Keil is an open, honest woman, and we have talked."

"*Guten Tag, Fraulein Mueller.*"

Louisa straightened and faced the speaker. *Otto.* She studied him for a long moment and noted a hint of slyness in the way he held his mouth. "*Herr* Wulff. What a great surprise. The last word from your parents put you in Essen with a bride. Did she journey with you? Is she well?" She leaned to one side and then the other to see if a woman accompanied him. "Allow me to introduce Anna Mueller, my Cousin Fredrick's wife."

After a few exchanges of polite, meaningless words, Louisa turned away to continue setting out the meal. *Why are Fredrick and Hans so long to bring the beer?*

"Will you dance with me, Louisa?"

"The band is yet to tune their instruments." *Why does he not say one word of his wife?* Louisa enjoyed all forms of music and usually danced with half a dozen or more different partners of all ages and abilities during the afternoon. But she pressed her lips and hesitated to encourage Otto. She looked forward to giving Hans another polka lesson.

"I would take great pleasure to waltz with you."

"Return later and ask again." She set a stack of four plates beside the basket.

"Typical Louisa, quick to speak her mind in plain words." Fredrick extended a full beer stein to his wife before turning his attention to Otto. He introduced himself and waited for a response.

"Wulff—Otto Wulff. I am a childhood friend of Louisa. She had her eye on my youngest brother. God rest his soul."

Hans presented a beer to Louisa and switched his gaze back and forth between her and Otto. Raising his stein, he addressed the physician. "You should try *Herr* Althoff's lager. Best beer in town. Reasonable price."

"You"—he pointed a slender finger at Hans. "You tell me Dietrich Mueller is not in Elm Ridge. You did not say one word concerning the pretty daughter." He edged closer until their toes were scant inches apart.

"*Herr* Dietrich Mueller is not in Elm Ridge." He glanced toward Louisa. "He died thirty-two days into the voyage. I do not lie."

Louisa watched the two men, standing in the posture of long-time enemies. *Hans is careful with his speech. Did Otto inquire directly about me?* She forced her lips to remain neutral. "*Herr* Wulff, if you settle in Elm Ridge, we will have many opportunities to speak. But now, I think it best you leave our group. *Bitte,* allow us to eat our picnic in peace."

Clamping one hand over the crown of his hat, Otto nodded to Louisa and Anna. "I will claim a waltz. You can count on it."

"Will he cause trouble?" Fredrick squatted near his son but kept his gaze on the physician's back.

Louisa sighed. "As a youth, Otto played tricks on people, especially the younger girls. I find it strange he did not speak of his wife."

Hans lifted a pickle from the jar. "People can change. The town needs a physician. By all accounts, the American doctor spends much time with the whiskey bottle."

Nodding, Louisa ate in silence. She listened to Fredrick talk of the new calves and paid extra attention to Hans's questions. *My friend is eager to learn.*

After the sandwiches were gone and the plates returned to the basket, Hans led Louisa toward the dancers.

"Do you remember? Will you listen to the tuba? Count the beat?" She stood before him outside of the circle.

"*Ja.*" He tilted his head. "*Ein...und zwei...und.*"

She set her hand against his, ignored the tingle of excitement where his skin touched hers, and stepped off at the beginning of the next phrase. "Quick step—long step." The moment she sensed a gap in the swirling dancers, she guided them into the midst. When the song's final note faded, she studied his face. "Why the frown? This is happy music."

"Dancing is both difficult and a pleasure."

"A few more lessons and you will find more pleasure and less difficulty." She smiled wide and repositioned her hands at the next polka's introduction.

Lifting her gaze from their feet after a turn, she noticed Otto headed toward them. She stepped too far and bumped Hans's foot. "*Bitte.* Pardon me."

A moment later, Otto tapped Hans on the shoulder.

Aware of a sudden chill in her fingers, Louisa gripped Hans tight.

"I wish a dance with the *Fraulein.*"

Hans looked first toward Louisa, then to Otto, and back.

My friend, Hans, is confused—not familiar with all the manners on the dance floor. She nodded. *A polka...in public. I do not wish to make a fuss.* Forcing a smile, she decided to ask the physician a few questions during the dance.

"*Danke, Louisa.*" Otto led her into the dance circle with flawless steps.

"You requested a waltz, not polka. I prefer you call me *Fraulein* Mueller." She held her lips in a small smile while a chill crawled up her arm. *Kindness and manners to all in public.* She recalled her father's advice. *Touching Otto is much like putting my hands on cool dough in need of much flour.*

He shrugged while continuing the dance.

She pressed her lips and arranged her words. "Tell me, *Herr* Doctor Wulff, does your wife wait for you in Essen?"

Shaking his head, he brought them to a halt on the band's final note. "Like you, death has taken someone dear to me. I find it painful to speak of the lovely Ernestine."

"Ah, my sympathy to you." The first notes of a familiar waltz filled the air, and she placed her left hand on his shoulder. "When did you last have word from

177

your parents? Are they well?"

He nodded. "Tomorrow, I will write and give my family the new address. What shall I tell them of you?"

"Uncle Horst will share our letters with your father. The friendship between the families runs deep." *I sense a secret, perhaps a falsehood, in your reason to be in Elm Ridge.*

"Is it correct you work in a bakery?"

Louisa twirled under his raised arm. *"Ja, mit Frau Keil."*

"Is this common in America, two women running a business?"

"I do not yet know what is common. Since *Herr* Keil's recent death, *Frau* Keil wished to continue the bakery. I work with her—kind lady, *Frau* Keil." One glance into his arrogant face and she held back any mention of enjoying the situation. To be honest, she missed the baker who hummed while working. His soft voice, with or without proper words, allowed her imagination to picture dough and batter thriving to music. However, each day the arrangement with Charlotte smoothed a little. She looked forward to establishing a pattern which suited both of them.

"I will not make my wife work in a shop. She will spend her days keeping a fine house and raising our children."

Louisa tipped her head in surprise at the force of his statement. "Ernestine, your late wife, did she keep a fine house? Did she knit your stockings?"

"She did all the proper duties—always tidy, *mein Frau.*" He settled his lips in a straight line.

"Kinder?" Children? She formed the question without pausing to think.

"*Nein.*" He narrowed pale, gray eyes.

She focused on his face. *Why do you avoid answers to family questions?* Once more, a childhood memory intruded. This time, she remembered the tall boy chasing younger students and frightening them with commands shouted in Latin. *Has he changed? Or learned to cloak the unpleasant?* She glanced at their feet and recalled the admonition to think the best until proven wrong. "Ah, the final chorus. You dance well."

"*Danke.*" He guided them to a graceful stop on the long, final note.

Louisa pulled her hands away and backed half a step. *I have practiced enough kindness and manners with Otto today.* "I go tend little Karl now. His parents will enjoy time to dance."

Chapter Seventeen

Louisa wiped the final mixing bowl. Nesting the crockery with two others on the shelf, she sighed. *Friday—a week and a day since* Herr *Keil's burial.* The bakery worked on a new pattern. Many things—the number of loaves each day and the schedule to prepare cakes, pies, and cookies—remained the same. The most immediate change, begun the day after the funeral, was the cast-iron kettle with the midday meal simmering on this stove instead of upstairs. "*Frau* Keil, *bitte,* come and eat your lunch. The customers arrive at a trickle this late in the day. I will handle the sales."

"And you? Have you eaten?"

"*Ja.* The moment the pound cakes went in the oven, I dished my plate." She glanced at the place setting and small crock of pickled cucumbers at the far end of the worktable. "The cakes will be done when the clock strikes the half hour."

Charlotte entered the workroom, lifted the plain white plate, and walked to the stove. Raising the Dutch oven's lid, she drew a deep, noisy breath. "Kraut, carrots, and knockwurst—a good, sustaining meal."

Wiping her hands on her apron, Louisa entered the sales area. She moved her lips in silence and used English numbers while inventorying the loaves, rolls, and cakes on the pass-through shelves. Business was good. Tomorrow, she needed to prepare an extra pan of cinnamon buns, a special order, with the scheduled Saturday items.

"Good day."

She straightened from counting ginger cookies in the glass case at the first word. Closing her lips on *Deutsch* words, she rearranged her tongue. "Good day, *Herr*...Mr. Black."

Without removing, or even touching, his stovepipe hat, he glared from a modest, five-inch height advantage. "I need to speak with *Frau* Keil—immediately."

Louisa glanced into the workroom.

Dabbing her lips, Charlotte stood. A moment later, she posed tall and proud in the passage between the two rooms. "What is your business today, Mr. Black?"

"Collecting payment—the entire amount." He displayed one flat palm.

Tick-tock-tick.

Does he expect Frau *Keil to pull a large payment out of her pocket?* Louisa held her breath and listened.

"Did you not receive the letter from my lawyer?" Charlotte held her head high and released English words at an irregular pace. "I witnessed him fasten a wax seal and hand the correspondence to his messenger boy."

"The letter does not matter. You broke the contract. Keil's bakery is to buy all flour from Black's Mill for an entire year."

"*Nein.*" Charlotte shook her head before she switched back to English. "There is no contract with you among my late husband's papers. Any verbal agreement you forced on him does not stand. Keil's Bakery will use the finest ingredients available. Flour from Gordon's Mill is better quality and lower price. I have told you before…you sell lumpy, coarse flour."

Mr. Black stepped toward *Frau* Keil, lifted one arm, hesitated, and returned his arm to his side. "This is not the end of it." He raised a hand and shook a finger toward Charlotte's face. "I'll own this bakery and all your equipment before the end of July. You filthy immigrants think you can take advantage of true Americans. Go back where you belong."

You take our money easy enough. Louisa pressed her lips before her thoughts escaped. According to snatches of conversation she overheard at the beer garden, Mr. Black led a small group of businessmen who attempted to charge higher prices to their non-English speaking customers.

"Firm, I stand." Charlotte crossed her arms at the top of her spotless apron. "No more flour from your mill will the bakery buy."

"Without flour— you will close. Gordon won't sell you a speck once I spread the truth about your husband. Tell me, was yours a legal union—or did he forget to marry you?" He leaned close to the startled widow's nose.

Louisa stood frozen.

Leo Black pivoted and strode toward the door. Halting after two steps, he turned to face *Frau* Keil. "Stay away from Polly. My little sister is forbidden to associate with the likes of you."

"Your sister"—Charlotte stiffened—"is a grown woman. She is a mother…a capable seamstress, making her own way in life. Her friends are her business, not yours."

"Not until she marries." He slammed the door.

Louisa shuddered. Each time Mr. Black visited the bakery, she felt the unease of air seeded with violence and hatred. Gripping the edge of the counter, she sought Charlotte's gaze. "I understand few of his words, but his anger is clear. Can he take the bakery equipment away from you?"

"The lawyer says he cannot."

Shifting her gaze to the clock, Louisa gasped. "The cakes." She pushed past a slightly dazed *Frau* Keil and snatched a towel on her way to the oven. "*Gute.* They are golden, not dark from the extra time."

Charlotte cleared away the remains of her lunch and sighed. "*Herr* Black will try to cause trouble. We must watch our words. He, and others, will seek an opportunity to ruin the bakery's reputation."

Louisa nodded and selected a long, sharp knife to loosen the cakes in the pans. Two of the fragrant cakes were special orders from regular customers. The third, she planned to take to Mrs. Cook as payment for her first two English lessons. "I will be watchful. You can trust me." A few moments later, while Charlotte was gone to the yard, Louisa heard the front door open. "*Ein minute.*"

"*Guten Tag,* Louisa."

She dropped the last pan in the dish water and turned toward the voice. *Has Otto sought me out? Why?* Wiping her hands on her apron, she crossed the workroom. She met him one step inside the sales area. "*Guten Tag, Herr* Wulff. Have you come for a loaf of hearty rye bread? Or perhaps a pastry is more to your liking this afternoon. We have apple turnovers fresh from the oven this morning."

"Neither." He removed his hat and shook his

abundant blond hair. "Supper at the tavern is sufficient for me. I came to ask you a question...to give you a warning."

Louisa blinked, collected her thoughts, and eased behind the counter. A little portion of her brain warned her to keep space between her and Otto. She rubbed her arms and banished the last of the gooseflesh raised by their previous visitor. Did Otto know Mr. Black? *Herr Wulff is new, less than a week in Elm Ridge, and I pray he has not made the unfortunate acquaintance with Mr. Black.* "What is your question?"

"How well do you know Hans Hoffmann?" He placed his hands behind his back and jutted his chin toward her.

"We are friends from the sea voyage. We...became acquainted...after Papa died." She closed her suddenly dry mouth. *What business of yours is my friendship?*

"Do you trust him?"

Trust. Weeks ago, before they departed *The Flying Gull,* Alfred asked her the same question. Widow Krause repeated the inquiry in New Orleans. Neither time did she have an answer. Now, after numerous short, careful conversations, three dance lessons, and the return of Papa's shoes, she wanted to trust Hans. The precious wooden clogs, returned cleaned and with the familiar sunburst pattern gleaming, proved honesty in one small thing. "He has kept his word to me."

"Does he speak of his family?"

"He has no family. His parents are dead. He came to America alone." She pressed her lips. Twice, Hans mentioned his mother's death. But he spoke little of his father, aside from describing him as a *harsh man.*

Otto placed his hands behind his back and glanced

toward the ceiling for a moment. "Have you proof? Have you viewed his traveling papers? What if he is telling lies? A man can invent a story to suit his own purpose."

"Liars answer to God." She stared into Otto's face and looked for hints of his purpose to this conversation. Dull, pale eyes met her gaze. *I see neither joy nor sorrow.* "Do you tell lies of your wife? A trained physician who does not state clearly how a loved one died makes me hesitant to believe all your words. Cousin Fredrick received a letter from our uncle in Hamm two days ago. In the paper, dated second of March, Uncle Horst mentioned your family—parents and brother. I read the letter myself and found not one word of your wife's death or any plans to emigrate."

"*Mein Frau's* death is not your business. The letter…my family might not have received word before your uncle penned it. You are aware of the hazards letters face during transit."

Louisa sealed her lips. Only a foolish person would repeat the doubts Anna voiced during a visit to town Wednesday.

A keen observer, Anna had likened Otto's smile to the trickster in a children's book. "You need to be careful, Louisa." The farmer's wife advised. "Listen to Fredrick. Your cousin is the man in your family."

"I always consider my cousin's advice. I listen to his words and add my own good sense until the decision feels true." Interrupted, she had let the matter drop. Drawing a deep breath, Louisa risked a glance into the workroom.

Charlotte quietly washed the last dishes.

"If you are not going to purchase any baked goods,

you may go. The bakery is closing for the day."

"Do not challenge me, Louisa. I will prove your trust in *Herr* Hoffmann misplaced." He lifted his hat from the counter, gave her a slight bow, and walked out of the shop.

Louisa sank to the stool behind the counter. The conversation with Otto left her more exhausted than kneading six batches of dough. A shiver passed across her shoulders. She rubbed her arms. *Do I trust Hans? Do I trust Otto?*

****

Friday afternoon, nearing the end of four days working at the stables, Hans unhooked the last of the traces. He laid the leather straps gently across the draft horse's wide back and signaled *Herr* Bergmann to walk the team forward. *The final wagon—the last team.* He sighed. *Before full dark, I will be relaxing in the tavern and smoking my daily pipe.* Within the previous hour, he finished distributing grain and hay to the stalls. He needed to check and wipe six sets of harness before he left for supper. He glanced toward the scattering of high, white clouds. Straightening, he started walking a circuit of the wagon.

The lowering sun sent shafts of light out in a burst of farewell.

Intent on checking the tailgate latches, he almost missed it. One of those last rays of sun made raw metal glint and prompted him to take a second look. *Mein Gott.* He traced the linkages with his fingers to confirm the sight. "*Herr* Bergmann." He scurried after the stablemaster. "On the wagon…important…you must see."

"Calm yourself. First, we care for the tired horses.

Wagon inspection comes after the animals are settled." He patted one Percheron gelding's neck.

The team, weary after a long work day, dipped lips into fresh water in the large stone-and-mortar trough.

"*Ja*. I understand." Hans lowered his voice and watched the horses' ears for indications of their mood. "The problem is the wagon brake. The flat piece where it meets the rod is worn away."

Herr Bergmann turned his full attention to Hans. "You tell me I made the afternoon deliveries with no brakes on the wagon?"

"I do not know how long. But the linkage is broken now."

"Trip to the levee after the noon packet could have been my last." Crossing himself, the older man muttered. "These"—he indicated the two draft horses— "go in the far stalls on the west side. They will pick the right one. Be sure to put the harness away clean and proper. I will go and check the wagon again."

Hans nodded and accepted the bridle leads from his boss. A moment later, he addressed the animals in a soft monotone. "Good water after honest labor. After your drink, I take you inside. In your stall, you find a little grain and much sweet hay. Minus your harness, either *Herr* Bergmann or I give you good brushing. You will settle for the night without the dirt and sweat of a workday." A short time later, Hans wiped a horse collar before he hoisted it to a numbered peg.

Two drivers worked in nearby stalls. While brushing their teams and checking for signs of injury to the animals, the men spoke low, sparse words.

Herr Bergmann returned to the stable, took a careful look at each of the horses in their stalls, and nodded to the drivers. "A word before you go. Be sure to check your wagon brakes extra careful before you start in the morning."

"*Ja,*" the shorter of the two men replied. "Every load, I walk a circuit with a sharp eye."

"Continue your good habit." The stablemaster lifted a brush and paused by a stall door. In a soft voice, he addressed Hans. "*Danke.* Finish the harness and take your leave."

Hans swallowed. *Am I dismissed after less than a week?* From his point of view, he followed directions. He clenched and released one fist and won a brief battle not to strike the older man. *Have I failed to do my tasks to* Herr *Bergmann's satisfaction? An honest man does not argue with his employer.* He grasped the final set of traces and rubbed sweat and dirt off the leather.

"Starting tomorrow"—*Herr* Bergmann entered the stall housing one of the Percherons—"be here at six o'clock, when the first church bells ring. You are required to work one Sunday per month. Pay is equal to construction crew wages. Do you accept the terms?"

Hans felt a great invisible stone roll from his chest. He smiled, nodded, and gave silent thanks. "*Danke. Ja.* I work for you. Elm Ridge—this stable—feel like good place—steady employment—make a real home."

"*Gute.* Our business is settled." The stablemaster brushed the draft horse's neck and shoulder.

Hans stood in the alcove among the harnesses hanging on sturdy pegs and gazed at the peeled, log ceiling beam. *God is good.* He blinked surprise at the prayer. Long before he fled his father's house, he stopped praying outside of the church building. During his years of thievery, he thanked luck on the occasions he evaded the authorities, but he never gave a thought to God.

A short time later, Hans draped the final set of reins over a peg. His heart light with joy, he left the stable and headed toward the tavern. *A good day. If I am careful, I can save a little from my wages each week. Perhaps I will buy a pretty trinket for a special* fraulein. *I have a new reason to build a fine life in Elm Ridge. America allows*—nein—*encourages*—*a man to dream. I dream honest life brings reward of respect.*

****

"Amen." The congregation ended one of Louisa's favorite dismissal hymns.

Pastor Belker stepped in front of the altar, turned, and faced the assembly. Raising his arms, he spoke the final blessing.

Louisa hummed the sacred tune while waiting to exit the pew. Today's fair weather and a shorter-than-usual sermon lifted her spirits. She eagerly awaited a picnic in the beer garden. *I want to give Hans a waltz lesson today.* Nodding greetings to a young farm wife, she inched into the center aisle.

Plunk...clink. Coins landed on each other in the offering box.

He's staring. With a silent word of thanks for large bonnet brims, she fastened her gaze on the open sanctuary door. *Half a dozen steps to the cloakroom.* Conversation, at parlor volume, was permitted in the short, wide room. However, in fine weather, she preferred to refrain from speech until outside the building.

Clink. She dropped her customary offering through the slot.

"*Guten Tag, Fraulein* Mueller."

She startled at Otto's whisper near her ear. "*Bitte*—conversation can wait until we stand in the fresh air."

"When did you grow all proper?"

Delaying a reply until she gained the church entrance, she lifted her skirts a few inches with one hand. "I'm no longer the small girl in braids, running away from you on Hamm's streets. After you left for university, I grew into a young woman. My parents stressed the importance of kindness and manners."

"I noticed." He offered his arm and escorted her to the lawn. Here, on the sparse grass and spilling into the street, parishioners gathered in clusters, exchanging news of the week.

"Have you introduced yourself to the *Deutsch* business people?" She fussed with her light shawl to avoid his touch.

"*Ja.* I enter American shops, also. Several owners appeared to welcome my occupation. Illness and accident visit all parts of the community."

Recalling Mr. Cook's disgusted expression when another customer mentioned the American doctor, she pressed her lips. "You learn English?"

"Every day I try to add a few more words to my vocabulary."

"*Gute.* Good. Papa requested I learn. I find nice American lady to give me lessons."

"Are not the bakery customers *Deutsch*?"

She waved a greeting to *Frau* Hebing. "Immigrants and Americans both enjoy good bread and cake."

"You work very hard, Louisa. Bakery hours start so early, before sunrise."

"All my life, my family and I wake before the

roosters." She turned her smile to a laugh. "Physicians work long days. Are you not called out in the night?"

Otto shrugged.

Pressing her lips, she arranged her next words carefully. Asking for information about his wife, or life in Essen, caused Otto to respond with a vague answer and change the topic. "I'm curious why you chose to begin a practice in Elm Ridge. A man with your skill and training could have found a welcome in any of the larger communities where your steamboat paused on the journey from New Orleans."

"Cities do not suit me. After I learned of your father's intention to settle near relatives in Illinois, I determined to follow."

Louisa turned toward the street and spied Hans standing near Fredrick's team. *Good, I see Hans and Jacob Thayer speaking friendly. I believe the master carpenter does not wish ill to anyone, even former employees.*

"*Mein Vater* spoke often of a sincere wish for Wulff and Mueller families to join through a marriage."

"*Ja.*" She jerked her attention back to the doctor. "Often, our families spent long Sunday afternoons together. Hermann"—she blinked away the grief which surfaced. "Your brother was a fine young man. Often, in private, *Herr* Wulff boasted of Hermann's cooper skills. Were it not for army conscription, I believe we would have married and emigrated."

"*Mein Mutter*'s heart broke the day news of Hermann's death arrived."

Louisa thought back to the first time she called on *Frau* Wulff after her husband brought the official letter to the bakery. During the visit, Hermann's mother had prepared tea, recounted stories from her youngest son's childhood, and wiped stray tears. *Similar actions to other mothers who have lost children.* "To lose a child is difficult for a mother—and a father."

"*Und Bruder*—my world shifted the day I learned of little brother's death."

"*Herr* Doctor. *Herr* Doctor Wulff." An unfamiliar boy, wearing a Sunday suit and cloth cap, ran shouting among the dispersing parishioners.

Louisa's question about the timing of Hermann's and Ernestine's deaths vanished in her throat.

"Here"—Otto raised his arm and stepped toward the youngster. "What is the problem?"

"A fall—at the Catholic Church. My friend tumbled and hit his head on a stone." The boy panted.

"Awake?"

"*Nein.*"

"We go." Otto turned to Louisa. "I will join you at beer garden after I tend my new patient."

Louisa watched Otto stride away in the direction of the church where another portion of the *Deutsch* community worshiped. Moving her lips in a silent prayer for the injured child, she looked for Anna. *If we invite Hans to accompany us to the beer garden and leave promptly, I will have time to give him an introduction to the waltz before Otto can interrupt.*

Chapter Eighteen

Ignoring a short burst of voices when the tavern door across the street opened, Hans rinsed his face, neck, and hands in the horse trough. *Ahh—my muscles are sore this evening.* Today, midsummer, felt especially long, due to *Herr* Weiss's delayed return with the final wagon. Not more than ten minutes ago, while Hans cleaned the last horse collar, the driver and stablemaster departed to wives and homes.

He turned toward the river and admired the final light in the western sky. Twilight lingered on the longest day of the year. *My first summer solstice in America.* Images of village celebrations with music and dancing in the square arrived unbidden. *I found Midsummer Eve a good time to steal—while others partied.* Shaking his head, he failed to banish the image. He threaded his fingers through damp hair and moved his lips in silence. *Hans Hoffmann is an honest man.* A few minutes later, he entered the tavern. Gaining the proprietor's attention, he ordered beer and supper.

"*Herr* Hoffmann. Join us." Ernst invited him to the far end of the long table.

Hans settled on a plain stool, nodded toward Christian Giesel, the stonemason from the construction project, and addressed Ernst. "How goes work at the foundry? How many days? More than a week since I see you take supper at this tavern."

"No longer do I labor at the foundry. You were correct about the dirt. I think coal dust seeps through the skin. I work again for *Herr* Thayer. A man quit, and *Herr* Giesel"—he pointed toward the man beside him—"put in a good word for me. Now I learn to make rafters and roofs. More good luck came my way the day I changed boardinghouses. Christian rents the adjoining room, and the landlady includes a decent supper four days a week."

"*Gute.*" Hans started to form a question about the new lodgings, but a burst of laughter from near the entrance distracted the men.

A moment later, a long arm, covered in fine fabric, placed a black, low-crowned hat on the table. "Good evening, gentlemen—*Herr* Hoffmann."

Hans stuffed a large chunk of cooling turnip into his mouth. An instant later, he spared Otto a tiny nod. Twice this week, he and the doctor crossed paths on the street. Hans had left each brief encounter with a feeling of unease. *Does the doctor suspect my previous occupation? After this much time, would the authorities banish me to Europe? I like Elm Ridge. Working at the stable suits me. A dance lesson in Louisa's arms highlights my week.*

"The town square is quiet." Otto sipped from his full stein.

"*Ja.*" Ernst spoke for the group. "Americans don't give much attention to midsummer. They fill the square to celebrate Fourth of July with a large picnic and many speeches. They ring all the church bells at noon—no matter the day of the week."

Otto blinked three times quickly. "I do hear a little talk of this Independence Day."

"Grandest holiday of the year to Americans. Businesses shutter at noon," Ernst continued.

Hans listened to the carpenter's apprentice describe last year's celebration and failed to find a comparable day in Westphalia. Aside from church holidays, midsummer, and the occasional proclaimed Royal Day, festivals were local. *I must ask to escort Louisa to this American event.*

Sending the serving woman a smile, Otto accepted a plate of supper. "Do they welcome *Deutsch* to the fun?"

The fair-haired stonemason found his voice. "Speeches are all in English. Food and music bring all the town—and nearby farmers."

"I'll plan on it." Otto lowered his voice and looked directly toward Hans. "Will the horses demand your attention?"

Hans shrugged. Holiday or not, he expected the steamboats would deliver and collect freight. Therefore, at least one team and driver would be making limited rounds. Besides, animals needed food and water, no matter the day.

"Does not matter. Situations change. Young laborers come and go with every whistle of the packet boat." Otto grinned.

What does he expect of me? Since switching the passports on the ship, Hans lived an honest life. He struggled each time a stranger wore a fine watch chain. Walking past *Herr* Bergmann's empty office always sent a twinge to his gut. *The drawer with the receipts is guarded by a simple lock. I could open the desk in the time to breathe twice.* He fisted both hands on his lap. *The thief is dead. Honesty is difficult. Temptation winks each day from objects as varied as the church candlesticks and Otto's plump pockets.*

Christian extracted a *Deutsch* newspaper from his coat and held it high. "*Mein Bruder* send recent paper from St. Louis. I read. We discuss."

Half the men in the tavern gathered round with eager comments to learn news from the city.

Hans swallowed the dregs of his beer and eased away from the table. He enjoyed walking Elm Ridge's streets in the early dark more than sitting near Otto. *Why do I feel hate from his eyes? I have done nothing to interfere with the doctor's life. Does he think I talk and dance too much with Louisa? She is a delightful person—talented, intelligent, and pretty. I desire our friendship to grow and flourish. Into more?*

****

Two days later, Louisa stood at the bakery worktable. She inserted a large spoon into the lard crock and transferred first one, then a second, goose-egg-size portion into the bowl of flour and salt. *Hot today.* She turned a wrist and skimmed an arm across her brow before lifting the pastry cutter. *Work. Don't dawdle.* Forming her lips in a straight line to reflect determination, she cut lard into the flour. After each pass of the five blades in her right hand, she cleared the gadget with the blunt table knife in her left. Swipe...clear...swipe...clear. She allowed her mind to relax with the tempo of the work.

Hot should not surprise her. The calendar indicated early summer. She stood in a bakery and worked within a few steps of the large oven and modest stove. At this moment, cinnamon buns baked and sent a comforting scent into the air. Rhubarb, sweetened with fresh strawberries, simmered on the stove. *Monday baking includes a dozen tarts.*

When the lard particles in the flour were the size of beet seeds, she paused and relaxed her shoulders. Dipping a modest ladle into a small bowl of water, she sprinkled moisture over the beginnings of the pastry crust. In the next moment, she began to mix the dough with her hands. *A touch more water.* She used her fingers to dribble more moisture into the bowl. A blink later, she returned to mixing until she had a compact ball.

The front door closed behind a departing customer, and *Frau* Keil cleared her throat. "The tart filling smells delicious."

"*Ja.* The smell tempts me to save a little for my bread at luncheon." Louisa sealed her lips. A wise baker did not sample treats until the customers were served. If she ever wanted to run her own shop, she needed to remember the business lessons, in addition to the cooking.

"The rhubarb plant is generous this year. I think tomorrow you make *Herr* Keil's recipe for spring loaf cake with the tart fruit chopped fine."

Louisa cut the dough into three portions and began to roll the first into a generous rectangle. "Is it always so warm at the beginning of summer?"

Charlotte shrugged and rearranged the breads. "Today is warmer than most. I think we will have a storm before evening."

"Again?" Louisa took the circular cutter and pressed out four shapes. "The garden beds remain wet from Friday's storm. Does it not know how to rain without noise in America?"

Charlotte laughed.

While Louisa shaped the first tart shell against the small, round pan, she organized her words. "May I ask you a personal question?"

"*Ja.* No customers to overhear."

"What do you think of *Herr* Hoffmann? Do you trust him?" Louisa mixed her exhale with a sigh. Perhaps the widow's answer would stop her churning thoughts. The day Hans returned the wooden shoes, she expected the question of trust to vanish. Instead, doubt lingered in her thoughts each time *Herr* Wulff entered the bakery, tipped his hat after church, or danced the waltz at the beer garden.

"He is a pleasant young man. From where I stand, he is a hard worker. I think he likes *Herr* Bergmann's horses." The door squeaked open, and *Frau* Keil's attention turned to the new customer. *"Guten Tag, Frau* Muench. What is your pleasure today?"

Louisa removed the cinnamon buns from the oven and set them to cool under a clean linen towel. *Hard worker. Likes the horses.* She smiled and returned to preparing the tarts for baking. Yes, Hans appeared more cheerful working at the stable than on the construction crew. After yesterday's dance lesson, she thought he was ready to say something important after he completed a description of the new stallion at the livery. However, he spoke only one word before Otto interrupted.

Otto. She turned her smile into a frown. The physician managed to claim more than a fair share of the dances yesterday. At every mention of his late wife, he changed to a different topic. *Was the death of his spouse so painful?* She pressed her lips and thought of

Papa in the first weeks after dear Mama's funeral. *He never cried in my presence—like a good Mueller. He talked of her often, especially in the evenings.* Blinking, she banished gathering tears. No matter how broken her heart after Papa died, she experienced no trouble speaking of the many kind aspects of his nature.

Returning her thoughts to yesterday, she realized Otto spent considerable time in conversation with Fredrick. A shiver raced across her shoulders. The physician appeared to be making a friend of her cousin. However, if they were talking crops, weather, or even treatment of common injuries, why did the doctor glance in her direction so often? *Is Otto seeking permission to court me?*

"Nein," she muttered and placed the tarts in the oven. "I did not come to America in pursuit of a husband. I am a baker at Keil's in Elm Ridge, Illinois. One day, I will own a fine bakery and speak good English to my many American customers."

****

"Easy, Chief." Hans unlatched the gate and stepped into the restless stallion's stall. Until an hour ago, the recently purchased animal settled well in his new surroundings. This morning, from a little past seven o'clock to a quarter hour past noon, the horse was paired with the calmest of the geldings for deliveries.

While cleaning the final stall half an hour ago, Hans overheard portions of the driver's report to *Herr* Bergmann. *Lost the pace when a boat whistled.*

Hans held the brush and allowed the horse a moment to see and smell the tool. *"Ja.* I remove dirt and sweat from your back. Hot day. Nice to be in the shade." He began to groom the animal and recount yesterday's time in the beer garden in a soft, even voice.

Chief held his ears high, shifted his stance, and turned his head toward Hans.

"Easy, easy, my big fellow. Soon, you will take the sound of the steamboats in stride." Hans reached high and stroked the brush along the stallion's spine. "You are a fine animal. Your coat is as dark as the sky on a moonless night. When I finish the brushing, you will gleam like polished wood in candlelight."

A few minutes later, Hans glanced out one of the high, open windows. Dark, threatening clouds replaced the previous bright sunshine. Aware of the weight of the hot air inside the stable, he concentrated on keeping his movements even and smooth. If the one small patch of sky proved a true sample, a storm approached. He swallowed, continued brushing, and ducked under Chief's neck. *I brush from this side, stay between animal and stall door.* Could he vault the barrier, if necessary? He lifted to his toes, stretched, and made a long stroke across the stallion's hip. "We become friends—you and I."

Boom!

Hans froze with his hand holding the brush above Chief's back. C*annon? I have not seen any in the town square.* An instant later, he managed a breath and eased toward the gate. "American storm, my friend. Soon, the rain will start and cool the air."

Chief positioned his rump in a corner, stamped a forefoot, and shook his head.

"We finish grooming later." Hans alternated his attention between the stallion's ears and forelegs while he fumbled for the latch behind him. After he stood in the aisle and slid the pin into the hasp, he exhaled.

A gust of wind stirred dust from the plank floor.

One flash of lightning was followed by another until the thunder rolled like a band of drummers.

"Quick. Get the doors." *Herr* Bergmann hurried from the office and pointed at the large south door.

Hans turned and sprinted toward the wide opening. The instant he left the shelter of the eaves, he grasped the first of the three stones holding the sliding door in position. One after the other, he tipped the weights away from the building. Reaching the end of the barrier, he clasped the edge and leaned his shoulder against the heavy weight.

Whap! Rain slapped against his back like thrown from a bucket.

He staggered half a step forward and struggled for his next breath. Gathering his wits and strength, he pushed at the door until it started to move. The large, heavy panel moved by inches until the wheels on the overhead track gained momentum. With his next shove, the door moved easier, foot-by-foot rather than by inches. Abandoning his pushing when two feet of opening remained, Hans ran forward and slipped into the stable. He grasped the interior wooden handle and finished closing the door.

Sal, the carriage mare, whinnied.

A hoof thumped against the side of a stall.

Hans whirled. He glimpsed *Herr* Bergmann closing the window in an empty stall. Following his employer's lead, he entered the nearest pen. Soon, the stable was dim as a moonlit night, with thick, gray clouds visible through the two remaining open windows. He touched the gate of the carriage mare's pen.

"*Nein.*" *Herr* Bergmann grasped him by the elbow. "No time. She will panic and trample you."

He studied the usually calm horse.

Sal, a mild mare, stamped her feet, swished her tail, and twitched her ears.

A roar, different and louder than the thunder, filled Hans's head.

"Down." *Herr* Bergmann bellowed and sank to the floor.

Hans mimicked his employer. Lying on his stomach, holding palms against his ears, he felt the building tremble. *Gute Gott.* All the drums, whistles, and waterfalls in the world could not be this loud. He moved silent lips near the dusty wood in every prayer he remembered. "Is this the end of the world?"

After either a minute—or an hour—Hans became aware of *Herr* Bergmann pushing to his feet and dusting off the front of his clothing. He rolled and curled to a sitting position. In an instant, he sought the horses with his gaze.

The mare trembled at the far wall and stared with her head lowered.

Chief, the stallion, snorted and stamped.

"What—"

"Cyclone." *Herr* Bergmann cut off the remainder of the question. "Too close. We need to check for damage outside."

Hans followed his employer to the north door. Sliding the barrier open about three feet, he swallowed before stepping into a steady rain.

The stablemaster walked into the cobbled yard and turned a slow circle. "Wagon shed still stands. Tavern across the street escaped damage. The foundry's chimney remains tall and spewing dark smoke. I think the worst missed us."

Missed us? "Never have I heard so much roaring." Hans yielded to curiosity and walked into the street. Yes, foundry chimney stood thick and straight. The familiar buildings—the hotel, stores, and modest church steeples—appeared the same as during his walk to work several hours ago.

Two men exited the tavern, looked in all directions, and pointed to the northeast.

A weight settled on his shoulder, and he startled.

"I'm going to the levee to check on my crew and warehouse. Open both large doors, but don't enter either stall until the horses settle." *Herr* Bergmann adjusted his flat, wool cap and strode toward the levee road.

"*Ja.*" Hans added a nod to his reply. A moment later, he pushed the north stable door to the wide-open position. A light breeze replaced the strong, wild wind which previewed the storm. Looking west, he noticed a ragged hole in the clouds. "Come and gone in a hurry."

For the next hour, Hans worked alone. He opened the south door and the windows in the empty stalls. While putting out grain and hay for the soon-to-return teams, he found his soothing voice. He glanced frequently at the two horses and directed his words toward their stalls. "Yesterday, I almost told Louisa my secret. I want her to hear the difficult story from my lips. I do not trust *Herr* Doctor Wulff not to fill her head with his suspicions. He studies me at times as if he knows me from Westphalia. I do not recall him from my time in Essen. Each time he sits near me in the tavern for supper, I am tempted to leave Elm Ridge.

Am I a coward?"

Sal, the mare, snorted.

"Ah, my pretty." Hans crossed the aisle and opened one hand flat for the horse's inspection. "You feel better now. You promise not to tell others my secrets?"

The sound of hooves and wheels against the cobbled yard drifted to his ears.

Hans approached the arriving wagon.

Herr Weiss guided the team to back the empty vehicle into the long, low shed.

Standing well to the side, Hans chose careful words. "During the storm…did you find shelter?"

"*Nein.*" *Herr* Weiss set the wagon brake and signaled Hans to begin unhitching the team. "The rain caught us just after we passed the sawmill. These boys did well, but they needed a firm hand."

"I noticed a tree blown down."

"A tree's the least of it. Black's Mill is gone. Well…near to destroyed. The mill and dogtrot cabin nearby lost roofs. Water wheel is all busted."

"People?" Hans shivered with a sudden chill. Gripping a leather strap, he held his breath. *I wish no harm to any person.*

The driver spat on the cobbles. "Black—according to my source—the mill owner laid trapped under a beam. We almost got lucky."

Pausing in unbuckling the breeching straps from the wagon tongue, Hans remembered the flicker of dislike in *Frau* Keil's eyes the time one of the bakery customers mentioned the mill owner in conversation. *Black's wagon. Black's driver ran over Herr Keil.*

"The new doctor, *Herr* Wulff, treated the poor excuse for a miller after others freed him from the rubble. Broken leg, if the first rumor holds true. I didn't linger or leave the team. Animals are apt to spook for a time after a cyclone."

Hans returned to his work and soon signaled *Herr* Weiss to lead the horses to the water trough. *If today's story follows the pattern of most, by the time the tale reaches the bakery, Herr Wulff will be a hero. How can a poor stable hand compete?* He paused halfway across the yard. *When did Otto and I enter a contest? Louisa is a capable young woman, not a carnival prize.*

Chapter Nineteen

Early the next afternoon, Louisa transferred warm
ginger cookies from the baking sheet to a cloth-lined
tray. A tiny bubble of joy rose within her. The final
cookies for the day were in the oven. After she washed
the few dishes, she planned to don the calico sunbonnet
and her wooden shoes for garden work. While doing
physical work in fresh air, she hoped to sort the various
scraps of information from today's customers.

Currently, the story consisted of jumbled pieces.
Organizing a few of them, she assembled a frightening
picture. *I imagine terror when a team bolts and the
wagon crashes off the road.* She placed a calming hand
on her chest and muttered thanks for the farmer who
jumped free and suffered only scratches. Mr. Black—
she pressed her lips. Half a dozen customers described
the destroyed building in different degrees of detail.
One woman claimed to have sheltered in the root cellar
with the *Deutsch* physician. Otto—she sighed—he will
be a town hero.

She closed her eyes and imagined if the bakery,
rather than the flour mill, lay in the storm's path. A
simple prayer faded with a shiver. From the distance of
half a mile, the noise and threat of the storm scared her.
*Frau Keil locked the door and huddled beside me under
the sturdy worktable. Thank God, Charlotte is a
sensible woman.*

Louisa set the cookies on the lowest pass-through shelf and glanced toward the opening shop door. Curving her lips into a genuine smile, she stepped over to the opening between the rooms.

"Do you have cinnamon buns today?" Polly spoke in slow, clear English.

"*Ja.* Warm from the oven still," Charlotte replied in a mix of the languages. "How many?"

"Four." She displayed fingers as if necessary to confirm.

Moistening her lips, Louisa found an English greeting for one of the few Americans to come to the bakery at least once a week. "Madam Black, do you have news of your brother?"

"He will live—if infection does not set in." Polly beckoned her closer. Clearing her throat, she hesitated before speaking in slow, awkward *Deutsch* with an occasional English word. "He woke in the wreckage of the mill and screamed for help. Several people, sheltering in a root cellar across the road, heard him the moment they opened the door. Kind neighbors, they hurried to his aid. The new doctor, *Herr* Wulff, was among them. Do you know him?"

Louisa nodded. *Too well.* Deciding not to admit the extent of her knowledge concerning the physician until another day, she glanced toward Charlotte.

Polly set her shopping basket on the counter. "My brother complains of his care. According to the men who carried him to his rooming house, he cursed at everyone during the entire examination. I did not arrive until the doctor was tying the bandages. Leo, my brother, continued to mumble foul language to all in the room until the laudanum took over with sleep.

Complaining is his nature." Concentrating on the words, Louisa nodded. In her few encounters with the miller, he appeared to carry an invisible angry cloud. She heard loud threats spew from his mouth with the ease pleasant greetings crossed the lips of other business men.

"According to the witnesses, the doctor, *Herr* Wulff, behaved sensible. The landlady told me he called for warm water and good lye soap. She reports the doctor bathed the entire leg before applying bandage and splint. During all of the cleaning and treatment, my brother called for the American doctor."

"Did he arrive soon after?" Louisa recalled comments of the elderly man's fondness for whiskey.

"Nein." Polly shook her head. "During the storm, he slept in the tavern. The lad sent to fetch him looked at his condition and left without telling him where they had taken my brother. I tell you what others think. Mrs. Clark's customers call the American doctor a…quack— like a duck."

With the last portion of the message in English, Louisa puzzled over the words for a moment. "Is he not trained?"

Polly laughed. "My dear, little friend, in America a man wanders into a small town like Elm Ridge, claims to be a doctor, and practices the trade with more luck and slick words than skill and training."

"Otto." Louisa jerked a hand over her mouth. *Too late.* "*Herr* Doctor Wulff attended University in Westphalia. In our village schoolroom, he received the best marks in his class and made his parents proud." She dipped her gaze toward the floor. *My warm blush on neck and scalp reminds me I have said more than is proper.* An instant later, she detected a wisp of smoke. "Ach. The last ginger cookies threaten to burn."

Louisa fled to the oven, snatched a towel, and opened the door. Reaching inside, she removed the pan of spiced cookies. Eight disks with blackened edges confronted her. Heat from the oven joined the earlier flush from her speech and inattention to work.

"No worry, Louisa," *Frau* Keil soothed. "We will have a special, crisp treat with our tea."

With a large sigh, Louisa set the pan on an empty portion of the table. *A good baker pays close attention.* She glanced toward the clock and pressed her lips. The temptation to sweep the entire mess into the trash surged. *Nein. Dunking cookies.* She turned to retrieve a white china plate from a shelf.

"*Guten Tag,*" a familiar male voice greeted *Frau* Keil.

Ignore him. Thank him for treating Mr. Black. With each blink, she alternated the two options tussling within her mind.

"May I have a word with *Fraulein* Mueller?"

Louisa wiped her hands on her apron and walked to the workroom entrance. Opening her mouth, she closed it before a sound escaped. Otto stood beside another man. She took a moment to study the stranger beside him. The man stood middle height and displayed dark-brown hair and mustache. With an identical jawline and similar brown eyes, he appeared to be an image of Hans in a few years.

Bruder? She offered the stranger a small smile. "Welcome to Keil's Bakery."

Polly lifted her basket and tucked the cloth over her purchases. Turning toward Otto, she bobbed her head.

"I go to visit my brother. Shall I tell him you will call later, *Herr* Doctor?"

"*Nein.*" Otto spared the American a glance. "I left him a short time ago. He insisted on sitting, and his landlady loaned him a proper chair. You must make him rest and stay in the house today. I will call in the morning."

"*Danke,* I will be his nurse." In a swirl of stylish skirts, she nodded to each of them.

"Madam Black, be sure to bring your boy the next time you come to call. You are welcome any evening." *Frau* Keil continued to smile at the younger woman until the door closed again.

"We desire a private word." Otto pointed into the workroom.

Louisa shook her head and glanced toward Charlotte. Crossing her arms against the top of her apron, she decided neither man would leave the sales area. The burnt ginger cookies or unwashed baking tools were not their concern. "You may speak in front of *Frau* Keil. We stand in her bakery."

Otto shifted his position until he blocked the older woman's easy view of Louisa. "I want you to meet my friend, *Herr* Adolph Hoffmann of St. Louis. He immigrated from Arnsberg."

Arnsberg—Hans mentioned the village twice after I spoke of school days in Hamm. Louisa felt her heart skip a beat. She determined to pay close attention to every word. Perhaps the man in front of her was a relative Hans failed to mention. Often, when she asked questions about his life in Westphalia, Hans spoke place names without clarifying if he had lived in the place or only passed through on his way to another. He tended to prefer a colorful description, instead of specific names in his stories.

Aware of Otto's steady gaze, she glanced in his direction before settling her attention on Adolph. "How long have you been in St. Louis?"

Adolph shifted his gaze from the clock to Louisa. "Two years—I find the city lively and interesting. This spring, my younger brother planned to join me. We—older brother, father, and grandfather—trained in the leather and harness trade. Fashioning and repairing fittings remains a steady business, but opportunity for younger sons is more plentiful in America."

"Enough"—Otto interrupted. "Adolph and I have a friendship of several years. I stayed with him a week before continuing to Elm Ridge this spring. I...we...are here as a courtesy."

Courtesy? Louisa rolled the word around in her mind. *Good manners are not a quality I associate with Otto.* "Please state your business. The garden weeds grow every minute."

"Your friend at the stables—"

"Hans." She supplied the name before Otto could say another word. Narrowing her eyes, she focused on the physician's face. *What mischief do you plan?*

Otto moistened his lips. "Hans—yes—he answers to the name. I suspect he is a thief—of the worst sort. Adolph will help me prove it. If Hans is built of the character I suspect, he will be gone before sunset."

Louisa held her breath for a long moment. *Thief? Coward? Hans returned the shoes—and stopped a runaway team.* She shifted her attention to Adolph and reviewed the information at hand. *The harness maker had expected his brother to join him. A younger man who looked similar? A man who looked like Hans? Four young men often were together during the early weeks of the voyage. The quartet formed a tight group among the passengers taking air during fine days on the main deck. Two of them were younger, no more than boys fleeing to America before the army showed interest. The remaining pair looked so much alike her friend, Bertha, joked they could be twins. We buried one of the look-alikes the same day as Papa. Did it mean anything Hans spoke little about his family? Aside from stating his mother died and his father was harsh, did his family matter?* "My friend *Herr* Hoffmann will not turn coward and flee. He is an honest man doing honest work in America."

"And before?" Otto leaned closer.

"Westphalia is the past. I choose to remember it with fondness." She met and held Otto's gaze. *He stares with cold, accusing eyes.* Swallowing, she stiffened her arms against a tremble. "Others, who did not have a comfortable life, might desire to forget it. A new, fresh start—an opportunity to find a new dream— is reason to make the long, difficult journey to America."

"Don't complain I did not warn you." Otto turned, made a slight bow to *Frau* Keil, and stepped toward the door. "Come, Adolph, we go to expose an imposter."

Louisa allowed fragments of questions and portions of words to swirl. Staring at the floor, she listened to the men exit the bakery. *What if Hans was not born Hans Hoffmann? Who was he? Did it matter?* He treated her kindly and worked hard at the stables. She raised her gaze from her felt slippers to Charlotte. "*Bitte.* No questions. I have no answers."

212

****

Hans removed Chief's bridle and draped it over his shoulder. Slipping the halter onto the stallion, he checked the buckle and chin strap. "You worked hard today. *Herr* Weiss gave a good report." Sidestepping, he set the bridle over the door, paused, and lifted the brush. "*Herr* Weiss tends you well, but today, he was called on an urgent errand. I give you a good brushing while you munch your evening meal. You will feel refreshed after I remove the dirt on the outside." He chuckled. "You pay no attention to me—I am aware you are eager to fill your belly with grain and hay."

While he groomed the stallion, Hans crooned bits of lullaby. The soft words and even tempo of his voice tended to sooth restless horses. He glanced frequently toward the animal's head, checking the position of the ears for a sign of anxiety or fear. Perhaps his feelings were foolish, but he already felt affection for this new draft horse. The conversation between *Herr* Bergmann and the driver, positive on the beast's behavior in harness today, indicated the animal was settling into his new home. *Like me.* Hans lifted Chief's right front foot and checked for debris lodged between shoe and hoof.

"Exactly the man we want to see," Otto's voice boomed over the normal stable sounds.

Hans shivered, released Chief's foot, and scurried out of the horse's way. Setting a hand on the stall door, he glared at the physician. "Hush—men have no need to shout and disturb the fine animals." He glanced toward the horse and exited the stall. "What is your business, *Herr* Wulff and…?"

"You give fine advice," the man beside Otto spoke low and musical. "My name is Adolph Hoffmann. I

213

journey from St. Louis at the request of my physician friend."

Hans inspected the man more carefully. Blinking, he reminded himself this was not a glimpse in the shaving mirror with the addition of a few years—and a mustache. At a stray sound, he glanced toward Otto in time to see a faint smile cross his lips.

"We wish to speak with you." Otto widened his stance and crossed his arms.

"Go to the end of the aisle, by the half open door, and I will join you soon." Hans turned to Chief.

The horse, busy with his hay ration, shifted enough to rub one hip on the stall's side.

Gathering the bridle, Hans hurried to the tack alcove and hung the equipment on the proper peg. *Adolph Hoffmann.* He shivered in the heat. *I could fetch my money and possessions from my room and leave on the next steamboat. Where would I go? I have done no evil.* He glanced at the clean harness hanging ready for tomorrow's work and found a grain of courage. He moved his lips in silence. *Hans Hoffmann is an honest man.*

During his walk to the south end of the stable, Hans reviewed the contents of the small trunk which he lost in St. Louis. The tools and most of the clothing disappeared with the chest. His workmate rescued one shirt, in addition to the Bible, a letter, two pipes, shaving equipment, and a pair of spectacles. The letter tucked into the Bible was clearly written by the true Hans's brother and signed A. Hoffmann.

"What do you think, Adolph?" Otto leaned against the doorframe.

"He could pass. The nose is different. My brother

would have recognized me."

Hans advanced the final step and shrugged to feign little interest. "I do not understand."

Adolph cleared his throat and shot a glance toward Otto. "My younger brother, Johannes, planned to join me in St. Louis this spring. Three weeks ago, during Otto's final days in the city, I received a letter from our parents saying he left Bremerhaven in mid-January. Do you know of him? When did you set sail?"

"Hans, or Johannes, Hoffmann is a common name." He looked at each of them before settling his gaze on Adolph. *I will tell the truth—in part.* Glancing toward the underside of the loft, he sorted facts to find a logical beginning. "*The Flying Gull* left port on eighteen January. I did not become acquainted with all of the passengers."

"What name did your parents speak at your baptism?" Otto leaned forward.

Hans widened his stance. *I will stay silent rather than lie.*

Adolph stood quiet and roamed his gaze over Hans.

"Tell me, what trade did your brother practice?" Hans removed his cap and wiped his brow. During the motion, he avoided looking toward Otto.

"Harness making."

Nodding, Hans pursed his lips. *Tell the truth.* "I met your brother on the ship. He was friendly without insisting on knowing another's business. His death, on the thirty-second day of the voyage, saddened me."

"Did you steal his name?" Otto hissed.

Hans looked at the toes of his new wooden shoes, instead of shifting his gaze to the physician. Tucking his hands into his pockets, he hid his trembling fingers.

He will not accept any answer I give.

"The name is not the most important concern." Adolph pointed from his lips to Otto.

Gute. I also want Otto to remain quiet.

"What do I write our parents? Where is his trunk? Why did you not inquire for me in St. Louis?" Adolph opened his hands and displayed his palms.

Hans exhaled more than he knew his lungs could hold. Lifting his gaze, he looked Adolph full in the face. *All in Elm Ridge, Louisa, and others on the ship know me as Hans Hoffmann.* "Your brother died of the shipboard fever and received a Christian burial. After his death, I claimed his passport and trunk. My forged papers were poor and required a bribe to the boarding master in Bremerhaven. Rumors in the streets near the shipping company offices made me afraid America would not allow me to stay with the false passport."

"How do we know you didn't kill him?" Otto stepped into the small space between the other men.

Backing a step, Hans struggled for a calm voice. "He died of the fever." He failed to ignore sweat beaded on his brow. Directing his gaze to Otto, he moistened his lips. "Not all boys grow to young men in generous families with the opportunity to attend university. Some of us are forced to survive by our wits—perhaps a bit of stealing. I am not proud of everything I've done in life—but never could I do harm to a man."

Otto muttered and spat into the thin straw layer on the floor.

Hans switched his attention to Adolph. "Hans Hoffmann, born in Arnsberg, died of shipboard fever on the thirty-second day of the voyage. He and *Herr*

Dietrich Mueller of Hamm were buried the same morning."

"How do we sort truth from lie?" Otto growled.

"Let him speak, Otto." Adolph put a hand on the physician's arm. "My brother is dead. The story of illness, death, and burial is not difficult to believe. I saw men die during the voyage, as did you." He shifted his attention to Hans. "What happened to his tools and personal things?"

"Thieves—dishonest Americans." Hans focused on the plain, silver watchchain Adolph wore.

"All of it?" Adolph pushed his face forward.

Catching a whiff of peppermint on the other man's breath, Hans pulled courage into his voice. "Most—a few things remain."

"Show me. Johannes brought family treasures—the youngest son's inheritance." Adolph insisted.

Hans glanced toward the other end of the stable.

A driver, the last to return from today's deliveries, led a horse into a stall.

"I must finish my work." Hans backed a step. "Go to the tavern on First Street. *Herr* Wulff knows the place. I will join you after the animals are settled for the night."

Otto laughed. "You expect us to trust you? The word of a thief is worth less than a wheelbarrow of horse droppings."

Curling his fingers into fists, Hans controlled the anger surging through his body. "You have no proof. Perhaps I'm guilty of holding a dead man's property. Another man might name my sin as not seeking Adolph during my brief stay in St. Louis."

Adolph grinned. "I like your spunk, young man. I

think we watch the stable from the bench outside the tavern door until you finish work and join us."

"I will meet you in the tavern." Hans lifted his cap and skimmed an arm across his brow.

"Come, Otto. I buy beer."

Hans stood for a long moment and watched the pair walk away from the stable. *I know a way to the levee they cannot see.* Shaking his head, he turned and stepped into the familiar surroundings. *Nein.* He mouthed his decision a moment before he started to clean the final sets of harness. "I think best to face my enemy. No matter what Adolph says—I keep name Hans Hoffmann."

****

An hour later, Hans gave his landlady quick introductions to Otto and Adolph before he led them to his second-floor room. "Nothing inside you may not see." He opened the door and gestured the others to enter. He followed a step behind Adolph. Blinking, he imagined how the visitors perceived his simple room. Sparse, the space shared much with the cheap New Orleans hotel. A single window, open a few inches for ventilation, occupied space near the head of a narrow, iron bed. A stained washstand and wooden chair completed the list of furniture.

He cleared his throat. "The traveling chest and fine tools were taken in St. Louis. A fellow-worker managed to transfer a few of the trunk's contents into a sack before the angry stablemaster claimed my possessions." Hans walked the few steps to two short shelves. Retrieving the Bible and a cloth-wrapped bundle, he held them at shoulder height. "This is all."

Weighing the parcel in his hand, Adolph frowned.

"We open—now."

Leaning against the door frame, Otto crossed his ankles and arms while wearing one of his not-quite-a-smile expressions.

Inspects me as if I were a bug under a magnifying glass. Hans resisted the urge to wipe sweat off his brow.

Opening the Bible, Adolph scanned the inscription and smiled. "*Ja*—written in *Mutter's* hand." Plucking the paper from the center of the book, he nodded. "My letter, the one I filled with advice in August of last year." Loosening the string, Adolph smiled as the fine linen shirt holding the treasures fell away. "What are these—spectacles?"

Hans met the visitor's gaze. "Poor eyesight is noted on the passport. I do not recall seeing them on his face during the voyage."

"I must give little brother, Johannes, credit for a bit of cleverness." He set aside a plain razor, brush, and cup. Scooping a medium-sized porcelain pipe bowl from the fabric with one hand, he held it high for the others to see. "Ah, the family treasure."

"Tell us." Hans silently pleaded for no questions about the other pipe, the one of carved walnut, which he carried in his coat pocket and smoked each evening.

"Four generations have lived since this pipe was presented to our ancestor, a pastor near Essen." Adolph caressed the pipe bowl with one thumb. "Always, the youngest son inherits. After Mother's brother died without children, she saved the heirloom for Johannes."

"No money?" Otto tossed the words into the room.

Hans shook his head. "Steamboat—lodging—meals. Modest amount to begin."

"*Ja*—I believe. *Vater* clings tight to *Thalers*. The value was in the tools—and the memories in this." Adolph gestured to the items displayed on the bed. "Now"—he wrapped the family treasures once again in the shirt—"tell me of this St. Louis stablemaster."

Hans recounted a description of Mr. Covington. He remembered the street name and several details of the building, but the exact date of his hasty departure failed him. "Easter was past—one week—or two—the morning I buy ticket for Elm Ridge."

"I ask once again—tell me your baptismal name." Adolph tied the string.

"*Nein.*" Hans shook his head to emphasize his refusal. "I use common name Hans Hoffmann the day I set foot in America. No purpose to speaking the other."

"What do you tell others of your family?" Adolph raised his gaze to intersect Hans's.

"*Mutter* died the year I was four and ten. I fled *Vater,* a harsh man, soon after. No need to burden others with stories of my past." The advantage to the brief tale lay in the amount of truth. Prone to drink and violence, his father lacked respect among even the rough miners of the village.

"You deceptive worm." Otto pushed off, advanced, and grabbed Hans's shirt.

"Truth—new life in America. New land allows a man a new dream." Hans stared into the physician's eyes and chilled at the lack of life in the pale gray color.

"Let him go, Otto. *Mein Bruder* died during the voyage. I learned information to write to my family. Illinois grows and welcomes immigrants each week. I believe America is large enough to host one more Hans Hoffmann." Adolph stepped closer to Hans. "Never contact me or claim my family—understand?"

Hans nodded. *You ask a small price.* "*Ja*—I escort you out of this house." Later, Hans sat on his bed and propped his head with both hands. Muttering to the floor, he confided to the empty room. "Never did I dream the difficulty to be an honest man."

Chapter Twenty

Louisa inhaled the comforting scent of rising bread dough early the next morning. Counting, she ladled water into the coffeepot. She set the tin container on the stove and assessed the day. *Gute Tag.* While she pumped water a short time ago, she noticed a fair, summer sky. At this hour, the day resembled a blank piece of paper, unmarred by any unpleasant event— such as a visit from *Herr* Wulff. Holding her breath, she felt a shiver scamper across her shoulders. *Otto is a coward—he implies wrongdoing of another when the man is not present to offer a defense.* Gathering a few drops of water in her hand, she opened the oven and flicked her fingers. Listening to the satisfying sizzle of liquid hitting hot iron, she smiled. *Good. Ready on time.*

A few moments later, after she closed the door on the loaves of wheat and rye bread, she sensed a shadow outside the front door. While collecting the *Kuchen* pans, she looked past the sales area to the sidewalk.

A man paused at the door, knocked, and waved. "Louisa. Open the door. I wish to speak to you."

Hans. She exhaled tension hidden in her lungs. Otto's prediction didn't come true. Whatever happened between *Herr* Wulff, his friend from St. Louis, and Hans, the confrontation did not chase her friend from Elm Ridge. *Why did he come to the bakery before full sunrise?* She walked to the center of the vacant sales area. "We are closed. Only bakers and roosters work at this hour."

"*Bitte.* I must speak to you…before I go to work at the stables. The topic is very important."

She glanced at the clock and then the pans waiting for the sweet dough rising in the crockery bowl. "Wait—two minutes." Hurrying out the back entrance, she sprinted up the stairs and knocked on the apartment door. She wiped her hands and transferred a portion of nervous tension to her apron. Raising one hand, she prepared to tap again.

"Louisa. My goodness. Do we have a problem?" *Frau* Keil stood in front of her with a few wisps of hair not yet pinned.

"*Nein…Ja.* Hans is at the door."

"Go—let him in. I will join you in a minute."

Louisa fled down the stairs, through the bakery rooms, and snatched the key from behind the sales counter.

"I need to talk with you." Hans rattled the knob.

"*Ja. Ja.* Let go of the door. I need to turn key." She opened the door a hand's width.

Hans pushed the opening wider and slipped inside. Jerking off his cap, he faced her. "I need to tell my confession. You must listen to the wrongs I have done."

"Confession?" She stilled with one hand in midair. "I am not a pastor. I am a mere baker. Tell your sins to God." She re-locked the door and returned the key to the hook. "Is it a long story?"

"Complicated." He held his gaze on the floor.

Pausing behind the counter, she grasped the high stool and set the seat a few inches inside the workroom.

"Sit. I have *Kuchen* to prepare. Do not frown. I can use ears and hands at the same time."

Hans hesitated beside the stool and nodded a greeting to *Frau* Keil.

After a quick exchange of pleasantries, the widow filled the coffee grinder and set about preparing the morning drink.

"I-I…was not born Hans Hoffmann." He studied the cap in his hands.

Louisa dipped her fingers in soft lard and greased the first, round pan. "Johannes?"

"*Nein.*" He looked at each woman for a long moment. "Ulrich—not a word to another?"

Ulrich. She let the name rest in her mind for a moment. Snatches of *Herr* Wulff's accusations waited at the tip of her tongue. *Imposter?* She closed her eyes and held her breath for a moment until Otto's prediction of cowardice faded. In the next instant, she visualized the quartet of young men from early in the voyage. *Why? Is it true he fled a cruel father? Does he have no family? Or did his brother stand in this very shop yesterday?* Truth and possible lies tumbled over each other like fresh berries mixing with sugar. "Explain."

Hans told his story with many pauses and a little prodding.

Louisa pressed sweet dough into pans, spooned softened plums, and drizzled honey across the top while she listened. Many details were missing. However, his tone gave her confidence he told all she needed to know at present. Hans's tale reminded her of stories whispered by adults during her childhood. *Hans is not the first youngster to run from drunken and harsh parents. A great shame, and difficulty, to learn living with an uncle more miserable than his father.*

"My thieving days are over." He thanked *Frau* Keil when she handed him a mug of hot coffee. "I thought my crimes ended before I set foot on *The Flying Gull.* Then temptation...or opportunity...overtook me. I watched the man born Hans Hoffmann die. I swear to God in heaven—I did not aid his death. I took his papers because I feared the American officials would send me back if they discovered forged documents."

Sighing, Louisa looked carefully at the man on the stool. If sent back to Westphalia, he would languish in jail—or the army. Neither place resulted in either a long or happy life. She remembered portions of the letters Hermann sent to his family. Visiting the cooper's house, she eagerly listened to his parents share the writings. Hard work and harsh living filled army life. She blinked away forming tears. *I wish for some memories to fade.* But the image of the elder *Herr* Wulff entering the bakery on a hot August afternoon with news of his youngest son's death appeared clear. *Measles—a terrible disease—worse to die alone—far from family.*

"You know my life in Elm Ridge, Louisa. Forgive me for my many past sins. Rest my mind—assure me America is truly the land of new beginnings—new dreams."

She set aside the honey pot and wiped both hands on her apron. "Forgiveness is not mine to grant."

"Are you going to send me away?" He stood and set the cooling coffee on a corner of the worktable.

"*Nein.* I have no right to tell you where to live. I think"...she curved her lips into the first real smile since he'd knocked on the door. "I think I will hold my money close…lest you suffer too much temptation."

He opened his lips but released no sound.

A laugh? Or does he choke? "You are my friend. You are my student who needs more dance lessons." She shifted her gaze to his face. Aware of a pleasant warmth blossoming in her chest, she studied his clear, brown eyes. *Do I detect a trace of hope?*

"Until next time," he spoke over the striking clock. "I must hurry to the stables before *Herr* Bergmann and the drivers question why the first team is not wearing a harness at the water trough."

"*Ja*—I unlock door." Louisa followed him across the sales area.

The instant she set the key in the lock, she felt his coarser skin against her fingers.

Tugging their clasped hands upward, he bent his head and pressed a firm kiss on her skin.

Louisa sealed her lips and swallowed. Like ripples spread from a pebble dropped in a pond, she sensed warmth and calm spreading up her arm. Aware of Hans exiting and hurrying toward the stables, she stared at her hand for a long moment. *Others will hear my pounding heart.* Breathing deep, she stilled her lungs before a sigh began. "Ach, the bread."

****

Sunday, soon after the church bells proclaimed the end of worship, Hans entered Chief's stall. "My friend, do you enjoy watching me work today? While you lingered at the water trough, I cleaned out all your waste and sprinkled fresh straw. Now you reward me with this pile of dung."

The stallion reached for a whisp of hay on the floor.

Shaking his head, Hans left the stall and walked to get the wheelbarrow and fork. *Stable work is never done.* His boss displayed great trust by assigning him to work on his own today. Sunday duties included cleaning stalls, giving feed and water to the animals, and handling any customers who came to rent a saddle horse or the gig.

Entering Chief's stall to remove the fresh manure, he thought of his visitors this week. He pursed his lips and muttered at the memory of Otto and Adolph confronting him Tuesday afternoon, "*Herr* Wulff needs to keep his nose out of my business. *Herr* Hoffmann, you are not so bad as I feared. I have much to learn in my new life."

Wednesday morning, the harness maker had arrived at the livery alone. The request for a private word before Adolph boarded the packet to St. Louis sounded ominous. But it turned out well. Adolph expressed another round of thanks for the return of the heirloom pipe, inscribed Bible, and plain spectacles. Shaking hands a final time, Adolph lowered his voice and issued a warning. "Herr Wulff has changed since his brother, Hermann, died. He's determined to bind his family with the Muellers."

"*Herr* Bergmann."

Hans startled at the woman's voice. Tossing a forkful of waste into the wheelbarrow, he leaned over the stall gate and called toward the voice, "*Ein minute.*"

"Hans?" *Frau* Keil walked the center aisle with the skirts of her Sunday dress hovering scant inches above the dust and debris on the plank floor. "I see you have good reason not to be in church. Today is fine weather—pleasant for either picnic or beer garden."

"*Ja.*" He stepped into the aisle and latched the stall gate. "What brings you to the stables on such a day?"

"Do you have a horse and buggy to rent?"

He nodded. "We have a gentle mare trained for a gig. Can you drive?"

Frau Keil released a combination of snort and laugh. "The days *mein Vater* lay drunk in his bed, I drove the team of four from quarry to building site all day."

Feeling growing admiration for the widow each time he learned another fact from her past, Hans smiled. "Allow me a few minutes to fetch the horse and get her hitched." He hurried to the tack alcove. A moment later, he paused midstride. Frau *Keil brought guests—a woman and boy.* Glancing toward *Frau* Keil, he saw her nod. "I not take long."

A short time later, Hans led the mare, wearing her harness, toward the gig. As he passed *Frau* Keil, Polly Black, and the young boy, he touched his cap in respect and acknowledgement. *Not the guest I expect.* He backed the mare between the shafts and stole glances at the boy. Turning his attention to the harness, he secured all the fasteners. *The boy has bright copper hair. Where have I seen such a color recently?* After looping the reins onto the gig's seat, he grasped the bridle strap. A few moments later, he halted mare and rig in front of the women.

"She has a name?" *Frau* Keil presented a flattened hand to the animal.

"*Ja*—the mare is Sal. She is fond of carrot." He reached into his pocket, pulled out a carrot, and broke it into two pieces.

"*Danke.*" *Frau* Keil accepted one chunk and

beckoned the boy forward. "See this, Joseph. Sal's treat. Now open your hand, hold it flat, and you will make a friend for the afternoon."

The boy followed directions.

The mare moved her lips across his palm.

"Tickles." Joseph grinned.

"*Ja*—now you climb into the gig. *Frau* Keil will take you on an adventure." Charlotte guided the boy toward the vehicle's left wheel.

Hans stowed the basket and offered a hand to the American woman.

"Thank you. We have met. Do you remember?" She grasped her skirt with one hand. "I am Polly Black—from the dress shop."

"I recall." He thought on the message he'd taken back to the bakery. The entire errand did not make sense at the time. Several forms of address rushed through his mind. *Frau? Nein. Fraulein* was out of the question. He blinked and settled on an American word. "Madam Black."

Frau Keil pressed a golden coin into his hand before he assisted her into the gig. "We will settle the exact amount when we return. The question you are afraid to ask"—she gathered the reins and checked where the excess was draped. "Joseph is *Herr* Keil's son."

Hans opened his lips and froze.

Laughing, Charlotte slapped the reins and commanded the horse to move. At the last moment, she turned her face toward Hans. "The look of a fish is not good on your face."

Hans snapped shut his mouth. He backed a step to clear the gig's wheel hub. Never did he expect such a statement from a respectable woman. He stayed in the yard, watched them turn south on First Street, and shook his head. "One lady has *Herr* Keil's name. The other has his child." Hans muttered during his return to the stable. "How can they be friends?"

****

"*Ein...und...zwei...und...*" Louisa held little Karl's hands and encouraged him to move his feet. Aware of *Deutsch* greetings crossing in the air between Sunday beer garden patrons, she addressed her small student. "Again. Do you like the dancing?"

The child giggled and lifted his foot. "*Ein.*" He plopped to the ground. "Again."

Anna removed a tin from the picnic basket. "He is too young. You would have him dance before he walks steady."

"A person is never too young to learn dancing." Louisa sang the numbers again and swayed with her student. Breathing in the warm sunshine, she tipped her face to the sky and gave silent thanks for family. The scent of early summer blossoms wafted from a garden. Breathing deeply, she glanced toward the fair sky. *Perfect picnic weather.* She lacked only one thing— Hans's company. Tapping her foot to the melody in her head, she recalled his hurried visit to the bakery yesterday.

Before he'd taken the first bite of his lunch roll, he apologized for not being able to accompany her to the beer garden for another dance lesson. "*Herr* Bergmann has assigned me to work. The animals know nothing of Sunday."

"I invited a guest. Did you bring enough lunch to share?" Fredrick approached, carrying two full beer steins.

Louisa glanced from playing a finger game with the child. Pressing her lips tight, she felt her heart stutter and resisted the urge to frown. *Good manners and kindness.* Papa's advice for serving customers suited social situations also. "*Guten Tag, Herr* Doctor Wulff.*"

"*Bitte.* This is America. We have no need to be so formal among friends." He held out a stein for her. "Call me Otto. I will address you as Louisa."

She accepted the beer. Sipping cool liquid through the foam layer, she studied the physician. Her English lessons, with Mrs. Cook, included some discussion of new customs, including the use of Christian names among friends of brief acquaintance. She hesitated. A decision wavered like a blade of grass in a breeze. Hunting for kind words without encouraging familiarity, she studied his pale eyes. *Do I see friendship, mischief, or something more sinister?* "*Herr* Otto." She compromised. "You may call me *Fraulein* Louisa."

"Agreed." He smiled before taking a drink of beer.

During the picnic, Louisa watched the unspoken conversation between her cousin and the doctor. *He has charmed Fredrick.* While the topics spoken aloud over plates of seasoned rabbit, crisp kraut, and potato bread varied widely, she noticed *Herr* Otto did not mention his St. Louis friend. Herr *Hoffmann did not stay long in Elm Ridge.* Soon, her thoughts drifted to Hans's Thursday evening visit. She pulled garden weeds in the dusk, and Hans repaired the gate hinge. Their conversation had been casual and reminiscent of chatting with Hermann while picking plums.

"Tell us more of the cyclone." Anna alternated her gaze between Otto and Louisa before she handed her son a piece of bread crust.

Louisa swallowed a bite of kraut. "In a span of a few minutes, the air turned dark as dusk. The sound—frightful—louder and hurt my ears more than standing near a steamboat engine. *Frau* Keil and I wished for a better place than under the worktable to hide."

"These American storms can be fierce." Fredrick nodded. "Before arriving in Illinois, if a man had told me of such weather, I would have called him a liar. Now, after seeing clouds spin, I think anything is possible."

Otto swallowed beer and skimmed the back of his hand across his lips. "*Ja*—I pray never to see another storm like the one which roared past on Monday. After the Americans and I emerged from the root cellar, I saw a thin shingle embedded into a fence post. I would not have believed the tale from another. But I observed the oddity with my own eyes."

"I hear you treated the grist mill owner." Fredrick wiped his fingers on a handkerchief.

"*Ja*. As the storm approached, I stood, gawking at the clouds. Two Americans shouted and urged me to shelter in a root cellar with them. After the noise faded, we came out and saw the destroyed buildings. *Herr* Black lay trapped under a timber. He suffered a terrible fracture of his lower leg. Once the other men got him free, we carried him on a wide board to the nearest house. He swore with every step. I'm glad I understood only a few of the English words."

Fredrick laughed.

Louisa hid her smile behind one hand. She wanted

to giggle at the image of the loud, unpleasant American complaining to the men aiding him. Listening, she compared the picture Otto painted with words, to the man standing in the bakery, waving his finger at *Frau* Keil, and threatening to take ownership of the business. She gave a quick, silent prayer Polly would be correct and re-played portions of Friday afternoon's exchange in the bakery.

"My brother is not suited for the milling business." Polly had stated a fact clear to the other women. "His landlady and I urge him to accept the price the foreman offered. Even Mr. Rush, a man Leo admires, has told him to return to St. Louis."

"May I?"

Louisa snapped out of her reverie and noticed Otto's extended hand. The melody of a lively polka drifted over the beer garden. "The dance?"

"I asked twice while you were lost in thought."

Laughing, Louisa scrambled to stand. "*Ja.* I will give you one dance."

One polka turned into two, and an entire set. Louisa and Otto moved among the dozen couples on the flat, trampled grass. Both experienced dancers, they guided their feet in the steps without treading on the other. In the circle dance following the polkas, Louisa touched hands and twirled with many partners.

"Come—dancing makes me thirsty." Otto clasped her hand.

Withdrawing her fingers from his smooth hand, Louisa followed at an easy pace. "We send Fredrick and Anna to the dancing circle while we keep watch over little Karl."

"Excellent idea." He stopped, turned, and lifted her

hand. A moment later, he pressed his lips against the thin fabric of her summer gloves.

Louisa watched the kiss. *No heat. No tingle.* Fixing her lips in a gentle curve, she silently repeated Papa's advice. *Kindness and manners.* She contrasted her skin's reaction to Otto's kiss and Hans's quick caress. *One man lights my body with excitement—the other reminds my skin of a dribble of tepid water.* She pressed her lips into a tiny smile. *I keep this knowledge private.*

Chapter Twenty-One

Thursday, an hour after the bakery closed, Louisa sat on a ladder-back chair in the apartment above the hardware store.

Mrs. Cook occupied a similar chair across the corner of a square table. "Next page, please."

" 'The girl and the cat sat by the fire.' " Louisa closed the schoolbook and used a finger to hold her place. "It is helpful *Deutsch* and English letters are almost the same."

Mrs. Cook chuckled and blinked dark-brown eyes. Reaching to her left, she pulled a black, leather-bound volume close. "You are a good student—quick to learn. Next, I want you to read a few lines from this thick book. Open it to our Declaration of Independence. Today is a good time to introduce you."

"So soon?" Louisa pursed her lips. The few official documents in the Mueller household contained complicated words mixed with the familiar. The schoolbook she held used common words to tell of ordinary things—animals, houses, and farms.

"If you and I read the beginning of the proclamation today, you will better understand Mayor Gordon when he reads the document at the Fourth of July celebration tomorrow."

"The bakery customers talk of your holiday." Louisa spoke, slow and uneven. When speaking in

English, she needed to pause and hunt for the correct word. "A birthday for a whole country—the idea is new to me."

Eliza Cook smiled. "We are a growing nation. Immigrants, like your family, arrive every year and help settle the new states. Brave people, from the East and Europe, start farms and villages on the vast land between Missouri and California." She nudged the heavy volume closer to Louisa. "Has your cousin applied for citizenship?"

"I have not asked him. Is it difficult?"

"He needs to declare his intentions at the courthouse. The clerk can tell him the rules. I believe he needs to answer questions in English. A citizen with a farm can vote." Mrs. Cook tapped the black book. "Tell me about your English conversations since your last lesson."

Louisa set the slim schoolbook aside and opened the larger volume to the list of contents. "Polly Black, the seamstress, came to the bakery. We talked about the weather." Halting the main topic of yesterday's conversation on the back of her tongue, she glanced toward the ceiling. *I mix a few English words into the* Deutsch *with the American lady.* Yes, she repeated a few new English words during a discussion of Mr. Black's recovery and his plans to return to St. Louis. However, Polly used liberal amounts of *Deutsch* and gestures. "My errands are to the German shops."

"All of them?"

"*Nein*...no...I'm sorry. My tongue did not wait for my brain." Louisa found the proper page and studied the document's heading. "Two days ago, I came to your store to buy a new scrubbing brush. Mr. Cook speaks very fast. He complained about the high price of something—but I did not understand all of the words."

"My Henry." Mrs. Cook smiled. "When the price on a keg of nails increases by even two pennies, he complains for a week."

"Mr. Cook was patient when I counted my money." Louisa stood and walked toward the window. "Mr. Cook is a good man. You speak like a happy wife." She hesitated. *Is the question too personal?* "Did your family arrange the marriage?"

Eliza stood, pursed her lips, and blinked twice.

I have overstepped. "Pardon," Louisa scrambled for an English apology.

"I agree Mr. Cook is a good man. Yes, I am a happy wife." Eliza sighed. "As to the other—our families did not arrange the marriage."

"Is such common in America? No? In Westphalia, parents often arrange." She turned to face her tutor but glanced toward the floor when warmth climbed her neck.

Mrs. Cook cleared her throat. "I do not know how to explain—more than one way to select a husband—or wife. I have seen both happy and miserable marriages when the family approved. I witness the same among couples who ignored advice from others. Why do you ask? Is the young stable hand talking of marriage?"

Drawing a deep breath, Louisa directed her gaze out the window. *Blush is the curse of the fair-skinned.* "*Nein*—no. Hans is a friend. I teach him to dance." She clasped her hands and searched for English words. "Long ago, when I was in the schoolroom, Papa and his good friend, *Herr* Wulff, the cooper on the same street, agreed I should marry Hermann. He was a kind boy. I think we would have made a happy home. But the army took him…last summer…in August…he died."

"In battle?"

Louisa shook her head. "Measles." In a flash, all the events since the day the fateful letter arrived crossed her mind. *Not yet a year and my whole life is changed.* "His brother, the new physician, hints he wants to court me. He makes friends with Cousin Fredrick."

"Do you like him?"

"I am…confused. Otto does not have a calm nature like his younger brother. He not…open. Doctor Wulff's smile…I do not know if it comes from the heart. He is…sly." *Yesterday,* Frau *Hebing called him arrogant.* Louisa sighed. The butcher's wife voiced many opinions and most contained a large portion of truth. She drew a deep breath and stilled by the window. "Do you smell it? Smoke—heavy—not a chimney."

An instant later, a boy ran into sight. "Fire—fire—ring the bells."

One church bell rang. In less than a minute, a second signal sounded.

"Quick—follow me." Mrs. Cook abandoned the open book, stepped toward the door, and snatched a tin bucket.

Louisa followed. Pausing to grab two buckets sitting near the pump, she ran into the middle of the street beside Mrs. Cook.

By ones and twos, other residents exited homes and businesses to join them.

"The dressmaker's," a man shouted.

"Save the shop beside it." An older man stopped at the cooper's cistern and began to pump.

Louisa added her empty buckets to the growing

number beside the pump and lifted a full container. Handing the pail to Mrs. Cook, she realized an entire group of men and women passed precious water to wet the side of the building. She raised her gaze and saw a few brave men at the dress shop pump, scant yards from the smoking structure. *I pray all the people escape.* She blinked and passed another bucket of water.

Mr. Cook brought a ladder. Immediately, the men leaned it against the cooper's shop next to the burning building. In less than a minute, the first man scrambled up and started to wet the roof.

Louisa's world slowed. She lifted a heavy bucket of water and passed it to the person beside her. She turned right and repeated the motion, as her stomach grew hard as stone. Children dashed along the line, returning empty buckets to the men at the pump.

Where is Polly? Joseph? Is that Mrs. Clark?

"Faster," a man urged.

"More water." A woman's voice was lost below a horse's neigh.

"Wet those shavings," a man shouted.

Louisa overlooked the ache in her arms and lifted another full bucket. In the noise and smoke, she ignored the tears forming and seeping across her cheeks. She glanced at a small group of people gathered near the street. *Where are my friends?*

****

Hans led the two mares, Sal and Ginger, away from the farrier. The steady rhythm of eight new shoes on the packed earth street allowed his mind to wander. The first of the three drivers would be returning by the time he reached the livery. *If the work goes well, I will stop at the bakery and visit Louisa before I take supper at the tavern.*

Smiling, he lingered on a memory of two evenings ago, when he encountered her kneeling beside a garden bed. *Frau Keil invited us for tea in her apartment. Seldom have I felt so nervous.*

The widow had poured the steaming beverage into dainty china cups and served pound cake sliced thin as the tapered end of a shingle.

He held his cup with care and managed not to clink it against the saucer. While sharing the settee, he kept a hand width of upholstery visible between him and Louisa. *Many rules to remember to keep good favor with ladies. "Ja,"* Hans mused to the horses. *"Frau* Keil good lady—protects Louisa's reputation."

One of the mares snorted.

One church bell clanged, and in the next heartbeat, a second joined.

The other horse stopped, raised her head, and attempted to pull away.

"Whoa. Easy, my lovelies." Hans tightened his grip, stepped to the center of the street, and looked for anything which might have spooked the well-trained horses. *Was that?* He smelled smoke, not the usual scent from chimneys, or burning coal from the foundry, but a heavy, angry odor. An instant later, he spotted the gray mass escaping from a window on the corner. In swift motions, he secured the mares to the nearest rail. "Please, no people injured today." He sprinted toward the fire. Nearing the building, he became vaguely aware of others running in the same direction. He focused on dark smoke seeping from a window.

Hans arrived at the door the same instant as

another, taller man. Reaching out, he made one attempt to turn the knob. *Locked?* Backing a step, he raised one leg and kicked above the lock. The frame splintered under his wooden shoe.

"Is anyone there?" the taller man called out in *Deutsch*.

Glancing over his shoulder, Hans recognized the other man. He spared Otto a brief nod and advanced two steps. *I know this place.* Bolts of cloth on shelves and a dress form wearing a hat confirmed he stood in Mrs. Clark's dress shop. He coughed once, then yelled in English, "Hello. Answer us."

"Here." A muffled voice followed the word with a cough.

Otto hurried toward the source of the cry and squatted behind the counter. "I help."

"My boy." The woman coughed and struggled to her knees. Pointing toward the ceiling, she sputtered. "My boy." Facing the floor, she lost additional words in more coughing.

"I find boy." Hans heard his voice before his mind organized words. *Polly.* Frau *Keil's friend.* He sorted names for the red-haired boy. *Jack? Jacob?* Pulling a handkerchief from his pocket, he tied the cloth across his mouth. "Go." He tapped Otto on the arm. Stepping toward the drape, he pointed toward the door. "Take her. I look for her son."

The smoke thickened the instant Hans stepped past the heavy curtain. He swept his right arm in front of him, moved forward in cautious steps, and searched for access to the sleeping loft. After precious time, he felt his shin bump against a narrow, steep stairway. Feeling his way through smoke and tears, he climbed. "Boy—

call to me."

Crawling forward, Hans shook with fright. *The fire grows fiercer by the moment.* "Boy." He coughed and called again, "Joseph."

"I can't see." Child-sized coughs followed the weak words.

Hans crept toward the sound. A moment later, he discovered the boy hiding under a blanket. "I friend." He tugged the child against him. "Get on my back—hold tight." He paused for a coughing fit to pass and then laced the boy's arms around his neck. Turning, he lowered his head and searched for the stairs. "*Gott und Himmel.* God and heaven."

Flames licked the wall, blocking the stairway. *Thud.* A rafter near the chimney collapsed. Sparks danced against the roofing boards.

Hans swallowed smoke and fear. Another coughing fit seized him. Backing and turning, he spied a modest, rectangular window set less than a foot above the floor.

"I scared." The child sobbed next to Hans's ear.

"Wait. *Ein Minute.*" Hans pulled the boy off his back and pushed him against the outside wall. Standing, he kicked at the window.

Fresh air rushed in and fed the flames behind them. The floor grew warm to the touch.

Hans knelt. Reaching for the boy, he pulled him to his chest. "Come. We jump."

The child whimpered, wrapped his legs around Hans's waist, and clung to his neck.

Ignoring the intense heat on his back, Hans drew a breath of the best air available, pushed to his feet, and turned his back to the window. *Bitte Gott. Please God. Save the child.* He stuck his legs out the opening first.

Soon he eased the boy's small body over the sill and clung by his hands. "Hold tight. *Ein. Zwei.*"

Hans set the tips of his wooden shoes against the building. Pushing with every ounce of strength in his legs, he released his hands.

"Ahhh," Joseph screamed.

Loosening the boy's hands, Hans twisted. *How far to the ground? Will I crush the boy?*

Thump.

Hans lost every ounce of air in his body and rolled to his stomach. *Was the boy safe?* He heard his blood pound in his ears. Opening his mouth to breathe, he met a splash of water.

"Enough." A voice seemed to come from a great distance.

"Take the child."

"Move him—away from the building," a deeper, louder voice commanded.

Hans opened his mouth again, but before a sound emerged, the world shifted black and silent.

****

Louisa grabbed the handle of a full water bucket, turned left, and passed it to the next person in line. Shaking her head, she ignored the pain in both arms. She struggled for each breath. Raising her gaze, she thought she glimpsed Polly beside a shorter, stouter lady. *Mrs. Clark?* She moved another bucket from right to left.

"Look out, now," an American man shouted.

Thud. Hiss. A roof timber crashed. A brief fountain of sparks rose from the shop's damaged roof.

Louisa gasped. An instant later, she found air, wiped her brow with her arm, and resumed work.

243

"Mind the cooperage," a man shouted.

"Wet the shingles."

Louisa stopped trying to sort the voices from each other.

"More wa—my God."

Louisa raised her gaze to the upper window of the burning shop. A man, with a child clinging to his chest, hung from the sill for an instant. Then they were falling—separating—thudding into the dirt. *Joseph?* She feared her stalled heart would never start.

Instantly, a group of men surrounded the pair and blocked her view.

"More water. Don't slack off." The person beside her thrust another heavy, full bucket into her hands.

"*Ja. Ja.* We keep the line moving," she muttered and nodded. The important thing at the moment, since the dress shop looked beyond hope, was to save the neighboring building to prevent a larger disaster. She glimpsed Polly dashing across the yard with her arms outstretched. *Gute. Gute.* The reunion scene gave her new energy to pass the next bucket.

The next time she glanced toward the fire, she witnessed four men lift the fallen man and carry him out of the danger zone.

A half-grown boy dashed forward and retrieved a flat, brown cap and a pair of wooden shoes from the landing spot.

Louisa looked at the items the boy carried and then sent her gaze to the man the others lowered to the ground. *Why do they rest him on his chest? Flat cap. Wooden shoes. Brown hair.* "Hans?" She thrust the pail in her hand to the next person and darted out of the bucket brigade. Ignoring the shouts of the other workers, she sprinted toward the wounded man and sank to her knees beside him. She pushed back dark, wet hair and gasped. *"Bitte. Gott. Bitte."*

"Can you follow orders, Louisa?" Otto called from the other side of Hans.

"Ja." She added a nod, circled her fingers at Hans's wrist, and searched for his heartbeat's echo. As the soft, rapid vibration caressed her fingertips, she sighed. "He's alive."

Otto reached into one of his many coat pockets and pulled out scissors. "He will wake soon enough with the pain." He stared across the burned remains of Hans's shirt. "Fetch water and a rag. Keep the cloth moist while I work."

Louisa dashed to the pump and pulled a half-full bucket from a startled man's hands. "For the injured."

Following the physician's orders, she used her handkerchief like a sponge. Dip, dab, squeeze—she moistened the cloth ahead of Otto's fingers and scissors.

The physician lifted and cut the border of scorched and undamaged linen shirt.

She prayed in silence while her hands worked. Returning her gaze to Hans's pale profile, she dipped her rag into the bucket. *I forgive you all the times you step on my feet.*

Otto leaned close, the sharp scent of sooty cloth mingled with onions and beer on his breath. "Lower. Follow the burns."

Dipping her cloth again, she glanced at Hans's face. *Did an eyelid flutter?*

Otto snipped the last inch of cloth, and Hans's body shuddered.

Following instinct, Louisa reached to lift his head at the same time a series of deep coughs shook his body.

Hans expelled a glob of thick, black phlegm.

"Easy. Easy. You are safe now," she crooned.

Hans opened his eyes to slits and coughed again. "The...boy?"

"Joseph is safe." Louisa lifted her gaze for a moment and found her friends huddled at the edge of the street. "The boy is getting comfort in his mother's arms. Rest now."

Otto grunted. "Now comes the most painful part. It would be better if he still was unconscious." The physician lifted a small, burned portion of the shirt from the skin. "Louisa, you must keep it moist where I point."

She nodded and dipped her cloth. Pressing her lips, she watched Otto tug the linen and clip a mixture of skin and fabric.

"Ackkkkkkk." Hans screamed until the sound turned into coughing.

"*Ja*—hurts like the devil is dancing on your back." Otto pointed where he wanted her to dab water.

Louisa blinked away tears. *Please, don't die. I pray the pain will fade.* With shaking hands, she continued to moisten charred fabric as Otto lifted and snipped. "We be quick."

Hans convulsed with another coughing fit. With a mixture of cough and cry, he expelled more blackened mucus from his lungs.

"*Gute?*" She gestured toward the growing dark mass near Hans's mouth.

Without pausing in the procedure, Otto nodded.

"Smoke in the lungs—turns to sludge. He needs to cough it out before he will breathe normal."

Louisa pondered the physician's statement. *Is Hans similar to a chimney in need of cleaning?* She shook her head and returned her focus to bits of cloth clinging to fresh wounds. *Are those?*

A crash and shouts pulled her attention toward the building. Several men had pushed a portion of the shop wall and caused the structure to collapse inward. She saw three men still on the cooperage roof, wetting shingles. *Is the immediate danger past?*

"Louisa."

She tipped her head toward *Frau* Keil's familiar voice. Moistening her lips, she hunted for proper words. "I stay—tend Hans."

Charlotte pointed toward the knot of people in the street. "I am taking Polly and Joseph to the bakery. Do you have need of anything?"

"Ointment. Soft lard." Otto snapped the request.

"Bandages." Louisa touched Hans's hand to bring attention to the cuts and splinters.

"*Ja*—I bring all you ask plus good lye soap." Charlotte rubbed her hands against her apron.

Louisa smiled. Like many *Deutsch* women, *Frau* Keil used strong lye soap to clean every inch of the bakery, to scrub the laundry, and bathe her skin.

"*Ja. Gute.*" Otto positioned his scissors for another snip.

"Water," Hans whispered the single word before another coughing fit overtook him.

Otto shook his head. "*Nein...*wet his lips...none to drink."

Moistening his mouth before wiping his face,

Louisa leaned near Hans's ear. "You did a brave thing." She searched for better words. *How does a person put overwhelming joy and thankfulness into words? Hans saved Joseph.* "I praise God you live."

"*Ende.*" Otto leaned back on his heels and tucked the scissors into a pocket.

Louisa studied the exposed wounds on Hans's back. The fresh injuries glistened red and angry. Threaded among the new burns, injuries weeping a mixture of clear liquid and blood, she noticed crooked ridges—scars. She flicked her gaze to Otto, raised her brows, and pointed.

"Whip."

She caught the soft word by watching his lips. In an instant, she lowered her gaze to the wounds and blinked away a fresh batch of tears. *Father was harsh.* The simple phrase from Hans's lips returned. *Cruel. No better than the men driving slaves across the street in New Orleans.* She reached over and skimmed her thumb across Hans's cheek. *Rest. Heal.* Aware of a fullness in her chest, she feared the pity, respect, and an unnamed, new-to-her emotion would burst her heart.

Chapter Twenty-Two

The next morning, men prepared for the afternoon Fourth of July festivities by moving kegs and boards to make benches in the town square. Warm sunlight favored their work and entered the second-story window at Mrs. Winter's boardinghouse.

Images of summer insects droning in tall grass filled Hans's brain. He floated above the meadow and inhaled a hint of sweet fruit on a gentle breeze. Resting his cheek against a hammock, he trailed his fingers along the ground. *Ach.*

Pain sped from knuckles to shoulder.

Opening his eyes to slits, he steadied his gaze. One by one, he brought simple, familiar objects into focus. A square mirror hung over a washstand with a plain bowl and chipped pitcher. His unpolished leather shoes rested beside a wooden chair. *My room. Mrs. Winter's boardinghouse.*

Distant voices and a banging door roused him to the next level of wakefulness.

Sunlight. Mein Gott. I'm late. He held his breath while panic tightened his chest. He pushed his hand against the bare floor and bit back a cry. Pressing his lips with determination, he twisted his hips to roll to his side.

Pain, hot as fire, engulfed him.

Squeezing closed his eyes, he opened his mouth,

halted a scream, and panted. An image of his father raising the riding crop sent a tremble through his body. *I will not make noise and give satisfaction to the drunkard. Wait.* Opening his eyes, he looked again at the simple room. *I am in Elm Ridge. What hurt me?*

"*Gute.* The patient is awake."

Hans startled at the sounds of a firm footstep and male voice. "Who?" He licked his lips with a dry tongue. "Do I know you?"

"*Herr* Doctor Otto Wulff. Did yesterday's fire destroy your brain, in addition to the skin on your back?"

Hans watched the taller man set a low-crowned, black hat on the washstand. *Fire. Back.* A dress shop, a boy, and a smashed window returned to his mind as clouded images. *What do they mean? Where is the pattern? Yesterday? Burns on his back? The wounds hurt worse than...* Holding his breath, he shivered until the memory of the final beating vanished. "Tell me day and time."

Otto poured a small amount of water into a glass and stood inches beyond reach.

Finding a reserve of strength and pride in the presence of the physician, Hans levered into an awkward pose on the edge of the bed. *Never so painful to move.* "I remember you now—from same village as Louisa."

With a nod easily understood as approval, Otto pressed the drink into Hans's bandaged hand. "Today is Friday, almost noon. Sip"—he pointed to the water. "The laudanum I gave you last evening tends to leave a bitter taste."

A moment after one swallow, Hans coughed. Pain

attacked every muscle on his back. He dropped his head and studied the floor. *Please, God, or Satan, stop the pain. Never have I felt such agony.*

"Easy. Easy, my friend. I came to check your bandages."

"Work—the stables—I will lose my job." Hans straightened enough to attempt another sip of water.

"Nein. Today you rest—and tomorrow. I will speak with *Herr* Bergmann."

One touch from Otto on the shoulder and Hans slumped back in the bed. Bit by bit, thanks to the verbal prompts, the events of Thursday afternoon began to slide into a picture. "The mares—I tied them. In front of...by...I cannot remember." He exhaled frustration. The horses were important to the stables, the only animals trained for the gig and riding. "If they are lost—"

"I will make inquiries. At the moment, I need to look at your back." Otto pulled a pair of scissors from a coat pocket.

Hans tensed. *Burns? Bandages?* He steadied his breathing. "Private. You not tell what you see."

"The scars?"

Hans nodded.

Otto loosened a portion of the bandages. "Old wounds are not my business," he spoke low as he worked. "However, best I tell you now, your friend, Louisa, assisted in tending your burns. She is a good nurse."

"Ja." Hans closed his eyes for a moment. An image, Louisa wrapping his sprained foot on *The Perch,* returned to his mind. He did not want her to know of the scars. She deserved a friend who was honest and

whole—the sort of man he tried to be since taking his new name.

The examination felt like it lasted for hours. Hans drifted away from the pain twice and only returned to his senses after Otto asked him a sharp question.

"You are fortunate." Otto opened a jar of ointment.

"I do not understand." He opened his mouth to explain his back felt like a blacksmith found the place a convenient anvil.

The loud noon foundry whistle interrupted the intermittent conversation.

"The burns are not deep. With care, clean bandages, and a little luck, infection will stay away. You will be sore and stiff. However, in a few days, you will notice improvement and healing." Otto gave his professional opinion without a hint of emotion.

Hans envisioned the coins secreted in his coat pockets and his leather shoes. "I need to work."

"Again, I tell you. I will have a word with *Herr* Bergmann." The physician tied off the bandage.

"The boy…?" Hans blinked away tears when Otto assisted him to sit on the edge of the bed. "Images from the fire are like book pages out of order, but many include a young boy. Why?"

"Joseph Black." Otto pulled the plain wood chair close and sat within reach. "The boy's mother lives and works at the dress shop. He napped in the sleeping loft, and you were injured while saving him. You did a brave thing."

"Will I remember?"

"*Ja.* Memories improve after you eat and sleep. Today you must rest. I will have a word with your landlady. She is making a restoring broth, and you must drink two bowls of it before I return this evening."

"I am not helpless." Hans pushed against the thin mattress, paused with his buttocks an inch above the cushion, and willed his legs to make him stand.

The room spun.

Sinking back to the mattress, he gripped the flimsy pad and kept his scream silent. *Less than a full day in bed and my knees refuse to hold me.*

"Rest"—Otto leaned forward. Pushing to his feet, the physician returned the chair to its place and lifted his hat. "You have a choice. If I give you another dose of laudanum, the pain is less, but the dreams worse. Or, you can deal with the distress. I expect you have experienced suffering in the past. Which will it be?"

Hans shook his head. "No more medicine. I will manage."

"Until evening, then." With a nod, Otto walked to the door and left the room.

Hans sat on the bed and stared at his hands. Narrow strips of cloth bound each hand and wrist while leaving his thumbs free. *Louisa's work.* From the doctor's comments, he knew she had tended his burns and observed his scars. Would she scorn him for his past? What sort of boy, or man, allowed himself to be whipped like a criminal?

****

"One little pig...two little pigs...three little pigs." Louisa sang the counting song in English. Giving the batter for honey and walnut bars a final stir, she continued to the number five. With a glance to the clock, she pressed her lips. *With luck, all will be ready before the speeches begin at one o'clock.* A moment later, she pulled two square baking pans close and shifted her gaze to Joseph. "Why do we count with pigs?"

The boy, perched on a stool beside the washstand, shrugged his slim shoulders and opened his hands. "Mama sings the pig song when she counts my fingers and toes after a bath."

"Why pigs? Horses are a fine animal—smart—strong. Chickens would be good to count—or their eggs." She poured batter into greased pans and started to sing. "One little chick...two lively ducks...three fine cows in the barn."

Joseph stared with wide eyes. "Why do you change the words? Mama says, when I go to school I need to follow all the rules."

"This is a bakery—not a schoolroom. We can make our own rules." She coaxed the final drops of batter into a pan. The English words came easily talking to Joseph. The counting song was better than practicing with steps, or dishes, or even cinnamon buns. *Make our own rules.* The phrase returned, morphed into *Deutsch*, and back to English. *America's secret—citizens making their own laws instead of following edicts from a duke, prince, or king?*

"Do you always sing while you bake?" Joseph got off the stool and gripped the edge of the large, sturdy worktable.

Louisa nodded. *"Ja.* I like music. Does your mama sing while she sews?"

"Mama tells me stories. My favorites are brave men riding horses...and killing dragons and...other savage beasts. I want to be brave—like the men at the fire yesterday." He opened his eyes wide. "May I lick the spoon?"

"First, you step away from the oven. The door is hot." She pointed to where he should wait. In the next instant, she opened the cast-iron door and set the pans inside. Turning to the worktable, she handed him the wooden spoon coated with batter.

"*Danke.* Thank you."

"English, please." She made a mental note to ask Polly if she wanted her son to learn the *Deutsch* phrases he heard in the bakery.

"Is he pestering you?" Polly closed the back door, pulled off a calico sunbonnet, and stepped into the tidy workroom.

"We are singing. Speaking English—mostly." Louisa lowered her gaze as warmth enveloped her neck. *A sentence from my lips contains more* Deutsch *than English words.*

"It smells delightful in here—yeast, honey, and comfort. The scent makes my mouth water, even when my stomach is full," Polly spoke in slow, even English.

"We are in a bakery. The air is filled with good, hearty smells of home." Louisa carried the mixing bowl and other utensils to the pan of soapy water. "Today we close for holiday at the second foundry whistle. Treats in the oven are *Herr* Keil's special recipe. We take to celebration in the square and listen to speeches in English."

"Perhaps I stand near and offer snatches of explanation in my limited *Deutsch*?"

"Mama." Joseph stopped licking the spoon and laid it on the table. "Why is Uncle Leo in the bakery?"

Louisa turned toward the sales area and glimpsed Mr. Black, with his crutch, thumping toward the counter.

"Where are they?" Leo's harsh voice overflowed the modest rooms.

"*Bitte.* No need to shout." *Frau* Keil finished making change for a regular customer.

Polly hurried out of the workroom. "Good afternoon, dear brother. Have you walked the entire way from your boardinghouse? Should I fetch a chair so you can rest a bit?"

"Gather Joseph and your things. You're coming with me." He looked directly at his sister.

"We are staying in the bakery apartment at *Frau* Keil's invitation. We have no things." Polly's voice dropped to near a whisper on the final phrase.

Louisa listened to the brother and sister argue while she washed dishes. *No things.* Polly and her son currently had fewer possessions than the small sack Hans carried the day he stepped onto the Elm Ridge levee.

Soon after sunrise, Polly and Mrs. Clark had visited the fire scene. Some pottery and metal items survived the flames, but the modest building's wood furnishings and cloth dress goods were either burned or ruined.

"You belong with me." Mr. Black emphasized the last word with another thump.

Clearing her throat, Polly replied, "Joseph and I belong to ourselves. We will not move in with you."

"Why not? I live in a respectable boardinghouse." He rested one shoulder against the wall.

"Yes, and you make unnecessary demands of your landlady. We will stay here, with our friends."

"You are making a mistake, little sister. Not the first time you've gotten yourself in a mess by associating with filthy immigrants." Stabbing the air near Polly's face with one finger, he nearly dropped his crutch.

"Do not make your problems mine, Leo. Bernard and I had plans—good plans. You"— she perched both hands on her hips and leaned toward his face— "returned from six months in the West and disrupted everything. You are the one who locked me in my room and forbade even Madam Robineau, the landlady, from allowing me downstairs. For an entire week, long after Bernard departed St. Louis, you confined me like an exotic animal."

Waving her hands for Charlotte's attention, Louisa pointed toward the oven and then the clock. "Done at quarter past."

Frau Keil nodded.

"Come, Joseph." Louisa set the final clean dish on the worktable and offered her hand. "We will go to the pump and get another bucket of water."

"Will you teach me to count in your language?" Joseph moved a finger from one clean spoon on the table to another.

"I will ask your mama—later." She snatched the faded sunbonnet off the peg and reached for the wooden bucket. *Mr. Black is wrong to tally Polly's sins in front of Joseph.* She did not need to understand all of the English words to know it was wrong to discuss such a topic in front of *Frau* Keil and within hearing of bakery customers.

A few moments later, Joseph grasped the pump handle. "I help."

"You need to grow taller and stronger before you can fill the bucket by yourself." Louisa moved his

257

hands closer to the handle's middle and gripped the end. "Shall we count?"

"*Fraulein* Mueller." *Frau* Hebing stepped out of the butcher's building and waved a paper. "We have good news today—a letter from Werner."

Werner. She smiled at the thought of the tall, scholarly young man. Often, when his mother came into the bakery, she would mutter worried words. "Is he well? Has he found work?"

"*Ja. Ja.* I read to you." *Frau* Hebing smoothed the paper against her ample bosom.

"*Dearest Family. Forgive my leaving without a proper farewell. I am well and living in Memphis—in Tennessee. I am a tutor for three children of a wealthy businessman. The city is busy with immigrants from all parts of Europe. Many Negros, slave and free, live among us. Soon I will apply to the fine school in this city and continue my education. I miss all of you, but I dare not return to Elm Ridge. I was blinded by Mr. Black's money. The plan sounded like a simple thing— scare* Herr *Keil to pay money to the miller. Surprise and sadness overtook me by the result of one push into the street.* Herr *Keil's death was not my intention. Please forgive me. I pray God to give me courage to live better. Your son, Werner.*"

Louisa exhaled relief. With her next breath, she drew in happiness from the letter and the sunshine. "*Gute. Gute.* Will you share the letter with *Frau* Keil?"

The butcher's wife nodded. "I go now to invite her. I will make a pot of tea to share and let her read the letter."

"Best to wait another minute—Mr. Black arrived to argue with Polly." Louisa glanced toward the door.

"We attend holiday celebration today."

"*Ja—gute*—you will meet many new people. This year I do not have heart to attend." *Frau* Hebing shifted her attention to Joseph. "Ah—new bakery boy? Is your mother the young seamstress?"

Joseph looked at his bare feet for a long moment.

"My new friend does not speak *Deutsch*," Louisa replied. She mixed enough English words with *Deutsch* to manage an introduction.

Late in the afternoon, Louisa greeted Mrs. Winter. "I come to visit *Herr* Hoffmann. How is he feeling today?"

"He is in a sour mood." The diminutive American widow led her into the large kitchen and lifted a thick, white bowl from a shelf. "The *Deutsch* doctor visited him this morning and forbade him to leave the house. Not that he could walk to his room's threshold at the moment."

"I brought him a few fresh bakery treats." Louisa indicated the basket hooked over her arm. "The butcher added a chunk of good, hard sausage to give him strength."

"I add another portion of warm, hearty broth to the tray—only take a minute. Visit him. You know the room?"

"*Ja.* Yes." She switched to English. "I was with the others yesterday." A few moments later, she paused at the open door to Hans's room.

He lay facedown, sprawled on the narrow bed. A trace of wound seepage showed on his bandages.

Moving her gaze, she studied him in sleep.

Dark-brown hair pointed in every direction above a smooth brow. Uneven stubble darkened his cheek, and his lips were parted a fraction of an inch.

Handsome. Brave. My friend will recover. In a few weeks, he will hold me in the dance, and I will feel much joy. She became aware of her heart speeding and doing a little bounce within her chest. *Manners and kindness. I think he requires a large portion of each.* Lifting her fist, she knocked on the door frame. "Hans. Wake up. I brought food to accompany Mrs. Winter's fine broth."

****

Sunday morning, Hans gripped the smooth wood of the pew in front of him and held his breath until a pain passed. Listening to the pastor pronounce the longest of the final blessings, he moved his lips in silence. *I will not cry out.*

"Amen," the congregation responded.

Sinking to the bench, Hans unbuttoned his snug coat. Relief flooded his body. Careful not to allow his back to touch the rigid pew, he nodded to several acquaintances filing past.

Otto paused and stepped closer. "I did not expect to see you here."

"I cannot stay in my room forever. Tomorrow I must work." He refused to admit the struggle or pain involved in pulling his shirt over his head. *When a boy, I hid after each whipping.* He swallowed and blinked away the past. *I am a man—an honest man. I earn my way in America.*

"Remember—clean, loose shirt. Burns need air to heal."

"*Ja,* I remember. Easy to say. Difficult to do." Hans thought of the two shirts he owned. One, which he wore today, was a generous gift from *Frau* Keil. The garment, made of fine cloth, hung large on him—ideal according to the physician. Yesterday, he forced himself to walk to the laundress and redeemed his second shirt. Worn and dingy, the garment bound across his shoulders without room to let out the seams. *Perhaps* Frau *Keil will sell me another of the late baker's shirts.*

"I'll see you tomorrow—late." Otto leaned forward and paused.

Hans, attentive, anticipated another word of advice or caution.

Retreating in silence, Otto turned and nodded to a farmer.

After a few moments and several worshipers passed, Hans pushed to his feet and joined the thinning line. Reaching into his pocket, he fingered his coins. He didn't have much money left after paying Mrs. Winter a week's rent from four days' wages. With a sigh, he extracted two small coins from the depths and dropped them into the offering box.

Stepping into weak, midday sun, Hans tugged on his cap and scanned the crowd for Louisa. The moment he spied her straw bonnet, he smiled and descended the church steps. "*Guten Tag, Frau und Fraulein,*" Hans addressed the butcher's wife and Louisa.

"You have more color in your cheeks today." Louisa smiled and eased toward Fredrick's team and wagon.

"I give credit to the good cinnamon buns a charming young lady delivered to my boardinghouse."

"They were a trifle." She lowered her gaze toward the tips of her black half-boots peeking from the hem of her gown.

"Perhaps to you." Guilt of past sins pressed on him. He could never repay the kindness shown by his friends in the past two days. Pausing in front of Star, Fredrick's mare, and the gelding hitched with her, he struggled to keep emotion out of his voice. Tentatively, testing his shoulder's movement, Hans reached to pat the mare's cheek. "I treasured your visit and feel shamed you were witness to my weakness."

Louisa turned to face him. "Will you rest today?"

"*Ja.* Today I have no energy for dancing." He tipped his gaze toward the overcast sky. "The weather makes a poor day to visit the beer garden."

"Fredrick's neighbor is coming for dinner. He is a widower with three children."

Hans studied her face. *What emotion is in her eyes? Does she give the hint of a smile to me or thoughts of this eligible father?*

"*Nein.*" She shook her head and set the cloth flowers on her bonnet into a gentle dance. "My cousin is not playing matchmaker with this man. Anna calls the invitation a Christian duty and charity. His youngest is a good playmate for little Karl."

"I wish you a pleasant day." Hans mixed relief and sincerity into the words.

Star explored his chest with her nose, searching for a tasty treat in his pockets.

He leaned back. At the pain of the action, he sucked in his breath.

"You have spoiled her." Louisa presented her flat hand to the horse.

Hans glanced in all directions to assure they could have a private word. "I mean to ask you. I do not remember how I got home after the fire. Did I walk?"

She laughed and shook her head. "*Herr* Wulff gave you a dose of laudanum before the men lifted you into a cart. You were babbling nonsense all the time. Two strong men guided, half-carried, you to your room. Only after you lay on your bed, did the doctor allow me to put bandages over the ointment."

He swallowed. "How many? My back...the scars?"

"The men who helped you to your bed had little interest in old injuries. They did not linger, examining your burns."

"*Gute.*" He closed his eyes. Warmth, a blush of shame, crept up his neck, and he held his silence. *Will she walk out of my life the moment my burns heal? A fine young lady has no reason to continue friendship with me. I bear too many deep wounds, in body and soul, to imagine ever holding her in a dance again.* Glancing toward her face, he realized she was interested in something behind him. Turning, he saw Otto in earnest conversation with Fredrick.

"Hans—look at me."

He kept his sigh small and faced her. Educated Otto, a familiar figure in her life since childhood, suited the intelligent Louisa. He struggled to earn a living and read the songbook. *Should I leave Elm Ridge?* He ignored the ache in his back and straightened. No, he would stay. The stablemaster treated him well. The town was a good place to grow roots.

"I want—" She stepped forward until their shoes almost touched. "Hold me like we are finishing the waltz."

He blinked. *Hold her? Waltz?* Even if she hummed the tune, he did not have energy to dance. *Was a dance, or embrace, proper to consider on the street in front of the church?* Staring, he closed his lips.

She lifted his bandaged left fingers with her right hand and set her other hand on his right shoulder. In the same instant, she rose on her toes and brushed her lips across his mouth.

Wait. More. Aware his lips quivered with desire and a blush sped to the top of his ears, he was unable to move. *One touch of her lips and my fingers and toes tingle—begging for more.*

Quick as she'd kissed him, she pulled her head back and lifted her hands. Pressing her cheeks, she formed a perfect circle with her mouth for an instant before turning.

"Louisa," he spoke to her trim, straight back.

Giving him a glance over her shoulder, she smiled. "I go and ask Fredrick to give you a ride to your boardinghouse."

Chapter Twenty-Three

A full week later, at the hour the sky hinted at Monday's sunrise, Louisa hugged little Karl quick and tight.

The boy, a bundle of energy, squirmed to be let down.

"Off you go." She set his feet on the floor. "Now be a good boy for Mama and Papa."

"I hope you understand my position." Fredrick lifted his work cap from the peg beside the farmhouse's kitchen door.

She nodded. "I understand you have no reason to deny Otto permission to court me." A little shiver raced up her spine at the memory of the final waltz at the beer garden yesterday.

After Hans had left their picnic early, Otto claimed more than a fair share of the dances. She found it difficult to deny dancing with a person with such a good sense of rhythm. She moved without fear her feet would be trampled—unlike with erratic Hans or the enthusiastic Hebing brothers.

Dancing I can accept. She lifted her shawl from a peg. *He had no need to kiss me.* His press of lips against her mouth in a public setting startled her heart into missing two beats. *'Twas a cold kiss—unlike Hermann's so long ago. Or the bold peck I gave Hans last week.* Often, in the hours since the waltz—and kiss—she tried to imagine life with the physician. Each time she looked him in the face, she saw a hint of the trickster. Memories of the pranks he played on the younger children at school refused to fade. She could not imagine sitting in his company on a winter's evening and enjoying laughter or quiet conversation.

"He asked for more."

Fredrick's voice jolted Louisa to the present. "I am grateful you refused his request for marriage."

"You speak very plain on the topic since your arrival in Elm Ridge." Fredrick stepped into his wooden shoes. "The more I think on it, the less eager I am to hurry your marriage. I hold you in high regard and will not force you to live with a man you do not desire."

Louisa settled the light shawl across her shoulders and tied a tidy knot. A moment later, she pulled on her leather half boots. "*Danke.* Marriage...if it is meant for me...will come in its own time. This summer, I have much to learn in the bakery. My head is full with all the fine points of the craft. Polly and Mrs. Cook help me learn English—an important promise to Papa during his final day. Many things in America...the number of wild storms...how fast the laundry dries...the sense of urgency in daily tasks...are different than life in our Westphalian village."

Fredrick nodded. Crossing the porch, he stepped to packed dirt. "Are you sure you want to walk? I could harness the team. Anna would drive you into town."

"*Ja.* Three miles is a good, healthy walk. *Frau* Keil does not expect me at the bakery until seven o'clock this morning." She stepped from the porch and looked toward the east. A light gray sky hinted at a fine day. *I will use my hour walk to organize my thoughts on recent events.*

With a final nod, Fredrick walked toward the cattle grazing near the barn.

"Louisa—don't forget to take the eggs to *Frau* Keil." Anna hurried across the porch with a shallow basket.

Karl clung to his mother's skirts, running on short legs to keep pace.

"*Danke.*" Louisa accepted the gift. Lifting the cloth from the treasure, she counted. "Ten—the bakery will make good use of these."

Anna gathered Karl into her arms. "We will walk with you to the main road. Tomorrow afternoon, we plan a trip into town. I will have enough butter after today's churning to trade for sugar."

"I will save you a loaf of wheat bread."

"Do not let Fredrick push you into marriage. My husband has a good heart, but he does not always understand what is important to another person."

Louisa smiled. "Each time we discuss the topic, I think he sees my determination to be a baker with clearer eyes."

"God go with you, Louisa." Anna stopped and perched Karl on the stump which marked the turn from the main road to their lane.

Releasing Anna from a quick hug, Louisa adjusted the basket on her arm and set off along the road. With each step, she turned over bits of last night's discussion and placed them beside events of her busy week. After conversation with her relatives, and good sleep at the farmhouse, much of the past was sorted, but she still had a few things to clarify. In the same way she would make a list of items to prepare in the bakery, Louisa focused on the people causing the most confusion in her mind.

Polly. You are my new American friend. I watch you go from one household task to another without a word from *Frau* Keil. All the while, you stay aware of Joseph. The bakery is more lively and cheerful with your presence. Thanks to you, I have become acquainted with Mrs. Clark, a fine American lady. Both of you are very talented with the needle, and I understand how the dress shop prospered. I am pleased you plan to rebuild.

Herr Wulff. Louisa sighed. The physician remained too secretive about his wife and life in Essen. His lack of a clear explanation of his decision to immigrate and follow her to Elm Ridge left her unsatisfied. *Too many secrets.* She smiled at the memory of his praise for her nursing skills. "I see tending the injured and ill with a mixture of necessity and dread. Too often, the ill did not recover. I miss you, Papa." She ceased her whisper and made a hasty sign of the cross. A moment later, she frowned at the unbidden memory of Otto's sudden kiss on the final note of a waltz.

Hans. Aware of a smile forming, she stepped with a lighter heart. Pressing tight her lips, she remembered the kiss she stole a little more than a week ago. Never would she have expected to be so bold. Or for her mouth to beg for a repeat. In his presence, she wanted to defy the rules and hold his hand. *Do you trust him?* Alfred's question from many weeks ago returned. Louisa caught sight of a shoe tip and moved her lips. *He returned Papa's shoes. He confessed to taking another man's name. I trust him to tell the story of his scars at the right time.*

Glancing to both sides of the road, Louisa spotted a landmark. Soon she would be at the halfway point. Then it was a quarter mile to reach the short lane for the Adams' farm. Comforted by the chirping songbirds, she hummed the chorus of a folk song. *I will be at the bakery before they unlock the door.* She turned her thoughts to the week's baking. Concentrating on planning the cakes, pies, and tarts for the coming days, she barely heard the gentle sound of a horse and rider approaching from behind.

"*Guten Morgan, Fraulein.*"

Louisa froze. *Otto?* Gathering her wits, she turned her head and realized Otto rode almost even with her. She swallowed the mixture of fear and surprise in her mouth and took another step toward town. "*Guten Morgan, Herr* Doctor Wulff."

"So formal. I thought you agreed to address me as *Herr* Otto? This is America. We are friends. Are we not?"

She walked forward and stayed silent. *I will not allow one stray mutter or mumble to escape my lips.*

"Your cousin, Fredrick, granted me permission to persuade you to be my wife. Did he not tell you?"

"*Ja*—we discussed. I understand he gave you boundaries." She listened to her heartbeat shift from soft to louder than a large drum. An instant later, she turned her gaze to the edge of the woods. *I see the elm and oak growing so close no light passes between— halfway to the bakery.*

"Did you spend the night at Fredrick's farm?"

"On Sunday, I often stay with my relatives." She sealed her lips. Since *Herr* Keil's death, she seldom spent both Saturday and Sunday nights at the farm. This

269

week, *Frau* Keil volunteered to make the bread sponges and do the early morning work. Polly, eager to be useful, agreed to help with the early sales. *Otto is moving to this side of the road.*

"Ride with me. The horse is strong and can carry both of us."

"*Nein*—I walk for health of mind and body. You go ahead." *Run, run, run.* She became aware of each breath coming quicker than the last. She forced each step to be steady and even. *A woman cannot outrun a horse.*

"I will not leave you alone on the road."

She swallowed a mouthful of panic and urged her feet to take larger steps. "What sort of business has you riding toward town this early?"

"Medical business."

"At a farm?" Without turning her head, she glimpsed the horse's nose.

The animal drifted closer.

"*Ja. Herr* Altmann's arm injury turned bad. Last night, I amputated the putrid limb. Due to the late hour, I stayed with my patient until first light."

Nodding, she recalled the Altmann family's tidy buildings half a mile beyond Fredrick. "Farming will be difficult with only one arm. I will add the family to my prayers and ask *Frau* Keil to do the same."

"I do not wish to talk more of my patients." He halted the horse.

I do not wish to speak with you at all. She clamped her jaw before the insult escaped. "You must be weary. Are you not eager to get to your lodgings after such a long night of work? Go ahead."

"Ride with me, Louisa."

She detected an unwelcome insistence mixed with his words. Hurrying her pace, she stepped ahead of the mount's nose and put firmness in her own voice. "Go—I know the road well."

An instant later, he dismounted and wrapped one hand around her upper arm. "You are mine." He stepped in front of her. "Mine—you will come with me."

"*Nein—nein—nein.*" Ignoring the eggs spilling from the basket, she jerked free and sprinted forward.

He caught her within a dozen steps and grasped both her arms. "You are mine."

Louisa sealed her lips. *He pushes his face with foul breath too close.* She moved her foot and attempted to stamp on his leather boot.

Whap.

As her head tipped to the side, she felt the sting of his leather-gloved hand on her cheek. She blinked and sighted his open hand raised to strike her again. *Mein Gott.* She struggled for breath through her surprise.

Appearing to change tactics, he tightened his grip on her arms and pushed her backward. Two steps later, he forced both of them off the road.

"*Nein. Nein.*" She twisted her body in an attempt to shake off his grip. *He's too strong.* She swallowed for courage and watched his lips shape into a twisted, evil grin. He forced her to walk backward deeper into the woods while keeping his hands tight on her upper arms.

Louisa stumbled on downed branches and tree roots. Looking from side to side while keeping her face directed at him, she searched for landmarks. Without planning to, she opened her mouth and released a scream into the quiet forest.

"Stop it." He pushed her back against a large tree.

"*Nein.*" She drew a breath and sought the road with her gaze. The horse was out of sight, but by the location of the new day's sun, she knew the direction.

Otto lifted her arms against her will until they were stretched above her head.

Twisting right, she encountered a root with her foot.

"Spirit. I like a woman with a little fight in her." He grasped both her wrists with one hand and lifted her chin with the other. "A kiss. We start with a kiss."

Louisa shook her head and tipped her face.

For one instant, he lost hold of her chin.

She viewed his waistcoat straining at the buttons.

He jerked her head, giving her no choice but to face him.

Closing her eyes and sealing her lips, she felt his mouth against hers. Bitte, *God help me.*

He brushed his tongue across her seam, insisting on entry.

Nein, nein, *he must not.* She clenched her jaw. Flexing her knees she jumped high and broke the kiss.

Whap. He slapped her cheek again.

Bad to worse. Blinking back an unbidden tear, she watched Otto fumble one-handed with first her shawl's knot and then the top buttons on her dress. Bitte, Gott. *Forgive me for what I plan to do.* Pulling moisture into her mouth, she glanced at his cold eyes and spat.

He relaxed his hold for an instant.

Without thinking ahead, she raised her knee fast and hard.

"Ach." He released her, backed a step, and bent over.

Run—run—run. Louisa sprinted between the trees toward the road. When her skirt snagged on a bramble, she ripped it free and continued running. Dodging a stump, she caught her foot for an instant. She jerked free from the shoe and kept going. A few large steps later, she burst into the open. Glancing for the horse, she spied the mare a few yards ahead, on the opposite side of the road.

She dashed toward the animal. Disregarding her racing heart, she snatched the reins and tugged the beast forward. "Come, horse—we stay ahead of trouble." She heard Otto thrashing his way out of the forest. *I must hurry.* Grasping the reins in one hand and lifting her skirt with the other, she ran down the road's center.

"Halt. Whoa," Otto shouted behind her.

Louisa ignored the commands and panted near exhaustion. *Another step, I must keep moving.*

The horse emitted an occasional snort but trotted along.

She did not waste time to glance behind her. Instead, she sprinted. *His voice is too close. How long can I keep this pace? Where is the next farmhouse?*

"Blazing smokestacks." A tall, thin boy dashed into the road from a fenced pasture.

"Help…help me." Louisa gasped for air. Dropping the reins, she half-stumbled the final yards to the boy. "He…he…attack…me."

"She lies." Otto snatched the reins. "She stole my horse."

"Then why the tear in her dress?" The young American straightened to his full height and parked his fists on slender hips.

Louisa inspected her dress and discovered the top

three buttons were ripped away. She reached up and gripped the edges of her Sunday frock. "I tell the truth."

"Don't believe her, boy. A woman does not know what she wants." Otto mounted the horse, slapped the beast on the rump, and trotted away.

"We go to the house." The boy waved toward a white, frame building. "My mother will allow you to wash…give you pins for your dress."

"*Danke.*" Louisa realized her breathing started to slow toward normal. She studied her savior. The lad looked no more than twelve, but he had strong arms from farm work. "Thank you. Thank you not enough to say."

A woman and two small children ran from a neat house toward them.

"Adams?" She waited for the tall boy's nod. "Mueller—I am cousin to Fredrick—farm on this road." She paused and blinked slowly to gather more of her wits. *Nein.* Closing her eyes for even a moment brought an image of Otto's twisted, evil smile. She shivered in the mild morning at the comparison of Otto's features to the devil's face in a religious woodcut.

****

Before Monday's sun totally cleared the distant tree line, Hans stood at the north stable door and watched the last team leave the yard. Pulling on the large, leather gloves *Herr* Bergmann loaned him, he glanced at the wheelbarrow, fork, and shovel.

You can handle the cleaning on your own. I will return from the levee in an hour. The stablemaster's words slid across Hans's brain before settling.

Setting the stall cleaning tools in the barrow, he lifted the handles and guided the container to the far end of the building. In a few minutes, he tested the stretch of his back's damaged skin. Push. Lift. Carry. Dump. Over and over, he performed the familiar steps of the task. Routine soothed him. Movement aided his healing. The day of rest after working short days last week built his strength.

After twisting with a heavy shovelful of sharp-scented droppings, he blinked back tears from the pain. Wiping a stained handkerchief across his face, he spoke to Sal, the single animal currently in residence. "She allowed a kiss. On her hand—in view of her family—at the beer garden." He savored the memory from yesterday. Prior to leaving the picnic to go home and rest his back, he bid Louisa a tender farewell. The brief moment replayed in his mind during the entire walk to his room and the evening hours.

An instant later, Hans slid the shovel under another pile of manure. "An entire week and I've not found the courage, or words, to mention the kiss she brushed on my lips. Instead, I sit and stare at the wall each evening while she changes the bandages. She's going to think I'm ungrateful." Tipping the animal waste into the wheelbarrow, he smiled. "The kiss was glorious. Louisa tastes sweet—fresh—light as flower petals against my lips."

The horse snorted, raised her nose toward the small window, and perked her ears.

"*Ja. Ja.* My stories do not interest you today." He returned to his work and fought the urge to rub his painful back. He bent to scoop manure and blinked away the sensation of skin one size too small. He finished in the first stall and moved to the one across the aisle. Slow and steady, he continued the work until the barrow was rounded full. Lifting the handles, he pushed the container toward the door.

Clop. Clop. The distinctive sound of a shod horse on the yard cobbles reached him.

"Ein Minute." He started to wipe his hands on his trousers and stopped at the sight of the oversize gloves.

"Where is *Herr* Bergmann? I wish to buy this horse."

Herr *Wulff?* Hans studied the dismounted rider silhouetted in the doorway. *"Guten Morgan, Herr* Doctor. *Herr* Bergmann is not here. You will need to wait for his return." He removed one glove to give air to his warm, moist hand. "You like the mare, Ginger?"

"How long?" Otto released the reins.

Familiar with her surroundings, the saddled horse walked to the water trough.

Shrugging, Hans held his expression even and removed his second glove. *I will not show pain—no matter he knows the full extent of my injuries.* "Hour…less….I can stable the horse, and you can return to do your business later."

"She's mine." Otto widened his stance and placed hands on his hips.

"The horse? You do not yet know the price." Hans did not buy and sell. The only time he handled money was when someone rented the gig or saddle horse on his assigned Sunday. His boss trusted him, but only the stablemaster purchased and sold animals. Each morning, walking past the office, he glanced at the desk. *Second drawer on the left is locked and holds the money. The thief died on the ship. I work for wages—an honest man.*

"Have you suet pudding for brains?" Otto lifted

one side of his mouth in a crooked smile.

Hans froze and trembled under the physician's stare. "Louisa?" he whispered. "She is not yours. She is her own person."

Otto laughed sharp in the quiet air. "*Dummkopf.* Louisa is mine. I proved it this morning."

"*Nein.*" Hans moved forward and grasped Otto's forearm.

"Is that what you think? Bah. Her cousin will beg me to marry her now." Otto jerked his arm free, pulled a golden coin from his pocket, and tossed the money toward Hans. "For the horse."

"Louisa." Ignoring the money on the ground, Hans dropped the gloves, stepped in front of the physician, and grasped Otto's coat with both hands. "Did you ruin her?"

"Close enough." Otto twisted his lips.

Gripping the fabric and ignoring the pain, Hans sidestepped in a small circle and forced the taller man back. "She is goodness." Breathing deep, he recognized anger surging in his chest. With unexpected strength, he propelled them across the stable threshold. "You are evil."

Otto paused a futile attempt to pry Hans's fingers from his jacket. He fisted his right hand, drew back his arm, and swung.

Hans ducked. Shoving the physician away, he bent at the waist while observing his opponent. In an instant, he aimed his left fist at the physician's gut and powered his right toward the jaw.

Punch. Retreat. Duck. Attack.

Survival techniques learned in dark alleys thousands of miles away took control of Hans's muscles. Twice he connected against Otto's jaw with enough force to send ripples of shock and pain up his arm.

Otto held his own.

"Oooof." After a solid blow beneath his ribs, Hans fought for his next breath. With his hands on his knees, he gathered air and strength. *He is distracted for a moment.* He charged. Continuing his momentum after contact, he didn't stop until Otto tumbled backward into the wheelbarrow.

Hans gave Otto one more solid hit to the jaw before backing away and gasping for breath. "Go...go...never...come...back." Careful not to turn his back on the man sprawled in the horse manure, he moved to the water trough and plunged both hands into the cool liquid. He hissed as the fresh injuries contacted the water. A few gulping breaths later, he gathered Ginger's reins. Standing beside the horse, he petted the animal's neck and spoke soothing words. *Dear beast, you calm me as much as I reassure you.*

"Imposter." Otto regained his feet and spat the word. Bending to retrieve his hat from the cobbles, he held his gaze on Hans.

Hans pressed his lips. Every muscle in his body warned against another round of fisticuffs. He stood his ground until the physician walked off the property. Then, pausing to recover the golden coin and the leather gloves, he led the mare inside the stable. "If he soiled Louisa...I will protect her honor. If she is willing, I marry her."

Chapter Twenty-Four

"You are kind." Louisa pressed a bundle containing a loaf of warm rye bread and a dozen of Saturday's cookies into old Mr. Adams's hands. Standing in front of the bakery in morning light, she understood words, even fresh bread, were small payment for the actions of his family.

The moment his daughter-in-law had escorted her into the house, she received care. First came fresh water and sweet soap for washing. Pins to close the top of her dress were fetched without a request. The boy, Ted, under a stern look from his mother, left to search for her shoes and basket and to tell Fredrick. The white-haired man harnessed a horse to the small buggy and had insisted on delivering her to the bakery's front door.

Moments later, she waved farewell to her new American friend and entered the bakery. *Will Fredrick's temper get the better of him?* "Not now. I work—calm myself." She hurried past an astonished Polly and skeptical Charlotte on the way to her private area. With trembling hands, she unfastened the pins and buttons on her Sunday dress. *I am safe—among friends.* She changed into a weekday dress and donned an apron. From one moment to the next, her emotions switched from shame, to anger, to pride. *Best to keep busy hands.*

"Two pies, the sweet apple filling is on the stove."

Charlotte set a bowl of sifted flour at the worktable's center. "Are you well?"

"*Ja. Danke.*" Louisa toyed with the measuring cup. "We will talk later—when no customers. I expect Cousin Fredrick will arrive soon. I do not want to become center of gossip."

Pressing her lips, Charlotte hesitated for three ticks of the clock. Giving a nod, she turned, entered the sales area, and exchanged a few quiet words with Polly.

Louisa added two large pieces of lard to the flour and salt in the bowl. Lifting the pastry cutter and a table knife, she set to work. Within a few expert strokes, the lard became smaller and smaller flour-coated bits. *Good to keep my hands busy.* She did not wish to talk of the morning's events. To be truthful, she did not want to think about them. But the fresh memories refused to leave her mind. *Later. After the customers dwindle— perhaps after the second foundry whistle—I'll tell my story to Charlotte and Polly.*

"Louisa." Polly guided Joseph past the worktable. "Today we all eat late lunch upstairs."

She nodded. Unless her stomach unknotted in the course of routine work, she would not enjoy even one bite of the finest bread and jam. She moistened her lips and raised her gaze an instant before Polly hurried out of sight.

"Where is he?" Fredrick stomped into the bakery.

"Lower your voice." *Frau* Keil set a cinnamon *kuchen* into a customer's basket.

Fredrick removed his cap and nodded. A moment later, he paused in the workroom doorway. "Where will I find him?"

Louisa raised her gaze from the pea-sized pieces of

lard. "I do not know where he went. I do not wish to see him ever again."

"I will find him." Fredrick stood with feet shoulder width apart and crossed his arms. "He must pay."

"*Nein.*" She turned the bowl one quarter of a circle and continued her work.

"He did wrong."

"*Bitte*—do not answer violence with force.*" She moved the pastry cutter with a trembling hand and raised her gaze.

Fredrick held his mouth straight. In silence, he maintained his gaze on her form.

His anger is hot. I need to tell the story myself before he will return to his usual, even temper. Abandoning the pastry bowl, she wiped her hands and sorted words. "I am safe. I escaped *Herr* Wulff and reached the road before he grabbed me a second time. The Adams boy saw the end of it."

"Wulff?" Fredrick widened his eyes and backed a step. "I-I…forgive me…I thought."

"Later, I tell the story only once." She dipped a gourd ladle into the small bowl of water.

Anna, holding little Karl by the hand, appeared in the workroom entrance. "What has the physician done?"

"Evil," Fredrick replied.

Tick…tock…tick.

"The bakery workroom while preparing pies for the oven is a poor place to tell my experience. *Bitte,* we must wait for a private time and place." Louisa turned to the oven and removed two kuchens topped with peach slices.

Anna looked from Louisa, to Charlotte, and back to

Louisa, before she addressed her husband. "Now is a good time to go buy your tobacco. Ask if we have a letter. Do not hurry."

"*Ja. Gute.*" Charlotte rearranged cookies in the glass case.

After Fredrick had gone, Charlotte addressed Anna. "Polly and Joseph are in the garden. Take your boy and join them. I will close for the day after the second foundry whistle. Together we discuss in the apartment."

A few minutes later, Louisa resumed making the pastry. Working the dough with her hands, flouring the smooth table, and rolling the pie crust allowed her to sort her thoughts. *My dress can be mended. My shoe and shawl, if we find them, can be repaired. I can get new ribbons for the bonnet. My reputation?* "I've done nothing wrong," she whispered to the crust while she pinched the edge around the rim of the first pie plate. By the time she spooned the hot, thick apple-and-cinnamon filling into the second crust, her mind rested more peacefully than since she set out for town at sunrise.

She cut narrow leaves of the remaining pastry and arranged eight in a sunburst pattern on each pie. *How will I tell Hans?* She swallowed another mouthful of anxiety. *I need to speak with him before he hears rumors.* Already, she listened while Charlotte pinched off a wild story brought by a customer. She braced her hands on the table while a tremble traveled from fingers to toes. *Would it be proper to seek him out at the stables?* She glanced toward the ceiling and listened to soft footsteps. *First, I must tell the people already gathering.*

Ten minutes before the second foundry whistle was due, Fredrick returned to the bakery. "I go upstairs. According to the postmaster, *Herr* Wulff rode the horse to Bergmann's."

Louisa stilled. *What if...* She rubbed her hands to banish a sudden chill.

Frau Keil finished serving the customers inside the shop. She walked the final lady to the door and turned the key. Returning to the counter, she bent to retrieve the cash box.

"*Bitte. Bitte.*" Muffled words and tapping signaled an impatient person.

Louisa closed the oven, glanced toward the clock, and then the large, front window. "Hans." She hurried into the sales area and took the key from Charlotte's hand.

He burst into the room before she opened the door the entire way. "Louisa—you are safe?"

She released a deep breath. *Joy—relief—I do not know names for all the good things in my heart at the sight of you.*

****

A short time later, Hans listened to Louisa recount the events of earlier this morning. A bowl of fine vegetables, simmered in ham broth, grew cold in front of him. He could not eat. At each turn of the story— each polite question from the others—he felt his stomach shrivel and sour.

"*Herr* Wulff sought me out at the stable." After his statement, he heard the soft tick of the clock.

"To check your burns?" Joseph blurted.

Polly shushed her son and directed him to show the younger child his collection of smooth stones.

"*Nein.* Otto returned the horse—claimed he wanted to buy the mare. But he refused to wait for *Herr* Bergmann's return before he bragged." He flexed his hand under the table. "I do not think he will boast of this morning again."

Louisa reached over and tugged his hand into view. "You need ointment on your knuckles. I will re-bandage your hands before you leave."

"*Danke.*" Words were not enough to acknowledge her kindness and strength.

"Today I fetched a letter." Fredrick pulled a square envelope from his coat pocket. "It is addressed to Dietrich. Do you want to read it, Louisa? Or should I?"

Louisa accepted the letter, broke the seal, and extracted a single piece of paper crowded with a bold script. She skimmed the lines to the signature. "*Herr* Wulff, Otto's *Vater,* writes to Papa." A glance at the date indicated this letter was sent while her first message from Elm Ridge still journeyed.

"*Greetings, my friend. I pray my letter finds you and your family well and settled into your new home in Illinois. My wife and I remain well. Business stays steady in the cooperage—plenty to support my second son and his growing family. I write a warning. The first Tuesday of Lent, our dear Ernestine, Otto's wife, arrived unannounced at our door. She was distraught, ill from travel, and expects a child near the end of summer. Over several days, she managed to tell us a distressing story.*"

Ernestine? Otto's wife? Hans felt the air in his lungs turn cold. *What sort of man claims a wife is dead when she carries his child?*

"The letter continues." Louisa adjusted the paper.

"My eldest son abandoned his family and brought shame to our name. Since his brother Hermann's death, Otto spoke of little else but your daughter, Louisa, my dear friend. As time passed, the fixation on her became more intense rather than less. Early in February, he left his wife and patients in Essen. A week after she woke to his absence, Ernestine received a note by messenger. That is how she learned he left for America. Ernestine, being without parents, sold off the large household furnishings and made her way to our family."

Louisa lowered the paper with a trembling hand. "I-I can read no more."

"The letter explains a great many things." Anna set a gentle hand on Louisa's arm.

"I should have harnessed the team and driven you into town this morning. I did not look to your safety, Louisa." Fredrick studied the floor.

"*Nein.*" *Frau* Keil pushed back her chair. "The incident this morning is not the fault of anyone in this room—not Fredrick—not Anna—not Louisa. The blame belongs to one person—Otto."

Louisa raised a hand and touched her cheek. "The story will spread in town. Passersby witnessed my arrival with Mr. Adams. People are sure to have loose tongues. I overheard speculation from two customers during the time I prepared pies. Gossip, a snake with many voices, will ruin me."

Hans drew a deep breath. "The rumor fire will have no fuel. After our conversation"—he displayed the fresh scrapes on his knuckles—"Otto left the stable. According to a reliable driver, the physician collected his traveling trunk and boarded the packet to Iowa."

"Coward," Fredrick ground out the word.

"*Ja,*" Hans spoke.

The others nodded agreement.

Will he return to Elm Ridge?

The clock struck the hour.

Louisa startled and pushed back her chair. "The pies."

"I will remove them from the oven." Polly stood and hurried to the door.

Hans lifted Louisa's hand before setting his damaged fingers over her warm flesh. From each point where his skin contacted her, he experienced a warm glow. He cleared his throat and intersected her gaze. "Louisa, I knew from early in the voyage you were the prettiest girl on *The Flying Gull.* Since then, you show me a kind and beautiful spirit. If you will allow it…if you are willing to risk association with a poor, humble stable hand…I will court you. I wish to protect you. You and I—we work to live a new dream in America."

Chapter Twenty-Five

April 1852

Louisa adjusted her hand on Hans's arm and paused outside the church door. Glancing toward the April sky, she breathed deeply at the sight of sparse, white clouds in a blue expanse. *The air is filled with the scent of new growth and hope. My heart overflows with joy.* She smiled and looked toward the river where a thin trail of black smoke marked one of the frequent steamboats. *"Ein gute Tag."*

"Today is the best day of my life." Hans guided her down the steps. "I remembered to speak my vows loud enough for the witnesses to hear."

She laughed. For the last three days, he worried aloud his voice would fail him. "You have made me a fortunate woman." Walking arm in arm, she sang her new name to the melody of an old folk song. "My name is Louisa Christine Anna Mueller Hoffmann. When we meet on the street, as *Frau* Hoffmann we greet. Within the walls of our home, titles are banished. Louisa Hoffmann makes hunger vanish."

"Clever." He grinned. "Today I have the most beautiful bride and also the most quick-witted."

"My handsome husband flatters me." She turned to face him and placed her hands on his pristine black suit. Studying his sparkling brown eyes shaded by a new, wide-brimmed hat, she decided his smile pleased her most. The slight curve of his lips urged her heart to fly. "You are the most handsome groom in all of Elm Ridge—all of Illinois."

"Treat. Treat," Karl begged in his high voice from behind Louisa.

"Hush," Anna replied. "First we walk to the new house."

Our house. Louisa hid her sigh. Thanks to *Herr* Bergmann, they were renting an entire house on Hickory Street. A four-room home in an excellent location—four blocks to the bakery and five to the livery. Lifting the skirts of her new, blue summer dress, she stepped on the plank sidewalk and stole another glance at Hans's profile. *My husband. He is kind. A good worker.* She would run out of numbers tallying the positive qualities of the man walking beside her.

"We are home, *Frau* Hoffmann." Hans scooped her into his arms and adjusted his hold on her before stepping on the simple porch. "Over the threshold we go, my sweet."

Louisa turned her head to better view his smile and looped her arms around his neck. Ignoring the bump of her new summer bonnet's brim against his stiff hat, she giggled. Pleasure and contentment surged through her. If Fredrick, Anna, and Karl were not mere steps away, she would rest her cheek against his strong chest.

"Here they are," *Frau* Keil proclaimed.

"Good wishes to the bridal couple," Mrs. Cook added.

Herr Bergmann laughed. "Do we need to sing?"

Louisa jerked out of her daydream and gasped at the number of friends gathered in the parlor.

Hans set her feet on the smooth pine floor. An instant later, he laced fingers with her.

"A happy day." Polly stepped forward, hugged Louisa, and then a startled Hans.

"You are all here. Who is minding the bakery?" She glanced from Charlotte to Polly and back again.

"All is good. *Frau* Hebing and Polly arranged to take turns so both can celebrate your special day." Charlotte hugged Louisa. A moment later, she looked Hans straight in the eye while shaking his hand. "You take good care of the best baker in Elm Ridge."

"*Ja.*" He nodded. "I mind manners and avoid lies to keep your trust."

One after another, their friends gifted them with embraces and well-wishes.

Old Mr. Adams clapped Hans on the shoulder and whispered into his ear.

The stablemaster kissed the back of Louisa's hand.

Giggling, she responded. "We owe you a great debt, *Herr* Bergmann."

"*Nein*—I make your husband work hard. He demonstrates a gift with the animals."

Louisa drew a deep breath. *Hans promoted to regular driver. He brought the news home Saturday.* "*Danke. Danke.*"

"Attention—attention, everyone," *Frau* Keil called over the babble. "We have a special treat for the newest married couple in Elm Ridge. Today we start a new tradition."

Mrs. Cook stepped forward and helped Charlotte move a privacy screen.

"Oh…my…a dream." Louisa laid her hands against her cheeks. "The gift is beautiful…so large."

289

She studied a three-tiered cake covered with a bright-white icing of egg white and sugar. Violet petals scattered among the short, stiff peaks added a soft, spring touch.

"These cakes are all the rage in St. Louis society." Mrs. Cook touched Louisa's wrist. "Together the bride and groom cut the first two small pieces. Then you feed them to each other. Wedding fun? *Ja.*"

Hans laughed. "What? A man is not able to feed himself?"

"Shall we try?" Louisa looked toward her groom. Spying the sparkle in his eyes, she widened her smile.

A moment later, with Hans holding a hand over hers, Louisa sliced into the cake's bottom layer. "A new tradition. A land of new experiences. A new dream."

"A bold adventure." Hans snaked an arm around her waist.

In a flash, a summary of varied experiences since she stepped off *The Perch* one year ago threatened to overwhelm her. She steadied her breath, refreshed her smile, and cut two tiny squares of cake. *Next year?* She glanced toward Anna. Her cousin's wife would give birth in a few weeks. *Will that be me next spring?*

Holding her gaze steady on Hans's smiling eyes, she lifted one piece of cake with thumb and forefinger and gestured for Hans to do the same. "Are you ready?"

Thank you for purchasing
this publication of The Wild Rose Press, Inc.

For questions or more information
contact us at
info@thewildrosepress.com.

The Wild Rose Press, Inc.
www.thewildrosepress.com

Hans continued to rotate his flat, wool hat and aim his gaze among the shoppers. "I give you, my friends, a word of warning."

Straightening her spine, Louisa prepared to remember every word. "What sort of warning?"

He lifted his chin and turned his head, looking again among the crowd in the center aisle. In the next moment, he focused on her. He cleared his throat. "Thieves and pickpockets roam this market."

"Oh, my." Widow Krause released her hand from the teapot. "Have you been robbed?"

"A minor encounter. I advise you to stay on your guard." He glanced over his shoulder.

Louisa moved one hand across her skirt. Skimming fingers above her pocket's opening, she patted the fabric until she touched the thickness of the second set of cloth pouches under her petticoat. She gave silent thanks for taking a few minutes at the boardinghouse to sew the majority of her funds, plus the precious passport and church papers, into the hiding place. "*Danke*. We will be careful. Will you?"

"I must go." Hans replaced his cap on shaggy, mahogany hair and hurried off into the throng.

"*Herr* Hoffmann is an unusual young man." Widow Krause poured tea.

Louisa stared into the crowd. Within two blinks, she lost sight of him. "Alfred does not trust him."

"And you? Do you trust him?" The widow leaned close.

She pursed her lips to delay an answer. When she looked into his face, she saw a friend.

Praise for Ellen Parker

"NEW DREAMS tells the beautifully rendered journey of Louisa, an immigrant in America. Superb descriptions provide a perfect glimpse into the 1850s. Louisa learns early on that hardship and opportunity often travel the same road. Yet her gritty determination shines as she follows a path to Elm Ridge, Illinois, and her New Dreams. Louisa has no time for a suitor, but maybe she'll reconsider after meeting Hans Hoffmann. These delightful characters made a thoroughly enjoyable read! Gift this novel to anyone who loves historical fiction or historical romance."

~D. K. Deters, author of The Texan's Favor

~*~

"Ellen Parker's NEW DREAMS will keep your attention and you rooting for Louisa and Hans to finally kiss. The storyline is accurate in the plight of German immigrants and Parker's use of German is easy to translate for the reader not familiar with the language. A great read for the lovers of sweet romances."

~Suzanne Seibel

~*~

"Exciting and engaging, NEW DREAMS is hard to put down. Louisa's and Hans's journey from Germany to America and a new life will pull you in from the first page to the last, leaving you wishing for more."

~Jane Yunker, author